"You'd think a church would be a safe place..."

Small towns are known for their characters and their secrets. When Angus McPherson comes to Shoestring, Texas, to look into the death of a fellow pastor, he finds an abundance of both. Angus forms an unlikely partnership with the newly elected Chief of Police, Hector Chavez. Together they poke and prod through an investigation that uncovers more affairs than a romance novel and a menagerie of folks withholding evidence. Meanwhile a killer stalks the sleepy streets of Shoestring, looking for the next victim, dead set on getting Angus out of the way...

Blood Under the Altar

a novel by

Mark W. Stoub

Bald Angel

BA

This book is a work of fiction. Names, characters, places and incidents are either products of the author's imagination or are used fictitiously. Any resemblance to actual events, locales or persons, living or dead, is entirely coincidental.

BLOOD UNDER THE ALTAR, a novel by Mark W. Stoub
www.bloodunderthealtar.com

Published by Bald Angel Books, www.baldangelbooks.com

First Edition, July 2011

Author Services by Pedernales Publishing, LLC.
www.pedernalespublishing.com

Library of Congress Control Number: 2011910259

ISBN: 978-0-9835736-1-6

Printed in the United States of America

Acknowledgements

I would like to thank my friends, colleagues, and family members who have read my book and offered critical advice and helpful suggestions along the way. Most especially, I want to thank Mindy Reed and my wife, Jane, for editorial assistance. And a very special thanks to Jose Ramirez and Barbara Rainess at Pedernales Publications for their helpful guidance in the production of this novel.

12·18·21

For Janie:

Soul mate is just the beginning of what you are to me

To Nancy

Here's to life's mysteries!

Enjoy

Mark W Bond

Blood Under the Altar

Chapter One: A Good Walk Ruined

THE OLD CHURCH loomed over Shoestring, Texas, full of dark secrets, battered and bruised by the all too human battles fought within its walls. Spring had arrived, a time when all nature breathes in the rebirth of hope. For the church, it was the season of Lent, generally a time of reflection and renewal. But *this* church turned its back on any chance for renewal and perpetually practiced the darker side of Lent, with its muted colors and dour emotions. The current pastor had been there four years, the fulfillment of a lifelong dream to lead a large, historic church. Little did he know that he would pay the ultimate price for that dream.

He loved to walk the old, long, dark corridors of this wonderfully musty building. He did not see the peeling paint or the falling plaster. All he saw was power, particularly in the sanctuary, the last place he visited each day before leaving. The tall ceilings and the large rose window in the rear gave off a kind of dark confidence, filling him with awe and satisfaction. *God may be found in the dark shadows, as well as in the light*, he mused. Most of the people he knew spent the majority of their time in the darkness.

He glanced up at the immense organ with its gleaming pipes spread out like a golden eagle. When he had first come here, this magnificent instrument was in bad repair, and he took on the task of raising thousands of dollars, restoring it to its original splendor. Whenever its sonorous tones filled this august space, he smiled as he thought of pastors in Austin who would give their first born for this organ. But it was his.

He made a silent prayer, the same one the High Priest Simeon offered up when Jesus' parents brought him to be circumcised on the eighth day, according to the law. Simeon prayed, *"Now let your servant depart in peace, for my eyes have seen your salvation."*

As he walked through the building, a sense of peace washed over him. Even though he was drowning in a sea of trouble, he felt more connected to the core of his being than at any other time of his life. He was where he needed to be.

Oswald "Pete" Anderson was troubled by so much, but sure of one thing. He was pastor of a large church in a small town, and his life was beginning to look up. He had been so out of control these past few years; he had begun not to recognize himself in the mirror. He knew his life had to be different now.

He wrestled the old door open, accompanied by sounds of a pain buried deep within the building itself. He was on his way to the Rotary Club for lunch, one of the highlights of his week. As he cleared the door and stepped out into the cool, crisp spring day, he heard a loud noise from above. He looked up and the last thing he saw was the building's large cement Celtic cross crashing down toward him.

THE LITTLE white ball sailed through the atmosphere like a miniature moon. Inevitably gravity worked its cunning magic, and the little sphere succumbed to forces greater than it could resist, coming back to earth, resting comfortably among the trees to the right of the fairway.

The peacefulness of the scene was lost on Angus as he watched the flight of his ball. "Bloody Hell," he growled, taking the driver in both hands and bringing it over his raised right knee, white knuckles gripping the club like an ogre about to crush a puny human. Angus seethed through clenched teeth.

To Angus the golf course was sacred space, as sacred as a confessional in the Catholic Church, and another reason he preferred to play alone. A cardinal rule for him was, "What's said here stays here." He would have to trust someone before he would risk being misunderstood.

He had never picked up the game in his native Scotland—they couldn't afford it, and his dad thought it was a waste of time. And now he wondered why he had ever bothered. But he reminded himself he did not come out here to play on the Champion's Tour. He came out here to meditate.

He loved his adopted country and never considered going back to Scotland. Golf, however, was a way for him to stay close to the land of his birth. The older he got, he found, the more he needed those connections. What he also needed was to get away from time to time. His job as the General Presbyter for Mission Presbytery, covering all of South Texas, was demanding and he needed time to himself now and then.

Angus McPherson was a tall man with a thick head of black hair and a suggestion of gray at the temples. In his early sixties, he was just a few years away from the age most people begin to think about retirement. But such thoughts rarely entered his mind. Angus was a man in love with his life, even though he found himself in the rough now and then.

He smiled with recognition as he approached his ball, lurking in the shadows of the live oak trees lining the fairway on eighteen at the Oakmont Country Club. "Golf is a good walk ruined." Angus remembered Twain's quote about this silly game. But the game also was teaching him to "play it where it lies," a valuable lesson, if only he could learn it.

As he approached his shot, he tried to remember everything the club pro had said about the set up, take away, and follow through. He'd read somewhere about the twenty-seven parts to the golf swing. Trying to remember each one just tied him up in knots all the more. There was an echo in his ear from the dim reaches of eons of his dad's voice screaming at him, "*What are you doin' that for, ya' eejit?*" which didn't help much.

He had gone through his pre-shot routine, and was near the top of his back swing, ready to uncoil all the force of his energy down upon the unsuspecting ball, ready to see it sail straight and far and true to its intended target just as he had envisioned it, when his cell phone rang. Startled, he dropped the club at the top of the back swing. He watched it fall to the ground as he grabbed for his phone.

The ugly red dragon of his anger was rousing to do battle again with whoever would chance to interrupt him. It was his wife, Angelica.

"What?" he snapped.

There was silence on the other end.

"Sorry, love," said Angus, instantly red in the face. "I was in the middle of my back swing."

"And how am I supposed to know that?" Angelica's hot temper true to her native Mexican roots flared back at him. "You know I never call you unless it's very important."

"Aye, aye, of course," Angus said, shaking his head. "What's the matter, *mi Corazón?*"

"That's better." Angus could hear Angelica's smile through the phone. She loved hearing Spanish spoken with a Scottish accent. "Francesca called. Said she'd heard the pastor in Shoestring had died; some kind of accident."

"Why didn't she call me? She has my cell number."

"She probably didn't want to *disturb* you," said Angelica. Francesca was Angus's secretary of ten years, practically a part of the family.

"I will take care of it, sweetheart. *Thank you* so much for telling me about this."

"I forgive you, but get a grip, Pancho."

"Aye, ma'am."

AS CHIEF of Police, Hector was about to see his first dead body. He had worked for the state highway patrol and had been on the scene of a few deadly accidents, but never as chief. He'd just been hired in January, so this was all new to him. He knew all the other policemen and deputies on the scene would be looking closely at him. He didn't want to screw up.

The long shadows of the church steeple shrouded the yard like an old woman in a black cape, hunched over with pain, while two deputies scurried around as determined as worker ants, taking pictures, measuring, and looking for evidence. Shortly after Hector arrived, the medical examiner pulled up in a late-model black station wagon. Philip Bliss, the M.E., was a middle-aged man with energy popping out of every pore. His quick, jerky movements made Hector think of a hummingbird.

Philip found Hector looking in the bushes. "Find anything interesting?" Philip asked.

"No, it's a clean scene," said Hector. He motioned him over to the body where a small group of town folk had gathered in shock and grief. "The blow to the head and the blood on the cross seem to be the only indications of what happened here."

"No signs of a struggle?"

"Nope," Hector said. "Louise Lassitor, the church secretary, said she heard a loud crash, came out, and found him lying here in a pool of blood. We took her statement, and a few others', but nothing solid."

Philip put on rubber gloves to examine the body. He moved the head from side to side.

"It appears, as you suspected, the blow to the head did it," he said. "But we'll know more when we get him back on the slab. I'll let you know if we find anything."

Hector knew this was going to be the longest day of his young career as Shoestring Chief of Police.

AS HE folded his phone back into his pocket, Angus found it hard to catch his breath, as if an anvil was chained to his chest. Suddenly, the light blue in the sky and the wispy clouds turned gray and lifeless. He waved to the group behind him to play through, as he sat in his cart to compose himself.

Death had stalked him in his native Scotland. When his parents died, he decided nothing was holding him back from his dream to come to the States. He had fallen in love with the idea of America and had longed to see if it could be true. The past shackled him as long as he stayed in the country of his birth. Only by leaving could he be truly free of death and the past, until now.

Sitting under the spreading live oak, struggling to regain his composure, he called Francesca.

"Hi, Franny," he said. "I heard you called."

"I suppose I could have called your cell, but I thought it could wait."

"A good friend of mine dies, and you thought it could wait?" As soon as he said it, he wondered who this guy was.

There was silence on the other end.

"I'm sorry, Franny. I guess I must be in shock. Is there any other information?"

"He was just in the office yesterday. He wanted to know about making a loan from retirement savings. He was asking some pretty strange questions for a man twenty years from retirement. It sounded like he was looking for a quick way to get some cash."

Angus took in the information with a certain amount of curiosity. He scratched his head and looked at his watch. "That is strange," he said finally.

"They think it was an accident."

"How did you hear about it?"

"The church secretary called me. She figured we needed to know."

"Did she say anything about a funeral?"

"Not yet. Everyone is still in shock, but plans are underway."

They said their goodbyes and hung up. He sat for a few minutes trying to see again the beauty around him. He wanted to hold it to himself, but all he collected was empty air and a feeling of being crowded in this open space. A deepening sadness engulfed him.

He decided not to finish his round. He drove his cart to the clubhouse, loaded his gear in his yellow Jeep Cherokee, got a soda from the machine, and headed for home. The ride was a wonderful way to end this troubling day. He had remembered sunsets in his native Scotland, but they were nothing like those he witnessed in Texas.

The clouds and the sun's reflection off them arranged themselves in a spectacular pallet of color. Yellows, oranges, deep purple, and shooting light spread out like a geisha's fan. Overcome with awe, Angus pulled over and gave his undivided attention to the wonderful canvas in the sky and whispered a little prayer of thanks as a single tear rolled down his cheek.

When he drove around to the back of their large home, he turned off the Jeep and retrieved his clubs for a good cleaning later. He vividly remembered his mother fighting a losing battle with dirt, especially with his father's eternally present coal dust. As a young boy, he vowed to continue the fight, for his mother's sake. It had something to do with order. After all, God was about bringing order out of chaos, and so would he.

He came from the garage toward the house, an old Victorian they had rescued from the wrecking ball. Angelica stood in front of the kitchen door with her arms folded over her chest, the light behind her resting on her hair like a halo. She was tall and slender with a pleasant shape, her long black hair pulled into a ponytail. Her intense hazel eyes cast a spell on him, making him fall in love with her all over again. Her accent had a hint of Mexico. Her parents had moved to Brownsville from Mexico City in an attempt to give her family a "better life." Her father had been a barber, and her mother cleaned houses for the rich "gringos" who took up residence in the city. Angelica was a wonderful blend of the exotic and the domestic, and Angus had fallen in love with her.

He showed her the score card and gave her a kiss, recreating their world once more.

"I'm sorry about your friend," Angelica said, smiling sadly up at Angus.

"Me, too. I wish there was something we could do for his family and the congregation."

"Well, we could go there for church tomorrow. I know having their 'leader' worship with them would be a great encouragement."

She saw Angus ponder that. Then in an attempt to lift his spirits, she added, "Afterward we could go to a little place I have wanted us to try–for Sunday brunch?" She lightly touched his shoulder.

Angus nodded, smiling, and went upstairs to take a shower.

THEY DID not ordinarily watch the evening news before turning in, but tonight they made an exception. Angus was anxious to see if they would have anything about the death of his friend. They didn't have to wait long. It was the lead story on each of the three local channels. They gave an "in depth" report (for all of sixty seconds) about Anderson's ministry in Shoestring and the circumstances surrounding his death. The reporter interviewed the police chief, Hector Chavez, whose department had ruled it an accident.

ANGUS WOKE promptly at 5:00 a.m., meditated, went for a five-mile walk with Eve, their Labrador retriever, past the horse barn and through fields, while Calvin, an old mutt, slept on the porch. Then he showered and wrote for an hour. He liked awakening to the darkness and living into the light. Such a habit gave him hope.

As Angelica continued to sleep, he began to fix breakfast. The cell phone rang, and he jumped. He had been lost in thought about Peter and why he had never known his first name was Oswald. Angus had considered him a friend, but he could not get to the small towns as often as he would have liked.

Angus was close to pitching his cell phone; they were so intrusive, so insistent, so demanding. He did not recognize the number on the screen, but his curiosity got the better of him, and he answered it.

"Hello," Angus said.

"Hello," replied a young female voice, hesitantly.

"Who is this?" snapped Angus.

"Well, Reverend, you're not being very gracious."

"May I help you?" Angus insisted.

"It's I who want to help you."

Angus guessed this woman must be highly educated,

and not from Texas, by the way she asked the question and her accent. "How so?" he asked.

"I have certain information the police need in order to see justice done."

"What are you talking about?"

"About the murder of Peter Anderson."

"I thought they said it was an accident."

"Never mind what 'they' said. I know for a fact it wasn't. It was murder." Angus heard her voice quiver with nervousness. She sounded desperate.

"How do you know?"

"It's not important. Just please don't let them get away with this."

"Who's 'them'?" He was starting to sound a little desperate himself.

She hung up. Angus saved the number in his cell phone's memory. "I take back everything I ever thought about you," he said out loud, looking at the phone.

Chapter Two: No Longer In Service

ANGUS DIDN'T KNOW what to do. He thought about the call. He detected the unmistakable desperation in her voice. It was an emotion quite familiar to Angus because he had felt the same way growing up with a father who didn't understand him, and worse didn't seem to want to try. He shook his head. *That was the past, this is now,* he thought. But her calm assurance in him made Angus even more nervous.

Angelica walked into the kitchen as the light from the bay window washed her in brightness. They kissed, she got a cup of coffee, and Angus told her about the phone call.

"Do you believe her?" she said.

"I have no reason not to. What would she have to lose?"

"Nothing. But what if she saw this as a way to get someone involved who was innocent. It would throw suspicion from her onto someone else."

"All that's very interesting, but I don't think so. I heard her voice. She tried to sound calm, but she was scared."

"But why call you?"

"Good question. She might be a church member, in which case she might know who I am."

ANGUS MADE a breakfast of blackberries, ham and cheese omelets, and toast, while Angelica got dressed. The bay window of the breakfast nook overlooked the deck and the woods with a creek beyond. He saw a doe grazing by the water, the rising sun silhouetting her soft brown fur in the light. Angus thought, *I hope this is a good sign.*

THEY ARRIVED in Shoestring for the eleven o'clock service. As they entered the large sanctuary packed with the faithful and the curious, a flood of memories enveloped Angus. He remembered how Pete was so excited about the process of raising the funds for the organ's repair. But it was more about bringing the instrument back to life. He himself was being reborn with each new shiny pipe.

Then he heard it, and he closed his eyes. The pews vibrated with the full throat of the instrument. Goose bumps spread over his body like a field of clover, and a tear formed in the corner of one eye. He looked over at Angelica who was looking at him, and they both smiled.

The service was traditional, yet upbeat. The associate pastor, Beth McKinley, was petite, attractive, and spoke with a soothing voice and pastoral manner.

"We gather on this Sunday like it's any other service. We worship the way we've always worshiped. We praise God with songs and prayers and reading and speaking God's word. In that regard, nothing has changed.

"Yet, we all know everything has changed. Our compass has been crushed. We are a ship without a rudder, a car with no steering wheel. We have lost our leader, and now we too are lost.

"In this loss, it is my hope that we can now worship and more appreciate the mystery of life and death, and what a tenuous line there is between them. I also hope that as we mourn the loss of our leader, we may more surely turn with courage and confidence to the one who gives us all life, our Lord and Savior, Jesus Christ. Amen."

Beth paused and came down from the central pulpit to stand at the foot of the chancel steps. Then she did something Angus had not expected but was pleased to see. She opened up the floor for comments from those who had gathered for the service, which was the largest of the year.

A tall, dignified looking man stood a few pews away from Angus and Angelica. "I am, along with most everyone I've talked to, devastated by what happened here last week. We can't believe it, and frankly we don't understand a God who would let something like this happen."

A large woman in the balcony stood. "I feel like we've been robbed. We were just beginning to get things turned around in this church, and now this happened. It's not fair."

A young man in the back stood up and said, "I'll tell you what's not fair. Pete, besides being our pastor, was a husband and father. Their family has been cheated out of his presence for the rest of their lives. And if we are any kind of church at all, we will make sure they are well cared for." Lots of buzzing conversation began after those comments.

A little girl rose from her seat and headed forward toward Beth. Beth took the microphone from the pulpit and gave it to her. "I am sad about what happened," she said. "I will always love Pastor Pete. He knew my name and always made me feel special and safe when we came here to worship Jesus."

Angus found himself strangely moved by the service. Yes, Pete was a friend, but it surprised him how deeply he felt the loss. Feeling others' loss was difficult as well. He tried to guard himself from such feelings, but now all defenses were down.

The next thing he knew, he stood and headed for the pulpit. He embraced Beth and turned to face the congregation.

"My name is Angus McPherson," he said in thick Scottish brogue. "I am the General Presbyter of Mission Presbytery. That means that all the Presbyterian Churches in South Texas are here with you today. You and I are connected. We are joined by our common faith and the practice of that faith. It means that when one of us rejoices, we all rejoice. When one of us grieves, we all grieve. Today we all are grieving with and for you. I am here to let you know you are not alone. My office and I will do whatever we can to help you move through this difficult time as best we can. Together. May God bless you and keep you, now and forever."

Angus smiled again at Beth. The congregation erupted in a sea of chatter as he sat down.

AFTER THE SERVICE, Angus spoke briefly with Beth who introduced him to several church leaders gathering around her as he approached. The first was Ed Kramer, the treasurer. Wilted lettuce would have offered Angus a firmer hand shake. Looking down, Ed whispered, "Nice to meet you. Just call me Judas."

"Excuse me?" said Angus, leaning in with his good ear to be sure he heard correctly.

Angelica smiled and said, "We saw that National Geographic Special on the Gospel according to Judas. Apparently he wasn't the bad guy we all make him out to be."

Ed took one step back and coughed loudly. Angus said, "They must trust you very much to handle all the money."

He shrugged and looked down. Angus looked at Angelica and nodded.

Beth introduced Jim Williams, a member of the session. "Heck of a speech," he said, smiling as he shook Angus' hand with enthusiasm.

Next to him was a man of average height, good looking, with graying temples who did not wait for introductions. "Tom Branch is my name," he said. "I am clerk of the session, and I'm sure we will be hearing from you many times in the near future."

Beth introduced the last person in the circle as Paula Snodgrass. "This is all so shocking, and we will miss Peter desperately," she said, smiling weakly.

Angus could not help sensing beyond the shock, beyond the grief, most of the people he had met were hiding something–he knew it in his bones. He was curious about the feeling, and would pursue it later. Beth accepted the invitation to join them for lunch.

THE PARADISE café, the restaurant Angelica had suggested, was a carnival of sights, sounds, and smells. They served food from the interior of Mexico in a pleasant setting with helpful wait staff. Angus took a deep breath and felt himself relax for the first time since he'd heard the news about Pete's death.

The atmosphere in the converted warehouse was light and airy. The tall ceilings were covered in tin, dotted with ceiling fans and soft lighting. The tables wore white linen with cloth napkins. A huge sandstone brick fireplace covered one wall of the large room. The ductwork and water pipes were exposed and painted in vibrant primary colors. A mixture of fun and formal, it rivaled the finest restaurants in Austin.

The place was bright and buzzing with conversation and a darting wait staff. Angus drank it in, surveying the table before him. Their exchange of small talk about life in a small town made him thirsty for this life. For the first time in a long time, he started to feel as though something was missing from his life. He could not place it, and would not dare to name it for fear something wonderful would change.

Beth let out a huge sigh like air wheezing out of a balloon. "I didn't think I was going to get through that service. Thank you so much for your words. Your being here made all the difference."

"You did a fine job. I was very impressed with how you handled it. You did exactly the right thing," said Angus, putting a hand on her shoulder.

Beth's eyes were ringed in red. After some awkward silence, Angelica got up, came around Angus, pulled up a chair beside Beth and gently took her arm in hers, until Beth seemed to relax.

A young woman in a white shirt and black vest came and took their order of three brunch buffets and scurried off to get their drinks.

ANGUS DECIDED he would try calling the mystery woman again. He excused himself and went outside. He got the annoying three-tone chime with the recorded message: "*This number is no longer in service. Please check the number or try your call again.*"

As Angus returned to the table, Angelica had a worried look on her face. He assured them he was all right. He had gone to make a call, and he relayed the results.

"But I thought all this was an accident," said Beth, puzzled.

"Well, this woman—whoever she is—obviously thinks differently," said Angus.

"What are you going to do?" Angelica asked.

"I think I need to tell the police about this tomorrow."

"Do you believe her?" asked Beth.

"I don't know what I believe. I believe it is better to check out her story, if possible. If this were a murder, those responsible must be brought to justice."

WHEN ANGUS received the bill, he tried to act as though nothing was wrong. It was not like he had to pay for it. His expense account with the Presbytery would cover it, but it still bothered him. Spending large sums of money was foreign to his nature. He had lived with this money anxiety for many years and overcame it with minimum effort. But the death of his friend and the possible violence involved added agony to his usual struggle.

The detritus of their meal lay around them, as they sipped the last of their champagne and coffee. "Beth, this has really been wonderful. You did a great job today, and I will come and talk with you and the session again soon."

"Thank you for coming, today of all days," said Beth. "You made a bad day bearable."

Angelica took Beth by the hand and said, "It was a pleasure meeting you, and if you need anything at all, like someone besides a Scotsman to talk to, please don't hesitate to call." They all laughed and parted ways outside the restaurant.

BEFORE LEAVING, Angus and Angelica decided to drive around Shoestring. It was a charming town of about 12,000 people and, obviously, the people cared for it. The buildings were mostly turn of the last century and even the new construction reflected the Old World charm. Most of the stores were of the antique variety or were specialty shops with names like "The Century Shoppe" or "The Cat's Meow."

The tree-lined lanes just off the square laced the street with sunlight and shade, giving off an air of protection. The huge, white houses spoke of money, stability, and elegance. They passed by a bed and breakfast with tall Doric columns and a wrought-iron balcony on the second floor. The large sign in the front read "The Colonel's Bed and Breakfast," followed by the name of the proprietors, Steve and Jan Smith, with a number to call.

They parked in front of the B&B with the hope of looking inside. Motels were so impersonal, while the B&B gave a feel for the people and the history of the place and treated guests to a fine breakfast which had always been their favorite meal. When the boys were growing up, they would spend all Saturday morning fixing and eating a sumptuous feast.

Angelica went to the door and rang the bell. A small woman with an open face answered the door. She greeted them warmly and ushered them inside after Angelica had explained who they were and why they had come. Jan was more than happy to show them around, explaining the different rooms and their price structure.

Jan told them the history of the house. The huge home was built for a doctor, his wife, and their twelve children. He died soon after they had moved in, and she raised the brood on her own.

When the children had grown and gone, she sold the house. It had fallen into disrepair, until the Smiths moved to Shoestring from Houston, thus fulfilling their dream of running a bed and breakfast. They had seen it and fallen in love with it, Steve being a Texas history buff.

As they were leaving, Angus thought about something he had learned from his years of visiting congregations. If you want to find out about a church, ask other people in town what they know about it. You might get a new and different perspective from those of church members.

"Did you hear about the pastor's death?" he asked. "It must be awful for them and especially for his family."

"My Sarah goes to school with one of their boys," said Jan. "It's terrible. The church has really rallied around them, though. I have several friends who go there. They are all very upset." She placed her hand on her chest in an attempt to hold back the emotion bubbling beneath the surface.

"I don't know what to think," she said, tears welling. "We came here from Houston hoping to get away from all the crime and the filth. But it followed us here. I didn't know the Reverend well, but my friends tell me things weren't good in the church. It seems they were always fighting about something. I thought a church was supposed to be a place where people all got along."

"You'd think," Angus said.

"Thank you for showing us around." Angelica suddenly spoke up. "We will surely have to come back and stay with you sometime."

THEY LEFT and drove around the quaint little square, hoping to locate the police station. Before long they spotted a plain, dirty-blond brick building with a flat roof and a sign out front identifying it as the "James P. Conklin Police Station."

Three white police cars were parked out front with "Shoestring Police" painted in light blue letters on the side. Angus went inside and found a large room with several desks on one side and a wooden counter running the length of the room. A thin young woman dressed in a police uniform sat at one of the desks. When Angus came in, she stood up and asked if she could help him.

"I am Angus McPherson," he said, "and I'm looking for Chief Chavez."

"He's out fishing," she replied. "He'll be back in the office tomorrow morning."

Angus thanked her and got back in the car and reluctantly headed for home. They had wanted to wait and stay at the B&B, but their lives and obligations in other parts of the region beckoned to them.

Texas in the spring is, as they say, "a whole other country." Washington has its cheery blossoms, Atlanta has its peach trees, but Texas has bluebonnets. Seeing a field washed in blue as far as the eye can see is heaven on earth. Angus called it the eighth wonder of the world and was grateful to God he was able to witness it.

THE NEXT morning, Angus woke with a start. Trying not to wake Angelica he got up, stumbling in the darkness, searching the room. He swallowed hard and finally found the pen and paper. He had a dream to write down and interpret.

The mystery woman who called him was chasing Angus down a dark, wet alley. He tripped and fell. The woman looked down at him. She was smiling, holding a knife that gleamed from the light of a street lamp.

When Angelica awoke, he talked with her about the dream. "What do you think it means?" she asked, rubbing the sleep from her eyes.

"I guess I am afraid of something," replied Angus. "I didn't think I was afraid of the woman, but of 'them.' Maybe I am afraid *for* her."

"What do you mean?"

"She warned us this death was not an accident. She said 'they' were dangerous. Maybe she's afraid she'll be next."

"You're going to see the chief of police today, aren't you?" she asked.

"Aye, I am," he said.

Angelica smiled, and Angus thought, *Everything is going to be all right.*

THE OFFICE where Angus worked was like every other corporate office in Austin. Angus knew on which side of the debate between business and ministry the denominational hierarchy came down, just by looking at this austere building. He thought the church had long ago sold its soul to the "corporate model" and he did what he could, every now and then, to buy it back.

The one-story structure spread out like an octopus on what had recently been a field of wildflowers. The office where Angus worked was a mixture of Southwest and Scotland. Pictures on the wall were of Angelica and the boys, now grown and gone, and the place they called home. On another wall, a Celtic cross hung along with the family crest and diplomas from his college and seminary, and especially his Ph.D. in Psychology from UT.

Angus was proud to be the first in his family to go to college. His pride was not for his accomplishment, but for the sacrifices his mother had made to help him achieve his long-held, elusive goal.

His window looked out at a Wendy's and a Taco Bell and a few scant bluebonnets that defied urban encroachment. Underneath the window a small bookcase held a Bible, several phone books, a Presbytery directory, a Bible Dictionary, and a one-volume commentary on the Bible. Angus felt called to the work he was now doing, in large part because he always thought ministry, to be effective, must be shared. He resolved to be there for ministers because a minister had been there for him. In fact he owed one his life.

He still considered himself to be a parish pastor. He was never more alive than when he was in the pulpit preaching, even though it rarely happened now. His schedule did not always allow it; he nonetheless wanted to be prepared for the invitation.

"So what did you find out?" Francesca asked, as she brought him his first cup of coffee. They had had this argument before about who brought coffee to whom, and he knew now not to go there. She just liked doing it, so he let her.

"Not much," he said. "We got a strange message from a woman, but otherwise, it was a pleasant drive, good food, and a very troubled congregation. I need to call the chief of police and ask around a little more."

"Line one," she said smiling. "The Shoestring Chief of Police, line one," she said, pointing at the blinking light on the phone.

"But..."

"His name is Hector. Chief Hector Chavez."

"Hello," he said tentatively.

"Hello, Rev. McPherson," said Chief Chavez.

"Please call me Angus," he paused, confused. "Okay, I'm really sorry, but did I call you, or did you call me? My secretary just handed me the phone and said 'Here.'"

The chief laughed. "You called me."

"Sometimes my day starts before I get here, so I can't be too sure. It's hard to catch up."

"I often have days like that," said Hector, reassuringly. "What can I do for you?"

"I was wondering about the death of Rev. Anderson," Angus said. "He's one of ours, and I was curious what you've found out about it."

"As I told the news media, our preliminary investigation shows it was an accident."

"Well, I received a communication from someone who said Rev. Anderson's death was not an accident."

He wanted to tell the chief she also said something about a mysterious 'they,' but then thought better of it. He couldn't be sure why he refused to share this information. He needed to trust his instincts more, and this seemed a good place to start.

There was a pause.

"As a matter of fact, everyone around here considered this case closed," said the Chief. "But I'm willing to look into it a little more, especially in light of what you're telling me."

"Well, then, I'm glad I called." They both chuckled.

"Why don't you give me this woman's number so I can talk to her myself?" said Hector.

"I would be happy to," replied Angus. "But I called her back and the message said, '*This number is no longer in service.*' It could mean she's in trouble, or worried she will be, and so dumped the phone."

Angus gave him the number he had found on his cell phone.

"Thanks for this, uh... Angus," said Hector. "I'll see what I can find out about it. Even if it's out of service, I might be able to get a name. The longer we wait, the harder it will be to find out who did this, if your source is correct."

"Thanks, Chief," said Angus. He paused and then said, "Oh, uh... there's something else. The woman said something about 'they.' 'They' were responsible for this."

"It's interesting. But it could mean several things," said the Chief. "And none of them can be very good."

Chapter Three: A Recurring Nightmare

THE GRAY-HAIRED OLD man runs through the darkened, wet streets of Shoestring, splish-splashing as he goes. Frantically looking over his shoulder, desperate to get away from whoever is chasing him, he finds himself trapped on top of a church roof. He has nowhere to go. Finally, someone pushes him off the edge of the roof, and he falls.

Ben Irwin bolted upright in a cold sweat, eyes wide open. "The dream again," he said out loud, blinking and rubbing blood-shot eyes. "I can't shake this dream."

He got out of the lumpy, storm-tossed bed he had slept in for the last forty years. Ben was a thin man with white hair and mustache. He had yellowing, crooked teeth, and bleary, brown eyes. He lived above the drugstore on Main Street in a three-bedroom apartment.

He walked to the bathroom and wiped his face with a damp washcloth. He thought maybe if he went to work, even though it was early, it would take his mind off the awful dream.

He brushed his thick, bushy hair, and his crooked teeth, then got dressed. His gray coveralls hadn't been washed since he couldn't remember when. After his wife died thirteen years before, he'd lost all interest in hygiene.

He closed and locked the door. He knew he lived in a small town where safety was assumed, but the reoccurring nightmare left him nervous. Locking his door seemed a prudent precaution against the crazies he imagined out there.

His feet knew where he was going before he did. Down the stairs beside the drugstore, turn left, one block down on the left, open the door to the "Golden Fork," walk in, and take the first table to the right of the door by the window. He always ordered the same thing—oatmeal, whole-wheat toast and jam, with a cup of coffee, small orange juice, and tall glass of water. This was his routine, this was his life.

"Mornin', Ben," a waitress said from behind the counter. "You're early this mornin'."

"Yeah, I know, Ruthie," he said. "I didn't sleep so well."

Ruthie was in her late fifties, thick and sturdy, built like a redwood tree. Ben came here to breathe in Ruthie, bask in the tired glow of a woman who he knew cared for him, but dared not speak it for fear they would have to act on it. It was not worth risking their friendship.

"That ain't like you, darlin'," said Ruthie with a frown. "I hope nothin's wrong."

"No, no," he said. "I'm fine. I'll have toast and coffee. I'm not hungry."

"Now, I know somethin's wrong. A man don't change what he eats in ten years over nothin'."

"I'm fine, Ruthie. Now go get what I ordered, and quit your mothering."

"If I can't mother you, what's a girl to do?"

"I don't know, but I'm sure you'll think of something."

"You know, I couldn't deny you anything." And she was off to deliver the order to a man Ben had known almost as long as he had known Ruthie.

His name was Andy. Andy Reynolds. He was a big black man with a wide smile and a laugh as warm as a strong cup of coffee on a chilly morning. He was a master at the kind of fare Ben craved, and since Ben could not boil water, Andy was the next best thing to heaven.

Soon Ruthie came back with a pot of coffee and two creams, just the way Ben liked it.

"Have you heard about what happened at the church?" Ruthie looked around with a conspiratorial, secretive glance, not really trying to see if anyone was listening, but to include them if they were not.

"Yeah," said Ben. "I've heard, read the paper too. It seems everybody's talking about it."

"Ain't it thrilling?" she said, with her eyes as big as fifty-cent pieces.

"If you ask me, it's a whole lot of nonsense." His eyes flashed anger and frustration, something Ruthie had rarely seen.

"Why, Benjamin William, you old goat. If I didn't know better, I'd say you were angry." Ruthie was unflappable and tough as a rust stain on an old kitchen sink.

"Oh, it's all these blow-hards," he said, sweeping his hand around the café, "spouting off stuff they know nothing about."

"Guilty as charged, your honor," she said, straightening up, with her hand raised, as if taking an oath before sitting in the witness chair.

"Didn't mean you," he mumbled.

"Yes, you did, and it's okay. Most of these people don't have anything excitin' to get 'em out of bed in the mornin'. My only sunshine is thinkin' of seein' your ugly puss at the crack of dawn every day. So if the juiciest thing to hit this town in decades carries us away, well, then, I'm sorry. I'm sorry for the whole town."

"Okay, okay," he said, "I apologize to you and to the entire town for having an opinion. Please go ahead and talk." He waved his hand dismissively and took a sip of coffee, wincing at the heat of it.

"Do you want to get up and shout it to the rest of the place?" she asked, nudging him good-naturedly with a twinkle in her eye. "Let me go see how your order's doin'. And would you like a glass of 'whine' with that?" Her tone flattened into a mimicking whine. "I'll be back in a flash." She disappeared into the kitchen.

He looked down at his coffee, bubbles forming and dissolving on the side of the cup. This diner was the center of his universe. If he waited long enough, the whole world would pass through these doors. He did not have to budge, because everyone else would travel and come back and tell him about where they had been. And for Ben, the stories were much better than the places themselves. The meaning people gave to the places they had encountered is what produced the real flavor.

He had been married before, to the love of his life. They were high school sweethearts and married soon after graduation. They moved away from Shoestring to seek their fortune in Houston, where he found it in the oil fields. They moved back with three kids, two cars, and big dreams about building a house on a bluff overlooking the river.

Margaret died of breast cancer, and he raised their three children the best he could. Now they were grown and gone and living in Houston. He did not have much contact with them. When she died, the heart went out of their family. So he sold their dream home and made the move above the drugstore, which he also bought, just in case.

Ruthie came back with his toast and jam, sashaying like branches in the breeze, with the confidence of a woman in love.

"Here you go, darlin'." Even though she called all her customers 'darlin', she meant it when it came to Ben William Irwin.

"So, who do you think done it?" she asked, sitting down.

"Done what?"

"Why, killed the preacher is what."

"I didn't know it was murder," he said. "The building's so old it's bound to fall apart sooner or later. Like a lot of us old things around here."

"Boy, you are behind," she said. "You'd better catch up. They stopped calling it an accident almost before they dragged the body away. The head of their church in these parts–a foreigner–is helpin' Hector on this one. He's the one who said it wasn't no accident."

"That's all you have to go on?" he said. "The word of some foreigner?"

"Well, I heard the other pastor there had evidence she withheld from the chief," she said.

"About what?"

"I don't know. About how it wasn't no accident," she paused. "I don't believe in accidents anyway. I believe everything happens for a reason."

"I do too. Carelessness, shoddy work, old age, and wear and tear. Those are reason enough for me."

"Wear and tear?" she said, her voice getting more intense. "A cement cross fell on him, for God's sake!" She paused, put her hand to her mouth and smiled. "Sorry. Anyway, how in the world would it fall because of 'wear and tear'?"

"I don't know," he said.

"Anyway, I get off at 5:00 today. Want to do somethin' later, sailor?"

"Sure, Ruthie," he said smiling. "Come by the station, and I'll take you to Lockhart for some real food."

The bell rang from within the catacombs of the kitchen as Andy emerged from the shadows of the secrets inside. "Order up," he sang in his deep bass voice. "Hey, Ben, are you putting down my food? You know you don't have to eat here."

"Yes, Andy, it's me," said Ben, laughing. "I'd eat someplace else, but no other place would have me."

"Yeah, I guess we all have our crosses to bear," said Andy, shaking his head, returning to the secrets within the kitchen.

Ruthie stood, stuck out her hand and flashed him all five fingers, and mouthed the word "five," as she left to take an order to another hungry customer, leaves falling in her wake.

ANGUS GOT to Shoestring about noon, swung by the Paradise Café, ordered the best thing on the menu twice, and headed over to his office. The Chief's office stood out like a geek at a prom queen convention. Angus could tell this town took great pains to maintain its turn-of-the-century charm, but the Chief's office was just another ubiquitous blond box.

Hector Chavez, a young man of an impressive height with massive arms, dark hair, a bit of belly, and gray cowboy boots was sitting behind a standard-issue gray metal desk. The office was small and cramped, with a homey feel, nonetheless. Tacked to the cinder-block beige walls was a multicolored Mexican blanket with framed family pictures of an attractive woman and two small children—a boy of about six, frowning at the camera, and a girl in pigtails. On the opposite wall was a huge, small-mouth bass—about fifteen pounds, Angus guessed. A framed certificate from the Police Academy in Austin hung next to the fish.

Angus introduced himself, unpacked his offering, and they began to eat.

"They say," began Angus, "eating in your office is not good for your digestion or for your soul."

"You know," replied Hector, looking up with a glint in his eye, "you're right. Follow me."

Angus followed him down a long corridor out the back door and into the parking lot. They went down some steps to a park overlooking a little creek. Two picnic tables, a swing set, and a sad-looking neglected barbecue grill all looked like they hadn't been used in twenty years.

Angus and Hector set down the packages and heaved a collective sigh.

"This is more like it," said Hector, with a slow grin.

"So, I see you like to fish?" Angus started over again. "Where did you catch the lunker?"

"Yeah, there's a beautiful lake not far from here. Do you like to fish?"

"Yes, I do, but I go mostly for trout, and Texas is not known for its trout streams."

An awkward silence passed between the men who were not comfortable with small talk in the first place.

"I want to thank you for the information on the woman who called you," said Hector. "Of course, we don't know any more than we did before. We went over the evidence again—there wasn't much. I don't normally close a case so quickly, but it seemed so obvious to me. It is a ninety-year-old building, and there was a big crack in the cross already. There were some burn marks on it, and we're checking those out."

"We need to figure out who the woman is and what she knows," said Angus.

"Yes, we do," said Hector. "I'll let you know what we find out, if anything. I will reopen the case, though. That much is certain."

"I appreciate it, Chief," replied Angus. "Pete was a

friend of mine, and if I can help in any way, I want to solve this thing."

The Chief's eyes narrowed, regarding this tall, strange man. "Promise me three things, and I'll include you."

"Okay, what are they?"

"First, don't go off half-cocked, trying to solve it on your own. And second, when you find out something, let me know immediately."

"I will, Chief."

"And third, call me Hector."

Angus smiled, "Hector, it is."

"What can you tell me about the people in the church?" Hector asked.

"I know Pete and Beth, the Associate, pretty well. The rest are unknown to me." Angus paused. "What did you learn in your interviews?"

"We talked to Louise, the church secretary. She discovered the body and was pretty shaken by the whole thing. I think she knows more than what she told us. She was no help with possible suspects, which makes me suspect her."

"I'm headed there after we're done. I'll see what I can come up with."

"That'd be good."

"We talked to the wife. Again, not much help, and again, an iceberg."

"I've met Connie," said Angus. "She didn't seem cold to me."

"Not cold. There's more under the surface than what she shows."

"Did you learn that in your police training?"

"No, it's something my momma taught me."

"Your momma sounds like a wise woman."

"For a lot of my growing up years, my momma's street smarts were all we had to keep us going."

"Same here." The two men shook hands. Angus left, knowing he had made a new friend.

THE FIRST stop for Angus was the church, to talk to the secretary and the rest of the staff. As he swung his yellow Cherokee out of the parking lot onto the main street toward the church, he noticed the darkening clouds overhead. "Rain," he said. "We need it."

RAIN FELL the day his father died. It shocked him to remember it today. He died when Angus was thirteen, in a mining accident. His father was a distant, surly sort, but Angus loved him in spite of how he treated his mother. He remembered marking the day of the funeral as a day of freedom for her. His father had abused her terribly, and Angus had never forgiven him.

He remembered feeling guilty because he enjoyed his time with his father on the river, going after trout. He told his mother how he felt one day, and she told him not to worry. He did anyway.

Another of his dad's desires was travel. It was his dream to go to America. He had a cousin who lived in Texas, and he'd always wanted to go and visit him. When Angus did look him up, the cousin wanted nothing to do with him.

Angus worked in the mines in the summers during secondary school, and after he graduated, worked there full-time for two years. Then his mother succumbed to loneliness and a broken heart and died. Angus stayed with an aunt and went to university at night, working during the day. It was exhausting, impossible work, but he was determined. He carried weighty memories of both parents and always felt conflicted and unsettled about them.

He felt a call to ministry about then. His dad despised the church. Said it was for weaklings and cowards. Angus reasoned he said this because his mother was a devout Presbyterian.

He remembered the year before his father died when he was twelve. They had had a huge fight about his becoming confirmed in the church. His dad wanted nothing of it, but his mother won the argument, and he was confirmed along with several of his friends.

He remembered how alone he felt–the kind of alone you feel in a crowd of people who neither care for you nor know you are alive. Then he recalled saying a little prayer and a strange sensation coming over him. He knew what he had been doing was preparation for what was to come. He knew God had called him into the impossible work of ministry.

When he came to Texas years later on a mission trip to the Rio Grande valley, he decided he would stay. Only here did he feel free to be what God had called him to be. He went to seminary in Austin and then took a small church in Cuero.

He decided he wanted a further degree, so the church allowed him to pursue a Ph.D. in Psychology at The University of Texas. He chose psychology because of something his mother had said.

"I've always understood God," she said one winter in the living room of their tiny, soot-filled house, the fireplace blazing with the only heat available. "The real mystery to me has been people. I've never understood why people do what they do." He still had not figured people out. In fact the more he learned, the less he understood. But he did appreciate more and more the mystery of discovery.

ANGUS PULLED into the church parking lot and as he was about to get out of the car, he felt a thick, black fog creep across his brain. It scared him, so swift and thorough was its fury, as if he would be lost forever. He sat back in the seat, praying it would go away.

Chapter Four: Old Ghosts

THE RAIN FELL like daggers as he ducked for the cover of the large oak doorway of the church. As he ran he looked up and saw the hole where the cross had broken away from the front of the roof. He found a door and as he opened it, the sound was full of pain. A musty smell greeted him as he entered the dimly lit hallway. A glass case on one side had trophies from softball, volleyball, and bowling tournaments. There was nothing, Angus noted, after 1989. The floors were a dark brown vinyl with scuffmarks everywhere. He thought about an old adage among his colleagues in ministry, "The most impossible job in the church is not the pastor's, it's the custodian's." Nobody was satisfied with how clean a church should be. Now, he thought, it was as much an existential concern as it was a practical one. But it looked like the job was too much for the current custodian.

Then again, Angus guessed, *buildings grieve, too. But this one had been grieving for quite a while, by the looks of it.*

A plaque stuck out from the wall like a street sign. Below it an opaque glass window above the wood door indicated the church office. The doorknob looked 150 years old and as Angus opened it, the hinges creaked with age. He stepped inside.

He entered a large room with an "L-shaped" counter between him and two old desks, a copier, and a fax machine over by the window. A coffeepot sat on top of one of three rusty green filing cabinets, standing side by side like soldiers.

At one of the desks sat a woman in her early forties, with relaxed features. Angus noticed the look of grief about her as he stepped up to the counter.

"May I help you?" she said, not smiling, but pleasant.

"My name is Angus McPherson. I'm from the Presbytery Office," said Angus. "I would like to talk to you and Beth and members of your church about the unfortunate accident involving your pastor."

She looked down at her keyboard for a long second.

"I can't believe such a thing could happen to so wonderful a man. It is such a shock. No one can understand it." Tears wetted her lashes.

"It's hard to imagine." Angus shook his head, looking down. "Had you known him long, Miss ...?"

"My name is Louise, Louise Lassitor. Like I told the police, I have been the secretary here for seven years, seven good years. It's a shame they have to end this way."

"Are you leaving?" he asked.

"What's the point of going on?" she said wistfully. "Let the new pastor start fresh with a new secretary. All the old ghosts will be put to rest then."

"Old ghosts?" repeated Angus.

"Oh, quite a few old ghosts are wandering these halls, Reverend." Louise looked around as though she could see every one of them. "If these walls could talk, there would be a lot of embarrassed people with egg on their faces."

"What do you mean?" Angus asked with interest.

"Let's just say, I've seen things some people would not want spread around."

"Like what, for instance?"

Louise smiled and cocked her head to one side. "Oh, things they wouldn't want sung in any hymn, that's for sure."

"If you're leaving," Angus decided to change his tack, "what would you do?"

"I've been a church secretary for ten years, three years before I started here. Churches are always looking for good help."

"It sounds like you enjoy working in churches."

She shot him a quick glare, and then relaxed. "The work's not stressful, and I get to feel as though I'm doing something worthwhile with a bit of a challenge. And the pay is decent, although I wish I got benefits."

"So, you liked working here?"

"Pastor Pete was great to work for." She smiled for the first time. "Never a cross word, always very encouraging. He was always very...uh...passionate about his, um, work. It made it, you know, thrilling just to be around him."

"It sounds like you cared for him a great deal," said Angus.

"I did, very much," she said stiffly. "He was the best boss I ever had. The other people in the church, um, they could sometimes be pretty demanding. They'd sometimes give me stuff to do for a meeting that night. They never really appreciated me. But Peter was always respectful. We always worked so far ahead; getting everything done was a pleasure."

"Did someone in particular do that kind of thing?" he asked.

"Well, Tom Branch–he's the clerk of session–he'd do it all the time," she whispered. "It used to drive Peter to distraction."

"Thank you so much for being so open with me about all this. I see you're really hurting, and you cared very much for Pastor Pete. In fact, if I didn't know better...I'd say the two of you were more than close."

"How dare you say such a thing! He had a wife and children. I respected that man more than anyone on this planet. I would never do such a thing, compromise his standing in the community. He could have been fired for something like that."

"Sounds like you've given this a lot of thought," said Angus, reaching over the counter to give Louise a tissue. "I'm sorry if I've hurt you, but the police need all the information they can get if they're going to find out who did this." He pulled out his business card and set it in Louise's quivering, outstretched hand. "I understand that you cared for Peter a great deal. If you'd like to talk some more, or if you think of anything else, please let me know."

Louise looked at the card and then back to Angus. "Please don't tell Connie or anyone at church if you don't have to."

Angus looked calmly at this frail, trembling bird. "Don't worry; your secret is safe with me, Lass." He touched her shoulder. "I wonder if Beth is around so I could talk to her too."

BETH MCKINLEY was a native New Yorker whose clipped speech was twenty times faster than any Texan could expect to hear or understand. She was short and nicely proportioned. Beth had the look of one who ran track in college, and continued to run because it made her feel better. Her blond, perky good looks were matched with serious blue eyes. She had been the associate here for three years, but was yearning for something else, something more. Angus knew she was thinking about going back to Princeton for a Ph.D. so she could teach in a seminary.

Today she wore a blue jeans dress and red, long-sleeved blouse, with a white belt. She looked like she was headed for a square dance on the Fourth of July. Something happens to people who come to Texas unprepared. *In Texas, you either become very real, or you become a caricature of what you think the culture requires,* Angus thought.

Her office was a smallish space–white walls, tall ceiling, with a ceiling fan suspended and slowly turning. The desk took up most of the space with diplomas on the wall from New York City College and Princeton Seminary.

She was a collector of angels. Angels of all types and descriptions festooned every crevice and corner in the cramped space. She was single, so there were no family pictures except one. There was a picture of her and her black lab, wearing a red bandana. When people are infected with the disease, even animals are not immune.

"Hello, Beth," said Angus. She was seated at her desk, typing on her computer. "I see we're very patriotic today."

"Oh, this," she said, looking down. "I have to go to the Senior Center today, and I thought this might be a fun outfit to wear for them, get 'em talking."

"Excellent idea." There was a slight pause. "How are you holding up after what happened?" asked Angus. He smiled at what someone might think, listening to them together for the first time. Her clipped New York banter and his Scottish brogue made a strange brew of speech.

"I guess I don't know what to feel," admitted Beth. "It all happened so suddenly, none of us have had a chance to process any of it."

"I thought you did an excellent job with the congregation on Sunday," said Angus. "I know that wasn't easy, but you did it well."

"Thanks, Angus." Beth smiled broadly. "That means a lot, coming from you."

"I mean every word," Angus said. "You know, no one would object if you took some time off. You'll need it."

"I actually thought about it," she said, "and the session recommended it, but I really think they need me now more than ever. At least until we get some distance from this horrible thing. But later, yeah, I'd like to take a break."

"Well, you know best," he said. Then after a slight pause, "What can you tell me about Peter's death?"

"Just what I told the police. I didn't know about it until Louise came rushing in here to tell me what had happened."

"Then what did you do?"

"I went to look for myself."

"What did you see?"

Beth opened her middle desk drawer and pulled out a church stationary envelope marked "cloth." She handed it to Angus. He opened it and saw a piece of black fabric. It seemed to be a blend, the kind worn in a suit, smooth to the touch. Angus rubbed it between his thumb and forefinger.

"Where did you get this?" Angus asked.

"It was lying next to the body, I'd say a few feet away," she said. "I know what you're thinking. You're thinking 'Why didn't you leave this for the police?' You're thinking I'm withholding evidence. I watched *Matlock* growing up; I know that much."

"I'm thinking that same thing exactly." Angus's voice was strained.

"I'll take it to them. I knew you'd be here soon, and I wanted you to see it first."

"Why?" He knew the answer before she'd said it. But he'd learned it helps people heal when they supply their own answers. Although, at times–like now–this holding back was the hardest work he did.

"Well, it obviously belongs to a piece of clothing torn during the fall. I checked the body, and there was no torn cloth. So Pete was killed, and this must be from the killer's clothing."

"That's all the more reason to take it to the police." He started to press her. "If it belongs to the killer, he could have burned or destroyed the garment by now. If you had given it to them, they might have had something to go on."

"But what if it belongs to one of the members?"

Bingo, thought Angus. "You were hoping to protect the church from any adverse publicity?" Angus said.

"Well, yes, if this got out, it would damage the church's reputation for years," she pleaded.

"Well, Beth, it's too late. It's already gotten out," said Angus. "We talked to the owner of a bed and breakfast in town, and she's talking about it. And if she is, rest assured there are others. Besides, you know it's impossible to keep something this sensational quiet in a small town."

"Oh, I know," she said, crestfallen. "I guess I wasn't thinking too clearly."

"I remember once when I was a wee lad," smiled Angus, lapsing into his brogue. "Me ma' came down with a cold, a measly cold, mind, and the next day all me mates were sayin' how sorry they were me ma' was sick. And it was just a cold."

Angus paused. "What damage it will do will be done. But what you must not do is stop the truth from coming out. I'll take this to the police, and I'll have to tell them where I got it."

"Of course you will. I see it was a stupid thing to do," she said. "I want to know who did this just as much as anyone, maybe more."

"I know you do," said Angus. "I just hope the chief doesn't press charges against you for withholding evidence."

"The police have been saying all along this was an accident," she said.

"Evidence is evidence, Beth. And besides, this is quickly moving from an accident to something else."

"Why, what else do you know?" she asked.

Angus reminded her about the phone call from the strange woman, and Angus' discovery of a discontinued phone number. Then they talked about how things were going in the church, how upset everyone was, and how anxious they were to put all this behind them.

Angus agreed to meet with the session in the evening. He also asked for the address and phone number of the pastor's widow.

A GROUP of people met that afternoon at the church in a rather plain room with a magnificent mahogany table at its center. Greg Lathrop was there as a representative from the Committee on Ministry to help the leaders make decisions about the future of the church. They had already started when Angus entered the room and sat quietly in a chair next to the wall.

Jim Williams was the first to stand up. "Angus, good of you to come; please sit at the table with us."

"Please don't let me disturb you," said Angus, moving his chair closer to the table.

"I was just telling them some of the things they'll have to do in order to get an interim in here, and then begin to find a permanent pastor," said Greg.

"I don't see why we can't save some money and let Beth take the helm," said Tom Branch. "She's very capable, and it won't be forever."

"Of course, she's very capable," said Greg, looking sternly at Tom. "But it's not fair to her or to you. She needs help to run a church like this, and you will need an experienced hand to guide you through these rough waters."

"I agree with Greg," said Angus. "It will be worth your while to find someone else to shepherd you through this time."

The others nodded in reluctant agreement.

"Okay, okay," said Tom, throwing up his hands. "I know when I'm out numbered."

Angus thought, *This room feels oppressively heavy. Is it just me?* As the evening wore on, he determined it wasn't just him. *This room is filled with old ghosts,* he thought.

Chapter Five: None of Us Is Safe

ANGUS WAS AGITATED and distracted as he drove home. He was exhausted from the long, trying day and the equally long and difficult trip home. He wouldn't get home until after midnight and would have to turn right around and do this all over again, bright and early in the morning. He remembered the Greek myth of Sisyphus who was cursed to push a boulder up a hill only to have to roll it down the other side, and then start the process all over again. Work takes over, he figured, one way or another.

But still, he loved what he did, and he loved his life. He loved Angelica and how she made him feel. He loved his three sons, and was as proud of them as any father could be. And, most of all, he loved God. God was the reason he was able to do all this. There was no explaining how real, how tangible, how connected he was to this divine presence in his life. Oh, sure, he'd preached about it, but people would come out of church, say 'nice sermon, Reverend,' and they would not have a clue what he meant, or what he was talking about. Nowhere in his life had he felt the comfort, acceptance, correction, and challenge as he felt with Jesus.

But there was the paradox. Only if you had this kind of relationship with the divine would you be able to understand it. Which is why Angus had chosen this work. He wanted everyone to have the kind of relationship with this "Holy Other" as he did. The one person he wanted most to share it could not—his dad. Whenever he was sad or grieving, his thoughts inevitably turned to his father.

As he pulled up the gravel drive to their home, he saw the light on in their bedroom window. He imagined how Angelica had tried to wait up for him. She had gone to the bedroom to read a book, but the book got heavier and heavier, as did her eyelids. And soon she would be fast asleep. This process never took long, only about ten minutes. But it made Angus smile at the thought of what she'd tried to do.

The jeep followed the gravel around the back of the house to the garage and drove in slowly. He was so tired it was as though he was not in control of the vehicle. He knew the first animal to greet him would be Eve, their young, yellow Lab, followed by Adam, the gray fifteen-year-old short-hair cat. Eve was still just a puppy and still learning the ways of the house. Adam was all too eager to teach her.

Adam was the most intelligent creature Angus had ever met. It was not just what he did, it was in his eyes. Adam knew so much more than anyone could ever imagine. As Angus made his way from the utility room to the den, he saw what his pets had been doing. Adam had taken the shirts and towels from the clothes hamper and spread them all over the house. He used them for pillows wherever he felt like resting.

Eve left some of her gifts spread throughout the room. Torn up boxes, shredded newspapers, and cereal cartons greeted Angus as crunches on the carpet. He cleaned up the mess, all the while wondering why they'd got this new nuisance in their life, but glad for it nonetheless. As he made his way to the bedroom, it was just as he had thought. Angelica had her glasses just barely on her face, her head back resting on the pillow, the book on her lap, breathing the breath of sleep. Angus took her book and glasses and placed them gently on the nightstand. He got ready for bed, climbed in, and then reached over his lady in repose and shut off the light.

The dawn came too early for Angus. As was his custom, he punched the snooze button several times to get a few extra minutes, but this never did any good. He never really got any extra sleep once the alarm first went off. All it did was prolong the inevitable. He made coffee, fed the animals, and looked in on the llamas in their pen, and then he meditated. He decided he did not have time to go for his walk on this chilly morning. There were just some things he did not feel like doing. Besides he had to be on the road soon if he was going to make Shoestring by ten o'clock.

He showered and dressed, and then took Angelica a cup of coffee. She stirred in their king-sized bed, stretched and turned toward him. Her hair was tossed to one side. She looked at him through half-opened eyes and smiled a dreamy smile.

"Mmm, you smell nice," she said, kissing him.

"All the better to have my way with you," he smiled.

"Yeah, right," she laughed, drinking her coffee. "You were working late last night."

"Yeah, I met with the session." He sipped his own coffee.

"What do you think?" she asked expectantly.

"I don't know what to think. I don't know about Pete's family. Something is strange there. Beth says she has a list of folks who had it out for Peter. She wants to go over it today after the funeral. Then I'll meet with the chief again.

It promises to be another full day, and I probably won't get back until late again."

"I'll keep the light on for you," she said. "Let me get a good look at you, so I can remember what you look like."

They stared into each other's eyes for a long minute, and then Adam jumped on the bed and rubbed against Angelica's bent knee. She petted him, and his purr filled the room.

Angus rose from the bed. "I haven't been in the office for two days. Franny is not a happy camper."

"I give you permission to buy her some flowers," Angelica offered, smiling. "Your women need some attention paid to us to keep us happy."

"I'll tell her you said that."

As he stood up he saw a green chef's apron on the floor with the words "Have you hugged a Presbyterian today?" emblazoned across the front in white letters. Angus held it up to show Angelica, "Look what the cat dragged in." They laughed. "I've always wanted to say that."

"Adam wants you to protect yourself," said Angelica. "And so do I."

"Aye, I will, I will." Angus nodded. He came over to Angelica's side of the bed, sat next to her, and kissed her tenderly. "If I'm going to get there before the funeral, I'd better get going. You have an interesting day, and maybe we can do something fun this weekend."

"How would you like to go canoeing down the Pedernales?" she asked. "I think Michael will be free this weekend. Maybe he could join us."

"What a great idea! We could make a whole day of it, shore lunch and all."

Angelica gave a dreamy nod and turned over and fell fast asleep.

INSTEAD OF BREAKFAST, Angus had decided to fast. He did it once in college and once with the youth group in Cuero. He made a choice about this when he was on spiritual retreat last year. The director of the retreat had suggested Protestants do not know how to pray, and when significant events occur in our lives, we need to find meaningful ways to mark them. He decided he could give up food for one day out of respect for a fallen colleague.

He made a call as he was getting in his Jeep for the long trip to Shoestring.

"Franny, Angus. Sorry to call you at home."

"It's okay, Boss," said Francesca, wiping sleep from her eyes.

"I'm on my way to Peter's funeral," he said, "and I'm going to be at Shoestring all day again. I'll be in the office tomorrow, I promise."

"I'm glad you called," she said. "Aside from hearing your wonderful voice, you had two calls; one from the chief. He said something about a phone number you gave him. The other was kind of strange. She asked for you, but wouldn't give a number where she could be reached. She just said it was urgent."

"How can I reach her if I have no number?"

"The mystery of the ages, my captain," Francesca mused with a slight edge.

"I guess I'll have to wait for her to call me. It's funny, but she has my cell phone number, so why didn't she call me?" He thought about one of the persistent challenges of ministry–waiting. He would sew a seed in the minds and hearts of people, and then would have to wait to see if the idea would bear any fruit. Most of the time it did not. But it didn't stop him from throwing the seed out, trying to water it, and waiting to see if anything came of it.

"Another mystery," she said. "Maybe she didn't want to bother you at home over the weekend."

"Yes," he said, "but if it's as urgent as she said, she wouldn't worry about bothering me."

"Well, I'll run the office, and you attend to the mysteries of the universe. Frankly, I like my job a whole lot better than the one yours is shaping up to be."

"Thanks, Franny. I'll see you tomorrow. Take care of yourself."

"I will if you will."

"I'll be fine."

They talked about the finance meeting scheduled for in the morning. Bryan Reynolds was the treasurer. Angus always had a love/hate relationship with "bean counters." He admired the organization and head for details Bryan was blessed to possess. Bryan was a good friend who took the financial problems of the Presbytery personally, and did not hold Angus personally responsible. Angus understood the collective nature of the "business"—he hated how the word was applied to ministry—but could not seem to avoid it. He could, however, put it off until tomorrow. *Let today's trouble be enough for today,* he thought. *So the Bible says, but it still is news.*

His cell phone rang just as he was turning onto the main road to Shoestring. He answered it.

"If you don't act quickly, another person may soon be dead."

Angus applied the brakes, jerking the Jeep to the side of the road. A mixture of anger and dread flowed through his veins like lava.

"I tried to call you, and your number had been disconnected."

"It's not safe. I'm not safe. None of us is safe."

"Why won't you let me help you?" pleaded Angus. "I can't help you if you don't tell me your name."

There was a long pause. "Maureen, Maureen Sullivan.

I'm taking a huge risk trusting you. If I'm dead tomorrow, it will be on your conscience. There is no stopping them."

"Who are 'they'?" asked Angus. "And how do you know them?"

"Look...these last five years have been hell. If I don't play this just right, I could be in a lot of trouble. And one thing I've learned over the years is how to survive."

"But that's all the more reason to go to the police—"

She hung up.

HECTOR CHAVEZ arrived at his office by 7:30 in the morning. He could not sleep. Murder was not something he could get used to in his quiet little town. He had grown up here, raised his kids, and had many friends and a big family around him for support. He felt grounded here. His parents had come here as domestics and day laborers, and they liked it. He liked it too.

He got the idea of running for chief of police from his uncle who always talked about the opportunities in this country.

"*Hijito,*" he said. He always called him 'little son' even after Hector was a grown man. "The only opportunity we had back home was to be poor and a nobody. Here we may also be poor and a nobody, but at least you have the chance to change if you believe it hard enough."

When he was a child, Hector believed him with all his heart. But as he grew up, he started to see what this country could do to people who looked like him, especially his father. His father was only five feet six inches tall with a huge heart. He was generous beyond his means, which meant he was often in debt. But all it got him was a clear conscience. His dad was worn out and used up by the time he was 60. They said he died of a heart attack, but Hector knew he had died of a broken heart.

So for those reasons, the promise and the pain this country caused him, he decided to dedicate himself to upholding its laws. He had been on the ten-member police force for twelve years when the previous chief was about to step down.

It was Buzz's idea for him to run. He remembered the time like it was last week. It was a rainy day, and they were having lunch in the chief's office. Buzz was a large man with balding hair and a thick handle-bar mustache.

"Hector, you really like this stuff, don't you," he said.

"Well, my mother made the best chicken salad in the world, but yeah, I do get this a lot," Hector said, looking at his sandwich.

Buzz laughed his deep belly laugh. When Buzz laughed the whole station shook. Mirth just bounced off the walls.

"I meant the work," he said. "You are the first one here and the last one to leave. You're always coming up with ways to save money, be more effective. And if there is something to investigate, like the kid's disappearance, you are like a bloodhound."

Last year, a child was taken from the school. Hector interviewed the family and the mother. She had divorced the year before. No one knew where the father was. But Hector got his last known address and interviewed the neighbors and his ex-con buddies until he found him in New Mexico with the child. It was a first-rate piece of detective work.

"The only thing I don't know," said Buzz, "is if you can handle the politics."

"You mean, in your job?" Hector asked.

"That's exactly what I mean," said Buzz. "I know somebody who's looking to help get somebody elected, and he wanted me to pick him. I think you're the guy. But can you stand the politics?"

It was true; he did not care much for running for office. While he did meet many wonderful people who made his job so much easier now, dealing with the inter-departmental headaches, the mayor and the city council, and the state board were a pain. But he had learned to take those things in stride. He even had gone fishing with the mayor a couple of times. While Hector cared for all the people in Shoestring, he could not say the same about all the politicians.

HE COULD think of little else besides the murder. He reviewed the evidence in his mind. There was the murder weapon—a cross, no less. The victim's hair and blood were on it, and some trace residue of something, maybe an explosive. There was the piece of torn cloth, but it did not tell Hector much of anything. He and his men had combed the area thoroughly and found nothing. They had interviewed people in the neighborhood and found no witnesses. He had thought about calling the Feds in to help, but that was an avenue of last resort.

He was staring at the ceiling, running through all this in his mind when Max, the desk sergeant, popped his head in the door to tell him he had a call on line one.

"Hello, Chief, this is Angus McPherson. I'm on my way to Shoestring for Peter Anderson's funeral."

"Yes, I'm running escort duty for the procession to the cemetery, so I'll see you then; and I understood you wanted to see me afterward?"

"Aye," said Angus. "I have some more evidence. Well, it's not evidence as much as it is Beth's hunches about who might have it out for the Pastor. I wanted to go over some of this with you."

"First she holds out with the piece of cloth, and now she doesn't tell me she suspects several people," said Hector. "I've got to have a serious talk with her."

"I told her the same thing. I assure you, we want to cooperate with your investigation one hundred percent."

"I'm sure you do."

"But that's not why I called, Chief."

"Oh, what's up?"

"Well, the mystery woman called again. She told me there was more to this than meets the eye."

"Then what?"

"She just hung up on me again. She was able to tell me her name this time. Maureen Sullivan."

"Did she say where she was from?"

"No, I was lucky to get her name. Whatever she's seen, it's frightened her pretty badly. She said again how there seems to be some kind of conspiracy, and how her life is in jeopardy. She was very reluctant to give me her name, but I think she recognized I was her last best hope to get help. I certainly hope you can find her in time."

"Me, too, Reverend," said Hector, "me, too. Did you get her number? I mean I know you tried to call her before and the number was disconnected."

"Please, call me Angus, and no, I didn't get her new number. Nor did I find out why she had disconnected the other number."

"It's all about being scared, I guess, Angus," said Hector. "It's amazing what you'll do when you're scared."

"It's also amazing what drives one person to want to kill another."

"Aye, Hector, it is."

Chapter Six: Eating with the Dead

HECTOR KNEW HE had some time before the funeral, so he ran the name Angus had given him, Maureen Sullivan, through the system. He found her address in Lockhart, some twenty miles away from Shoestring. He decided he would drive out there rather than call the local law. *There's no crime in looking,* he smiled to himself. It was much better to see how and where a person lived than to just imagine who they were over the telephone. After he had time to check out this first real lead in the case, then he would stop by and see the sheriff of Caldwell County.

Hector hated the telephone anyway. Silvia, his wife, could not stop talking on the thing, which was only one of the reasons he detested it. The telephone limited him too much. He could not size a person up just by talking to a disembodied voice. He could not see through the phone whether someone was nervous, or sweating, or agitated, or refused to look him in the eyes. Body language said so much more than words when trying to find the truth. The telephone hid those things from view, making his job all the harder.

The risk was not finding her at home. In fact the odds were good she would not be there. Still it was a chance worth taking. At least he could check out where and how she lived.

He might also be able to talk to the neighbors, but he would not do so until he had cleared it with Bill Person, Lockhart's sheriff, a good man, and a fine friend.

Besides, the trip would do him good. Lockhart had one of the prettiest courthouses in these parts. He loved any excuse to go see the late nineteenth-century Victorian structure. He was sad that Shoestring lost its courthouse to fire in the fifties. They replaced it with a futuristic art deco building; however, not the "future" Hector had hoped to see.

He made the drive easily enough, and was able to clear his mind of all distractions, as he enjoyed the Texas countryside—especially marveling at the sumptuous bluebonnets. Hector started getting an uneasy feeling as he was getting closer to where Maureen should be living. She had an address on the "other side" of town, where the houses were more run-down. He could tell there was a definite change as the colors went from bright yellow and green to gray and brown. In the best sections, each house had a distinct personality. In the worst sections, where he was traveling, all the houses had a dreary, depressing sameness.

However, something was different about Ms. Sullivan's address at 2217 Archer Street. A small ranch-style house built from the ubiquitous South Texas blond brick, the landscaping was meticulous and obviously well cared for. Two huge live oak trees graced the front lawn, standing sentinel on either side of the front walk. They cast large shadows that darkened the house.

Hector looked inside a window. What he saw there was the same care and order he witnessed on the outside, with a definite feminine touch.

Hector rang the doorbell and heard its sound roll around the interior like an echo through a canyon. A small calico cat came into the living room, leaped onto the coffee table in front of the couch, and meowed.

"A cat person," he said out loud and smiled.

Hector walked around the house. A chain-link fence bordered a big back yard with several pecan trees and one hackberry. He also saw a clothesline and an unattached one-car garage which had seen better days. Hector guessed it had not seen a coat of paint in fifty years. The window on the side was broken, and the shrubs around it were dead. It was as if two different people lived here. Hector didn't know which one he was looking for or which one he would find.

HECTOR DECIDED to stop by the Sheriff's office to see his old buddy, Bill Person. Bill's office was sparse and functional. Except for his official title, nothing in this office told a casual observer who he was. Bill himself was short, fat, and open. A quick smile, a flash of teeth, and a short hand greeted Hector as he walked into the office.

"How are you, old buddy?" Bill asked. "Long time, no see. What's it been, two, three years?"

"Not that long," Hector smiled back, "has it? It's only been a year or two."

"Oh, well, that's better," Bill said, motioning Hector to sit down. "My, how time flies..."

"How are things with you and yours?" Hector asked.

"Rebecca is six, just starting school, and spells everything in sight." Bill beamed. "Cody is four, just broke his arm chasing his sister on his new tricycle. He'll be fine. And Hannah is still teaching the little bastards, believe it or not."

"I can't believe it," Hector said. "My Maria is twelve going on twenty, and Jorge is nine going on five. Silvia is still working at the plant. Things are good."

"I'm glad, partner, I am," Bill said, indicating if he'd like a drink which Hector declined. "What brings you to these parts?"

"You heard about Pete Anderson's death?" he asked.

"Yeah, who hasn't?"

"Well, what looked like an accident is turning out to be something else all together," Hector said.

"How do you know?" Bill asked.

"Well, this minister, a fella named Angus McPherson, had a woman tell him there was more to this than meets the eye. I ran the name, and she's here in Lockhart. I checked her place out, but I didn't see anything. I didn't think you'd mind."

"Not at all, but I'm glad you told me about her," said Bill. "Who is she?"

"Maureen Sullivan. She lives at 2217 Archer Street. Does that ring any bells?"

"I can't say I've heard the name, but the address is in the rough part of town. Not a pleasant place to live."

"Yeah, that's the impression I got, Bill. But the strange thing is, the place doesn't look like it belongs there. It's so neat and well maintained."

"That's the thing about this town, there's a palace parked right next to a dump. Neighborhoods kind of blend together here. It's the strangest thing. It makes it easier for redevelopment, I guess."

"Yeah, I guess," said Hector. "Anyway, would you keep an eye out for her? I really need to talk to her."

"You bet, partner. But do you really think she'll come back if she knows people are looking for her?"

"I hope she'll realize you and I are her only hope of staying alive, if she's as worried about her safety as she seems to be."

"People do dumb things all the time. How else do you think we make our living? I'll keep my eyes peeled for her."

Hector looked at the clock, which read 9:15.

"Thanks," Hector said. "I've got to go, or I'll be late for my own funeral."

Bill laughed. "We can only hope."

BEN WILLIAM hated God. He never said anything to anyone about it, least of all to Ruthie. It was his private little crusade. He figured he would do what he could to further the cause; take his opportunities where he could.

This hatred he felt was not a disinterested theoretical kind of hate. This was no "death of God" debate on a college campus somewhere. This was murder. Ben wanted Him dead. But there was nothing, no one to kill.

"When you took my Annie," Ben said out loud, looking up, "there was no reckoning. Who brings you to justice? Who can handcuff you and drag you off to rot in the slammer? What judge, all dressed in black, will gavel you to silence and pass sentence on you? I know it's been ten years, but an Irwin never forgets."

He thought too about Ruthie. He knew he would have to put those thoughts to rest if he ever hoped to make a life with her. Someday.

He was putting new brake shoes on a 1990 Taurus. The shoe would not fit, and he tried to force it. His hand slipped, he cut himself, and blood began to pour out the cut.

"Dammit!" he said.

ANGUS ARRIVED at the church about an hour before the funeral. He found Beth and checked in with her. She was a nervous wreck.

"I hate to preach," she confessed. "That's why I became an associate. I like working with little kids and old ladies, but preaching. Ugh!"

"You'll do fine," Angus said.

"Oh, I'll do fine," she said. "I just hate doing it."

"Me da' once said, 'The hen don't like lay'n eggs, but they sure do taste good.'" His brogue was as thick as tar on a swindler's backside.

"And what is that supposed to mean?" she asked, with an edge of sarcasm.

"I don't have any idea, I just made it up, and besides, it made you smile."

The telephone rang, and Beth answered it. It was Louise, telling her the funeral home people had arrived with the body. Beth could hardly understand her through her constant sobs. Beth knew Louise needed some time off to get herself together. Beth needed some time too. But now she was in charge, and there was no time. The time was always now. She was the 'head of staff' until they found an interim. Everyone looked to her for stability and guidance, and both were in short supply. It was certainly more than she had bargained for.

She went to the sanctuary to talk to the funeral director about the service and the placement of the flowers. In the Presbyterian Church, the one rule about flowers was that they should not display "undue ostentation." Beth loved the phrase, and thought it was the right note to strike, but in this culture, especially in the face of a mysterious, violent death, ostentation is the first refuge of people with lots of money and little taste.

Flowers festooned the front of the sanctuary, dwarfing the cross and hiding the communion table. There were more flowers than seemed possible or necessary. How else could people show their grief and support those who suffered loss? Beth knew Peter would have preferred having the money spent on charity, such as the thrift shop he wanted to start. She had let the church know this was his request, but still the flowers came. Nobody much wanted the thrift shop, but nobody would object to flowers.

"Why don't we keep only a few of these up front?" said Beth. "Put some in the narthex, let Connie take some home with her, and send the rest to the nursing home for those folks to enjoy."

Clive Sorrel nodded, touching the knot on his thin yellow tie. "That's what we'll do," he said, thinking about taking back all those flowers, but Beth was in charge.

A THIN, serious-looking woman came into the sanctuary. She was statuesque, but bookish. She made her way up the back steps to the organ.

"Oh, Judith is here," Beth chirped to Angus. "Come with me, I want you to meet her." Angus followed close behind Beth as they ascended the steps. Judith was getting the instrument ready to play.

And what a grand instrument it was. The sixteen-rank pipe organ was as old as the building itself, but completely redone, thanks to Peter.

He had been a fine preacher, and only passable at pastoral care. But where he had really shone was in raising money. If not done correctly, asking for monetary gifts could create a lot of enemies. Some people felt squeezed, no matter how tactfully one asked them to share their bounty. Peter had been involved in fundraisers for Rotary and the city as well, so asking people for money came second nature to him. All of his colleagues seemed to recognize and appreciate his gift in this often thankless area. Well, almost all.

"Hello, Judith," chimed Beth. "I'm glad you could make it. This is Angus McPherson, the Presbytery Executive. He'll be saying a few words today too."

"Do you have an order of service?" Judith asked, shaking Angus's hand. Beth produced a sheet of paper out of her Bible and handed it to Judith, who looked it over and nodded.

"Looks good. The family didn't want to sing a hymn or anything?"

"I tried to talk them into it," said Beth. "Singing at a time like this is so...therapeutic. Some of the Gospel hymns straight from the black slave songs, for instance, give such gracious voice to grief that we take wing and fly..."

"Yes, yes," interrupted Judith. "But what do they want?'

"They want 'Amazing Grace' and 'For All the Saints' played but not sung. And Mary Beth is doing a solo, "Ave Maria" before the service starts. It was Peter's favorite."

"And you didn't think to tell me all this?" asked Judith. "It would have been good to let me know. I haven't played 'Ave Maria' in months. And you expect me to accompany her? She is so unpredictable; you never know what she's going to do."

"Oh, Judith, I am so sorry," pleaded Beth. "Things have been just crazy around here since Pete's death, and you're so professional. You spoil me, I mean 'us.'"

"Yes, yes, of course," said Judith. "I know. But next time..."

"Of course, of course, Judith," said Beth. "Again, I am so sorry."

"Don't think another thing about it." Judith frowned.

As Angus and Beth were leaving to return to her office, Beth leaned over to Angus and said, "That went well." They both laughed.

THE TIME for the funeral had come, and Angus was not surprised to find the place packed. Especially noteworthy were all the ministers who showed up. *When one of their own falls, they come out of the woodwork*, he thought.

Judith played the organ with grace and power. Mary Beth sang haltingly but got through it, and Beth's words were comforting even to the ears of a war-weary, crusty old man like Angus. She used the story of Cain and Abel, concentrating on the part about Abel's blood crying out from the ground where it had spilled. "God's care for us is so great," she said. "Even blood spilled against us has a voice. It will be heard. Justice will be done, and God will be satisfied. We can find comfort there."

Thunderclouds rolled in during the service like a horde of thugs on hogs, gathering for some mean and nasty trouble. The air was so thick you could wear it like a scratchy wool coat. Then the rains came and came. Worshipers huddled in the narthex at the back of the church as crowded as cattle around a feed trough, with wary eyes glued to the heavens.

At the conclusion of the service, Beth invited them to the graveside service, and then to the Anderson's home for a meal. As they filed out of the sanctuary, Angus noticed Bonnie Anderson and her little brother Andy coming down the aisle, arm in arm. Angus smiled. Rain often came without warning in Texas and with violence. For now, Angus was not worried either about the weather or about the Anderson children.

Hector pulled up in the squad car, the rain pounding the roof like tom-toms. He reached into the back seat for a slicker and struggled into it. Clive Sorrel came up to Angus.

"I've got another funeral at 11:30," he said, looking at his Rolex. "I don't want to rush us here, but what would a little rain hurt?" Angus thought of Noah's Ark, but didn't say anything.

"I'm not the one you need to talk to," he said, pointing at Beth. "She's in charge."

Beth's face flushed red. "Yes, yes. Yes, of course," she said. "What would it hurt?"

Just then Hector came in the door and shook like a shaggy dog. Beth came up to him and said, "We'll get the family in the cars, and whoever wants to join us may do so. Maybe by then, the rain will let up."

"That's fine," said Hector, looking at Angus. "We'll go real slow."

Clive found the family after getting umbrellas from the lead car and shepherded them to the white Cadillac limousines standing at attention outside the sanctuary door. Beth's blue Honda came after the hearse, followed by the family car. Others fell in behind them. Angus rode with Beth.

The funeral procession was a sight to behold. Cars stretched off into the horizon like a multicolored snake slithering through the countryside. Traffic had to be stopped at every intersection; that was Hector's job. Especially on long processions, sometimes cars lagged behind and got into an accident.

It sounded like an old joke. "How'd he die?" "He was driving to a funeral." But it wasn't.

Some cities did away with the procession, but then the graveside service would often be over by the time many of the mourners arrived. They would also miss out on the deviled eggs back at the house of the bereaved. Deviled eggs were always the first to go.

"I can't imagine going to Connie's house after this," said Beth, squinting into the rain-drenched windshield. "The thought of eating after burying a loved one has always seemed barbaric to me."

"I've always found it curious. People don't know how to act around the dead or those who are bereaved. So put a glass in one hand and a fork in the other to give them something to do."

"But it just seems so...insensitive."

"Well, it's been around for many years. It's called eating with the dead. Our ancestors used to do it, believing they got strength from their dead loved ones. They also did it to send them off into a better life. The size of the spread went a long way toward ensuring the departed a better place in the next life."

"It always comes down to power. Is there a connection between that and communion?"

"Aye, I think so," said Angus. "Remember how Paul scolded the Corinthians for coming drunk to communion? They thought this was the same kind of meal. But Paul said no. Jesus is the host of this meal, and as such, they needed to conduct themselves with some decorum, some respect. There is great comfort in a meal like that. It's assuring those left behind that we are not left alone."

The graveside service went as quickly as Beth could move through it. The mourners battled the elements and their emotions to keep body and soul together. Angus looked at Connie's face and could not tell where rain ended and tears began.

Chapter Seven: What About His Friends?

TIME CEASED TO mean anything, as Ben Irwin sat in the emergency room. *If I'd been seriously hurt, I'd have bled to death by now*, he thought. He had bandaged his hand with a dirty rag from work, but he had no choice. Filling out the paperwork, everything in triplicate, took another eternity. The charge nurse was polite, but insistent. Ben fidgeted. He would have to tell someone what happened, and he certainly didn't want to do that. He had been careless and did not like to admit it. Ben was proud of his long track record of safety on the job, especially in auto repair, where injuries were common. Now everyone would know, and they would want to know why. He could not possibly say it was because of the dream.

It was a small hospital. They had forty beds, an ER, and an operating room. It was built in the fifties. It had served Shoestring well for more than half a century.

Ben just wanted to get fixed up and back to work. It was the one thing besides Ruthie he could count on. Thinking about Ruthie made him smile, when not much in his life could. *Maybe someday I'll make an 'honest woman' of her*, he thought. In the meantime, he just smiled and waited.

But the dream would not let him rest. Somebody pushed him off a cliff, and he kept falling and falling. The smile quickly faded. What could it possibly mean? Why was he still dreaming it? How could he get rid of it? Should he talk to someone? Who? He was not crazy, and certainly did not want anyone to think he was. His first thought was to talk to a minister, but he quickly dismissed it. Of all the professions, he trusted ministers the least. They could and would say almost anything if it made them look good or fattened up the Church coffers. He imagined a group of ministers feeding on hog slop like a bunch of pigs. The image made him smile, for the second time today.

THE RAIN let up a little, enough for them to do the service. Angus always preferred the graveside service, so he could say his favorite prayer.

O Lord, support us all the day long
until the shadows lengthen and the
evening comes and the busy world
is hushed, and the fever of life is over,
and our work is done. Then in your mercy
grant us a safe lodging and a holy rest
and peace at the last; through Jesus
Christ, our Lord. Amen

It was always much smaller than the regular funeral service, and more intimate. He hugged Connie and Bonnie, smiling inwardly at the lilting rhythm of their names. He was always fascinated at what people named their children, and for what reasons. Connie had asked him to the lunch afterward, and he promised he would go.

When they got into the car, Beth dug into her purse and fished out a piece of yellow legal paper.

"I couldn't sleep one night," she said, unfolding the piece of paper and giving it to Angus. "So I came up with this list of people who may have had it in for Pete."

There were four names listed, with a brief description of why Beth thought they were important. Jim Williams–argued about the organ; Paula Snodgrass–counselee; Bob Duckworth–arch conservative; Jan Smith–Century Shoppe.

"What's the *Century Shoppe*?" asked Angus.

"Stuff celebrating the turn of the century; antiques and collectibles, that sort of thing. It's a very upscale, pricey sort of store."

"So why is she on the list?"

"Peter's dream was to have a thrift shop on Main Street to help poor people make ends meet. The only place vacant was the one next to the 'Century Shoppe.' Jan heard about it and got really upset. She came to see me one day, said she was worried about the kind of people it would draw to downtown; said it would hurt property values. I think it was mostly about her own prejudice."

"There are only four names on this list. There are some missing."

"Who?"

"What about his friends?"

THEY WENT directly from the graveside to Connie's for lunch. Cars gathered around the house like geese on a golf course. Angus always felt uncomfortable at these things. What is the right attitude at such times? Most of the time, you ignore what just took place and act as if nothing happened. Chatty banter about banal things seemed somehow out of place, but it proved to be the best way to get through an impossible time.

Everyone who was at the wake also attended the luncheon. The church provided everything for it. Deli meats, breads, potato salads of every description, and cakes festooned the dining table, which groaned to overflowing. And deviled eggs–these passages always had to include deviled eggs.

The family had not gotten back from the gravesite, but Connie's brother, Al Housel, let them in, and introduced himself and his family. The moment Angus shook his hand he knew he was in the presence of a car salesperson. Some people, you can just tell.

"Where do you live, Al?" asked Angus.

"I'm from Big D," he said as he pumped Angus' hand. Angus had been in Texas long enough to know Dallas was a 'whole other country,' and everything there, the biggest.

"I'm in sales. Used cars. I know. 'Would you buy a used car from this man?' But we provide a service. Did you know a new car loses forty percent of its value the minute you drive it off the showroom floor?"

"I grew up lucky to have a push cart to get around in as a lad," said Angus. "I haven't bought a new car since the first car we bought when I married. Nothing but trouble. Since then, I've had good luck with used cars."

"That's what I'm talking about, friend," he said. "Here's my card, if you're ever in need of a 'push cart.'" He leaned back laughing, pointing at Angus. "I loved that. Just let me know. I'll make you a real good deal," he winked.

People like Al were one of the reasons Angus got out of parish work. "Motor mouths" was the technical term they dubbed it in seminary. *Some people just don't know when to shut up*, he thought.

Angus fixed himself a plate of food and looked for a place to set it down so he could eat and get out of there. He understood the need of many parishioners to sit in the back pews of the sanctuary. He too was always looking for an easy escape route.

He found a place on the sofa in the living room. TV trays had been set out. So he put his plate and drink on one and sat down next to a Mexican couple who looked very much out of place in this sea of white faces.

The man was gaunt and old with crevices in his face the size of Palo Duro Canyon. His black hair seemed unnatural, slick and shiny. His liquid brown eyes were sad and betrayed a wish to be anywhere but here.

"My name is Angus McPherson," he said. "I am Pastor Pete's pastor."

There was a pause, the old man and young woman looking lost. They stared at each other, then at Angus.

"*No hablamos mucho inglés*," said the woman.

Then, without missing a beat, he spoke to them in Spanish. He found out their names were Jesús and his new wife, Juanita Morales. They had been married three years. He had been the custodian of the church for one year.

"*Pastor Pete me trataba muy bien*," said Jesús slowly.

"*¿Porqúe dice usted esto?*" Angus asked.

Jesús told him of coming to this country, looking for a better life, and landing in Shoestring. He had a wife and five children, and no job and no prospects. But Pastor Pete took them in, found them an apartment, gave him the custodial job, and was beginning to teach them English.

"What can you tell me about the day he died?" asked Angus in his best Spanish.

Jesús looked at him for a long minute. His eyes filled with water. "*Nada mucho*," he said. He looked down at his scuffed-up brown shoes, then at Angus.

"Pastor Pete was a good man. I heard about his death the next day. Very sad." He looked at Juanita and then at Angus.

"It was trash day," his wife said, in halting English. "He was taking out the trash and found a pair of rubber gloves. They weren't the kind they use at church."

"This was after Pete had died?" asked Angus.

"It was the next day. Jesús brought them home. He didn't know what else to do. They weren't calling it a murder then. But maybe you could take them?" said Juanita.

"I'd be happy to, but you need to go talk to the police. They need to know what you discovered," said Angus.

Juanita produced a plastic bag with yellow plastic gloves inside, and slipped it toward Angus, as she looked around slowly. Angus took them and looked straight at Jesús.

"Is there anything else unusual you can remember?" he asked sternly.

Jesús talked to the young, olive-skinned woman, and she translated.

"He said Louise," she whispered, "was acting strange. She was real nervous. Most days she acted upbeat, a real happy kind of person. But the day before Pastor Pete—he could tell something was wrong, something was bothering her."

"This is all the more reason to go talk to the police," chided Angus. "They need to know this."

"I want no trouble," said Jesús, struggling to speak.

"That's a good phrase to know," Angus smiled.

Juanita placed her hand on Jesús' hand, looked at him and said, "We need to do this for Pastor Pete." Then to Angus, "We will go tomorrow."

HECTOR HAD just gotten back to his office when the phone rang. It was Bill Person from Lockhart.

"Hey, Bill, what's up?" said Hector, sitting back in his cushioned office chair. *If he was going to have to spend time behind a desk*, he thought, *he might as well be comfortable.*

"Nothing you're going to like, partner."

"Did you catch old Seth drunk and disorderly under the viaduct again?" Seth Green was a washed out crop duster who hit the skids, but always seemed to survive, wandering between Lockhart and Shoestring.

"No, it's not Seth. This time, it's serious."

Hector took his feet off his desk and leaned forward.

"What is it, man?"

"It's about the woman you told me to look up."

"You found her, that's good work," said Hector. "What did you find out? What did she tell you?"

"She didn't tell us anything, partner." Bill sighed deeply. "She's dead. Strangled, most likely. Rope burns around her neck."

"Holy…." Hector caught his breath. "Was there any sign of a struggle?"

"Yeah, the place was pretty tore up."

"Where'd you find her?"

"At her place."

"Did you find anything else?"

"No, nothing."

"What about the cat?"

"What cat? I didn't see any cat."

"She had a cat. I saw it when I went looking for her. How long has she been dead?"

"Phil said it couldn't be more than twenty-four hours."

"Is he still there?" Hector asked.

"Yeah, but he's about done, going to take the body too."

"I'd like to come by and check it out. Two murders in the same county—in small towns—just don't make sense. Between us, we've had two murders all of last year."

"I thought you might say that. Let's hope we've made our quota," said Bill. "I'll hold things up 'til you get here. But you're going to owe Phil big time. He doesn't like to wait."

"Oh, I'll take care of him; don't worry." Hector put the receiver down hard. He banged around the office in a hurry to straighten up before heading to Lockhart.

He got up to leave and stopped in the middle of the room. The ceiling fan turned slowly two feet above his head. He took a deep breath, and let it out slowly.

His pulse raced and his throat throbbed with anger. He both feared and was angry at death's capacity to rob him of his peace and security. When his dad died, he was not sad or even near tears. His best friend had died, and he was angry. His father could not see Hector's children achieve the kinds of things a sharecropper could only dream about. Silvia's brother also died in a gang fight in Mexico. Going there for the funeral made him mad at his brother-in-law for choosing such a life for himself. He had gone into law enforcement because of experiences like these.

"*Death is the enemy*," his daddy used to tell him. Those words came flooding back to him as his eyes filled with water. Death was not about to defeat him until the last possible second. And death certainly was not going to become a habit in these parts.

His secretary, Pam Dexter, came in, looking around for him.

"Hector," she said, "there's an Angus McPherson to see you."

"I'll come out to him. I have to go to Lockhart and will be gone the rest of the afternoon."

"But what about these reports?" asked Pam. The reports fanned out from her desk like cards in a poker hand. "They're due next week."

"The state will have to wait. There's been another murder. It's in Lockhart. I'll take the Reverend with me. I'll fill you in later."

HECTOR WAS in a hurry. Sirens were blaring and tires squealing. Angus gripped the door handle tightly, blinking as they took a corner with a slight fishtail.

"What happened?" asked Angus, catching his breath.

"Maureen is dead. Strangled. I don't know if there is a connection, but it seems pretty obvious."

"Does to me too." Angus tried to digest the shocking fact. "Good God...She obviously knew more than someone could stand for her to know." said Angus, outraged. "A little knowledge is a dangerous thing."

"I've always said murder was the dumbest crime; but a murder to cover up another murder is two dumbs."

"And two dumbs don't make a smart."

Chapter Eight: In the Right Place

THEY RODE TOGETHER in silence for some time as men often do. Angus thought of the silence at creation. It was the silence between the notes that made the music. It was the still small voice from God that Elijah heard on the mountain. It was the silent temptation in the wilderness tormenting Jesus before he began his ministry.

Be silent before me, you islands!
Let nations renew their strength!
Let them come forward and speak;
Let us meet together at the place of judgment."
–Isaiah 41:1

"Why are we driving so fast?" Angus said finally.

"Excuse me?" Hector said, leaning over.

"The girl is dead. Why are you is such a hurry?"

"Seconds count," Hector said. "The trail will grow cold quickly. Bill wants to wrap this up and keep a lid on it. We both live in small towns. This stuff spreads like wildfire. And besides, he's keeping Phil there until we arrive."

"Well, I guess you'll have them talking after the way we left town."

Hector looked at Angus, then back at the road that stretched like a plumb line straight to heaven, populated by Indian paintbrush and bluebonnets on either side.

"Good point. Oh, well, they'll know soon enough."

Hector turned off the siren on those silent streets, but left the lights flashing and the speed high. Angus smiled.

BILL PERSON and the Medical Examiner were still there when they arrived. People milled about like ants in a feeding frenzy. The house was in chaos, a far cry from the way Hector had seen it on his first visit. The place was completely turned upside down. Broken furniture, overturned dressers, clothes, and kitchen utensils were strewn everywhere. And there was Maureen Sullivan–her head limp, her arms spread wide, and her legs tucked up underneath her.

Hector introduced Bill to Angus.

"What do you know?" asked Hector.

"Not much. No prints to speak of, except hers." He looked down at Maureen's body, now partially covered with a sheet. "Don't know if anything is missing, or what caused this mess. Looks like someone was looking for something. Don't have a clue as to what yet. Do know, pretty clearly, this is the murder weapon." He showed them a plastic bag with a red scarf inside. He also showed them the bruises on her neck.

Angus had seen dead bodies before, in his native land in a mining accident, but not like this. This was not an accident. Someone wanted her dead and set out to make it happen. Angus felt sick at his stomach, but decided he couldn't afford to be.

"Where are the shoes?" he asked instead.

"We haven't found 'em yet," Bill replied. "Unless she wasn't wearing any. It's funny, but her closet wasn't touched. It seems to be the only place that wasn't."

"You think whoever did this found what he was looking for and left?" asked Hector.

"That's about the size of it," said Bill, taking off his cowboy hat and wiping his brow with a handkerchief.

"But where is the cat?" asked Hector.

"We've been lookin' for it," said Bill "but so far, nothing. Not a trace."

"It's funny, but I don't see any water or food dishes," said Angus, looking around. "Any trace of the cat is gone," he said, looking at Hector.

Bill also looked at Hector quizzically.

"There was a cat here," Hector stressed, looking at both men. "I saw it with my own eyes."

"Maybe you just thought you saw it," Bill said, with a half smile. "You think she was killed because of the cat, and not for what she knew?"

"I don't know," said Hector. "All I know is I saw a cat here, and now I don't. It has to mean something, especially if every trace of it was removed. Someone went to a lot of trouble to make us believe she didn't have a cat."

"It beats me what a cat would have to do with this mess anyway," said Bill. "Well, gentlemen, I've got work to do. We're going to finish up here, and then interview the neighbors. We'll see what we can turn up. I'll let you know whatever we find out."

"Thanks, Bill," said Hector, shaking hands. "And thanks for calling me."

"No problem," said Bill. He turned and walked off.

"MISSING SHOES and a cat?" said Hector absently, as he settled behind the wheel.

"Yeah," replied Angus. "Would you mind driving around a little? Maybe we'll get lucky."

They did not find the cat, but they did find an enigmatic

town. Nothing seemed to fit. A fancy, well-kept house often sat next door to a run-down shack. There was nothing consistent about the place, and neither of them could put their finger on it. They decided it was time to go home.

"You do believe me about the cat?" asked Hector.

"Of course I do. And it's pretty strange they removed all trace of it. It must have meant a lot to somebody." Angus thought to himself, *I wonder why he cares if I believe him or not.*

ON THE WAY home they talked about what they had found out so far, which wasn't much. Hector told him about the cross and his interview with Louise, the church secretary. She had indicated she was so distraught she did not hear or see anything helpful to the investigation. Angus told Hector he also had talked to her, and he was sure she was not telling all she knew. Angus also told him of the loan Pete had inquired about the day before he died.

"What do you make of the loan business?" asked Hector.

"Could be blackmail," said Angus. "Someone knows something Pete doesn't want known."

"That's what it sounds like to me."

"I've actually got a couple of things I'd like to give to you," said Angus.

He had already given Hector the torn black cloth. Now Angus produced two plastic bags. One contained Beth's enemy's list, and the other held the gloves Jesús found in the dumpster.

"Where did you get this?" asked Hector, his mouth agape.

"Confession is not a sacrament in the Presbyterian Church, but rank does have its privileges, even with us," Angus smiled. "People tell me things they won't tell anyone else."

"Add the cloth from Beth, the missing shoes and cat, and the evidence is starting to pile up," said Hector. "But it doesn't mean anything yet. It's all so unconnected, it has no reference point, no purpose. It's all just random bits of nothing found next to each other.

Angus said, "It's our job to give it meaning."

After a brief silence, Hector said, "And why didn't they bring this stuff to me?"

"Fear, I guess."

"I have the right, if I find out who they are, to have them spend some time in jail."

"Aye, I suppose you're right, Chief," said Angus. "But I pray you won't exercise it."

FEAR MOTIVATES, Angus thought. He meditated on this idea in his car on the long ride home. It was six o'clock when he noticed the tank was almost empty. He often rode on empty just to see how far he could get, one of the last thrills of an aging hell raiser. But today would not be one of those days. He wanted to get home soon, and safely, so he decided to fill up before he left town.

Fear inhibits mostly. He continued his musing as he looked for a gas station. *It's what causes people to get stuck, to lose confidence, to run in the face of commitment. Fear makes us smaller than we really are. Awe does the same thing,* thought Angus. *But with awe, you somehow feel a part of what makes you small. Fear makes you small and keeps you chained to the smallness. Awe makes you bigger than you really are. Like when Angelica gave birth to their first son. Such awe makes you feel small, but in a big way.* Angus smiled at the thought. It was something his youngest, Michael, might have said when he was a boy.

"Fear of the Lord is the beginning of wisdom," or so the Bible says. Angus always had trouble with the verse. He had grown up with a fear of his father. Although he knew his dad loved him, he feared his unpredictability. When he was drunk, there was no telling what he might do. When Angus looked at his sons, he saw God's handiwork. When he looked at his father, he saw someone for whom God would have compassion. He knew the difference, and he thanked God he did.

ANGUS PULLED into the gas station, tired and weary. It had been a long, exhausting day, and the ride home promised to be more of the same.

The gas station was like something out of the forties. The pumps were antiques, slender, with the globes on top. The hoses were small, but the gas nozzles were modern. Angus pulled up to one of the pumps. An old man with a bandage on his right arm came out from under a car high in the air in one of the stalls of the garage. He ambled up to the car.

"What can I do ya' fer, mister?" the man shouted.

"Fill her up, please," said Angus.

"Eh?"

"I said, please fill up the tank," he repeated slowly.

"Fill 'er up. Okay, now I got it."

Ben Irwin bent to his task with a love born of practice. The repetition would have burned out those who hated doing the same thing every day. But Ben Irwin did not. The more he did what he loved, the more he loved what he did.

Angus got out of the Jeep and stretched. He went into the station hoping to find a cappuccino machine and a tasty snack, but he was disappointed. He saw instead an old-fashioned rusty coffeepot, which was still on, but empty. A candy machine had stale-looking cheese crackers and some gum. He lost his appetite.

"You're not from around here, are ya'?" asked Ben.

"No, I'm from the Austin area."

"You're a long way from home, Mister."

"Well, I'll be home by about eight. That's not too bad."

"What do you do, Mister, if you don't mind my asking?" Ben asked, as he washed the Jeep's windshield.

Angus did mind. He did not like to say what he did for a living. Most people didn't understand it.

"I'm a minister, a Presbyterian."

"You mean like the one who was killed the other day."

"The very same. I've been here looking into it. It is really tragic."

"That was real sad," Ben said, looking down.

"Aye, it was," said Angus. "But you have a very good police department, and they will surely find out who did this."

"Well, I hope they do...I hope they do," Ben said absently.

Angus looked over at the church, which seemed sad and majestic at the same time. Then he looked back at Ben.

"You wouldn't happen to know anything about what happened, would you?"

"Me, no." He shook his head. "No, I didn't see nothing. Hector came by, asked me the same thing. You know, I wish his kind would go back..." Ben looked down.

"Well, thanks for the gas," Angus said slowly.

"Thanks for your business," said Ben. "Are you the new pastor there now?"

"No, Beth McKinley, the Associate. She'll take over until they can find an interim pastor. I'm here to lend a hand until then."

"A woman?" Ben straightened up, shaking his head.

Angus paused for a moment, then started his car in a hurry to get out of there, and drove off into the dark night, without any light to guide him, and a seething anger at small minds in small places.

BETH WOKE early the next day, Monday. It was the first day she was to conduct a staff meeting as head of staff. Everyone would look to her for guidance and direction.

"But really," she thought out loud, "they know what they're supposed to do. All I have to do is hear what they're doing and encourage them."

She fixed her breakfast of toast and jelly, a cup of coffee, and a banana. She read the Austin paper at her cramped kitchen table, which also doubled as her desk; the bills and bank statements shared space with the sugar and salt and pepper. She lived alone in a one-bedroom townhouse on the edge of town.

She dressed, finished her coffee, gathered her books, and headed toward the door. The design in the door stopped her. It was in the shape of a cross. It's a wonder she had not seen it before. She thought, "I guess you see a means of support only when you need it." She said a little prayer for the day and for her nerves.

But she knew she had nothing to fear, really. They were all her friends—Jesús, Louise, and the DCE, Mary Roberts. She was particularly friendly with the choir director, Charlie. She hoped it would not pose a problem.

She had invited Tom Branch, the clerk of session, for his assistance. He was a "detail" person, which she was not. She sighed, knowing she would have to do both her job and Pete's for awhile. She knew she could lean on Angus who had already been a great help.

"Oh, Pete, why did you have to die?" she sighed as she got into her car. Death put his bony, cold hand on Beth's shoulder, and she shivered. She was unable to shake the feeling of the millstone around her neck as she drove to work.

BETH WAS not one to read the Bible devotionally. It was the inspiration for her work, the tool of her trade, and she was not in the habit of using it for personal guidance. But this morning was different. She needed some help just to get through the day. Beth did not care to watch TV, too passive; she didn't smoke or drink much, too expensive; besides which, smoking was just plain nasty. So she did not consider herself someone with an addictive personality, but she did love her Coke.

She drank Coke in the morning, at noon, in the afternoon, or late in the evening. It didn't matter. She had to have her Coke. She might make it through without her Bible, but not without her Coke.

When she got to work, she said hello to Louise who was still very fragile and weepy, then went to the Coke machine to get her morning jolt. She went to her modest office, closed the blinds, and shut off the lights. She lit a candle on the desk. The candle holder held a brightly colored angel made in Mexico–turquoise with touches of reds and blues and greens throughout. It was a gift to herself when she was first called to this church. After the committee interviewed her, she made a trip to south Texas. She found this angel candle in a little shop in Piedras Negras, just over the border.

"It's funny," she said out loud, "but this is the first time I've lit this candle."

She prayed for some minutes, silently. She listened to her breathing, in and out, regular and rhythmic as the waves of the ocean. This was strangely calming. Strange because she had never experienced anything like it before. She had never known and felt such calm, certainly not since her life had exploded in the last week.

Then she opened her Bible. She didn't care where. She was willing to give herself over to serendipity or divine intervention. She started from the back and opened it at once. She read what was there.

These are the words of him who holds the seven stars in his right hand and walks among the seven golden lamp stands. "I know your deeds, your hard work and your perseverance. I know that you cannot tolerate the wicked, that you have tested those who claim to be apostles but are not, and have found them false. You have persevered and endured hardships for my name and have not grown weary."

-Rev. 2:1-3

She always had difficulty with this book of the Bible. She hardly ever read it, and when she did she never understood it. It angered her that some preachers used Revelation to scare people. The sentence structure was just plain torture.

"*Tested those who claim to be apostles but are not...*" She read it again. Although she could not reconcile its meaning, the words somehow made her feel better anyway. She thought she could face what the day brought with a better attitude now.

ANGUS COULD not sleep. He was haunted by the image of the young woman's life so violently ended–her body twisted in ways it would not have been in life. He had seen dead bodies many times before. His dad worked in a mine where accidents were frequent occurrences. As a small boy, he would carry water for the workers as bodies were brought up from the mines, black and lifeless.

This one haunted him all the more because he felt guilty about her death. *Maybe I could have prevented it*, he thought as he lay, looking first at the stars in the cloudless sky and then at his beautiful wife. She slept with a wisp of a smile on her face, giving Angus a feeling of peace and serenity, helping him relax some.

But what about the last man he saw in Shoestring last night, the gas station attendant? What was his name? Angus had a terrible time remembering names. When you are in the people business, it is an inescapable occupational hazard. But he remembered other things well; appointments, scripture, stuff his ma' taught him.

And what's this guy's story? Does he know something? Angus wondered. *Why did I let him get me so angry?* He had met his type of bigotry before, and he seldom let it bother him. But before this, death was not involved. Now it was. He resolved to call Hector about it in the morning. In the meantime he would try again to get some sleep.

SHE THOUGHT she would keep it the way Pete had done it: a Bible reading, some discussion, followed by a prayer, and then they would take a look at the week's activity.

The scripture she chose was one of her favorites, Romans 12:1. "Present yourselves as a living sacrifice, holy and pleasing to God—this is your spiritual act of worship." *Worship is more than what we do on Sunday morning, much more. Every breath we take can be a prayer, every breakfast a communion, every bath a baptism,* she mused.

It surprised her really. She never considered herself a pious person; her calling was more service-oriented. But maybe Pete's death had broadened her perspective. Maybe now she needed to believe the stuff he said every week. In fact she was desperate to believe it.

Even though she was well prepared, she could not shake the butterflies dancing in her stomach. Peter made this look so easy, so natural; she would have to do the same. She did not know if she could pull it off, but she had to try. They needed a leader right now, and she was elected. There was no one else.

What made it especially difficult was the prospect of

a murderer lurking among them. She thought the killer might well be in the group that was about to gather.

The phone rang. It was the intercom. Louise was on the intercom.

"Yes, Louise."

"You're next, bitch." It was a man's voice.

"Excuse me?" said Beth, her heart beating wildly in her throat.

The line went dead.

Chapter Nine: The River Styx

ANGELICA HAD PLANNED it carefully. Michael, their youngest son, was a UT post-grad and soon would be leaving for a summer job in Arkansas. He was going to bring a girlfriend he had been dating, and they would make a day of it, floating down the Pedernales and then have lunch on one of the river's many islands. They had done this often when the boys were little, and the whole family got such a kick out of it.

But she knew no plan was safe around Angus. Something always happened to draw him away from what the family—*what she wanted* the family to do. He was not allowed to take his cell phone on these trips. Angelica wanted him to focus on them for awhile. Was she asking too much? She dared not ask. If she was resolute, she knew she would have her way.

Angus would have felt more like going on this adventure if he hadn't been so preoccupied. He could not shake the guilt he felt over the second death. *I could have prevented the senseless killing of an innocent young woman,* he thought. *They should have started a search for her as soon as she had gone missing.*

As he put on his swim trunks, he thought about the cold river water. *Am I crazy? It's early in April, and this is Texas where it's warmer, but the water will still be freezing.* "I must be desperate," he said out loud. "Maybe I should talk to Angie about this. Or maybe I should go with the flow." Angus chuckled at the particularly curious Americanism. '*Go with the flow.*' *That's what the day is about,* he concluded. *See what the water is doing, and go from there. If it's too cold, it's Angie's decision.* He'd do whatever she said. It was her day. He was in her hands, and he felt good about it.

Angelica stirred from her slumber like a cat, all stretched out and unwound, and watched Angus finish getting into his trunks.

"Ready for the big day?" she said, pursing her lips through half-opened eyes.

Angus kissed her gently.

"Got my trunks on. I'm ready to go. Michael went to pick up Jessica. I guess we'll wait 'til they get here."

"Well, let's get breakfast going, and they may be able to join us before we finish."

MICHAEL AND JESSICA arrived before they finished breakfast and ate what was left. Michael was taller, bigger, and darker than his father. He wore bright orange and white swim trunks and a tee-shirt that said "Keeping Austin Weird." Jessica was the opposite—small and wiry with furtive hazel eyes taking in all-new information. She wore a yellow tank top with shorts and old sneakers. Angelica explained how the day would go, and they were pleased with the plan. They loaded the truck with the picnic lunch, and put the canoes on the boat rack on top.

The canoes were their one concession to living on the river. It was not a big river; in fact during the summer months it was often impassible. But some of their neighbors insisted on getting bigger and bigger boats. And they needed a place to put them when they weren't being used, so a huge marina was being built closer to the dam, not far from their place up river.

Angus and Angelica had moved out here for the natural beauty and for the peace and quiet. Now both were being disturbed, which made them increasingly unhappy. They had attended a town meeting to protest the building of the marina, but it did no good. As Angus had learned, the developer with the deepest pockets always wins. Angus joked with Angelica after the meeting with the developers, "Pretty soon we may have to move back into the city to get away from all the crowds."

Or they might move to Mexico. Angelica had talked about the possibility before, but with Angus' work, and Michael still in university, it was impossible. She went to the Valley to visit her parents twice a year. Her father was getting on in years, and she knew she wouldn't have him much longer. She felt guilty sometimes thinking of what her mother was going through. She had three younger sisters and two younger brothers, all of whom lived within a few miles of their parents. But she was the oldest. She felt responsible; what could she do?

THEY LOADED up the truck and climbed in. Then they drove to the point they would put in the canoes and unloaded them. Michael took the truck and parked where they usually ended their trip, and drove the mini-bike back.

While they waited, they had a look around. Texas was hard, but beautiful. The earth here was red clay and limestone with scrub brush. Its beauty was in the elemental nature of the place—so basic, so essential. Angus had never known a purer place. The sky was bright with promise, and hawks circled, endlessly searching. He loved hawks; the power, the freedom, the mystery. He considered them as spiritual beings.

Jessica saw a little lizard and jumped. Angus and Angelica laughed at her surprise. Jessica looked at them with a puzzled expression, which evolved into a smile, followed by a hearty laugh. She was strictly a city person; luckily, Michael was happy anywhere. Angus and Angelica were glad they had found each other, but Angus worried that they were so much in love so early in their lives.

Michael made it back, and they loaded up the two canoes and headed out. They enjoyed these mini-vacations; trips down nature's highway. Just breathing in the crisp, dewy morning air was something of a religious experience. But because the boys were grown, these trips grew more and more infrequent. It was just not the same without them. In fact, Angus had contemplated selling one or both of the canoes. But he did not have the heart to talk about it with his wife. She got much more attached to things than he did—especially the things that reminded her of their sons.

The river, however, had not changed. Yet it was never the same river; it was always in flux. What had not changed was the beauty of it and its effect on Angus. He soaked it in. So much of his life was spent going against the flow, trying to fit people's expectations with what he felt called to do. Here he felt just the opposite. He fit into the natural flow of the place. He had a sense of freedom and awe he could not, did not, find anywhere else. He felt alive again.

A fish jumped as they paddled their canoes silently down the brown expanse. They were able to paddle side by side comfortably, without much extra room.

"This so feeds my soul." Angelica broke Angus' reverie.

"Isn't it marvelous?" Angus affirmed. "I can't think of a better place to be than right here, right now."

"It sort of puts things into perspective, doesn't it?" Michael said from the other boat, his voice echoing off the red walls lining the riverbed.

"Aye, it does," said Angus.

They stayed quiet for some time.

Angus started thinking about the events at Shoestring. Pastor Pete's death was tragic enough, but then what were they to make of the death of the woman who warned them of more to come? He started feeling responsible for it again. The shame was real. She came to him for help, and he couldn't help her. She died anyway.

A fish jumped about twenty feet from the canoes, startling the occupants. Angus, on instinct almost, got his rod out and started casting at the splash in the water.

"You're not going to start fishing now, are you?" chided Angelica.

"Well, sure I am," protested Angus. "How else are we going to have a shore lunch?"

"We'll eat what we brought," Angelica said, matter-of-factly. Then she bowed her head and grinned like a little girl. "Okay, but just a few, all right? We don't want to be here forever."

After a little while with no luck, they were off again. They were making good time, a result of all the spring rains which made the current swift and sure.

They managed to pass the time amiably, talking about graduation plans and life at UT. Michael wanted to study physics and possibly go on for a doctorate so he could teach in a university. This surprised Angus.

Jessica wanted to complete a master's in elementary education. They saw their life together, but were hazy on the details. When pressed by either Angelica or Angus, they were about as open as a rusted door on a storm cellar. Angus suspected something more was going on, but did not want to spoil the day applying the "third degree" to the situation.

They ambled down the river looking at all the scrub oak, hackberry, cedar, and cypress trees lining the river. A stately gray heron took flight over the meandering canoers.

Angus was in awe at the sight and said a silent prayer of thanks for the chance to witness such a beautiful creature in her habitat. He took a deep breath and exhaled slowly.

But it was still hard for him to be present with them in this little outing. He never liked to disappoint Angelica, and having time with Michael and Jessica was a rare treat. Fight as he might, however, his mind was elsewhere.

He was haunted by the phone call from the frantic woman and her cry for help. *She must have known she was in grave danger,* he thought. *What more could I have done? We all failed her.*

This was all so foreign to him. Nothing like this had ever happened to him before. When he was a boy in Scotland, he'd heard whispers about a friend of a friend committing suicide. A classmate was killed in the Vietnam War, and there was the terrible mine accident when he was a kid. Death had been a natural—even expected, even hoped for—part of a merciful end to a struggle going on too long, needing to stop. But this was different. This death was personal. It happened to someone under Angus' care. In a sense, it had happened to him.

Violence was for TV news and cop shows, neither of which he liked much. Angelica was positively allergic to such fare, and Angus grew into the same aversion. Angus did not want to die, but if it was necessary, he knew he would be ready. His faith prepared him, but nothing had prepared him for this.

If only the woman had been more forthcoming about what she knew, maybe then they would know more about who was behind all this. He resolved to talk to Hector about her first thing in the morning. It would be difficult to find the time because he was soon to be the featured speaker at a mission conference put on by the Presbytery.

Angus began to wonder if he was becoming obsessive. This case consumed him. Every pore, every ounce of energy, every waking moment called for his undivided attention. However, the job he was called to do was in the way. He had responsibilities to perform, and he could not escape them, try as he might. He urgently needed to talk with Hector, but fulfilling expectations was more important for him right now. Since becoming involved in these murders, he wrestled with himself much more than usual.

He heard a splash by the bank and looked to see a turtle slide into the water.

"Look!" he said, pointing at a dead log protruding from the water. Another turtle dove in, causing more ripples in the water. Light shimmered off the water's ridges, widening from bank to bank. A half-dozen smaller turtles sunned on the same log.

"Thank you," whispered Angus under his breath. At times like these, he pitied those who did not believe in God. Thanking someone for the little serendipities gracing the day filled a hole in a soul with depth and richness. Angus believed this with his whole heart.

"The six apostles," said Michael, laughing.

"Yeah, the other five are out fishing," said Angelica.

"Weren't there twelve?" asked Jessica.

"Aye, but not after Jesus died," said Angus. "Judas betrayed him, and then took his own life."

"I'm sorry I asked," said Jessica, a bit crestfallen.

"Oh, don't mind him," laughed Michael. "Dad always does that. He always tells the truth, no matter who he hurts."

Angus laughed and slapped his paddle on the water sideways sending a wall of water splashing, glittering in the gathering day. The silver spray filled with the colors of the rainbow, infused with hope and trust, landed hardest on Jessica, but Michael got wet as well.

Jessica shook in surprise and laughed out loud, soon followed by Michael. Then, as if choreographed, they launched a counter attack. Soon, and for several minutes, the river erupted with splashing and laughter and wet clothes.

Angelica smiled, knowing her husband could rest for these few minutes from worry about murder and what it would mean for the church in Shoestring. *Mission accomplished*, she thought, as she treasured the moment.

Soon they found a sandy shore where they made land and started a fire. Angelica and Angus started unpacking the lunch as Michael and Jessica tried to dry out their clothes and went looking for wood. Lunch was trout almandine, potatoes au gratin, and a garden salad, with a nice bottle of chardonnay.

"I'm scared, Angus," Angelica said, as she got the containers out of the chest and arranged them on a red and white checked tablecloth laid out on the bank.

"Scared of what?" Angus asked, a little shocked. He had only seen her scared twice in their life together. The first time was twelve years ago when she saw Michael slip while diving into the river. He nearly hit his head on the nearby rocks, but survived unhurt.

The other time was when she gave the sermon on "the gifts of women" Sunday. Public speaking was not one of her gifts, but one rarely said no to her Pastor. She worked very hard on the speech, and on the day she delivered it, she was a basket case.

"I'm afraid this whole murder thing is going to involve you in some way," she said.

"Lass, I'm already involved. I have to help where I can." He wanted to tell her about the guilt he felt over the death of the woman, but knew the best thing right now was to concentrate on her fear and not compound it with his own. "I want to see it to a good conclusion. I want to stop this thing from going any farther. I promise I'll be careful."

"Oh, I know you won't do anything foolish, but the murderer isn't worried about your safety. In fact, he wants to do you harm," she said. "They have professionals hired for this sort of investigation. You don't have to take these kinds of risks. It's not your job."

His anxiety and her worry were combustible material. He got defensive whenever they talked about his job. It was one of the reasons he got out of the parish. She always worried when he stepped on someone's toes, and he never understood how to talk to her when that happened.

"You've got to let me do what's right here, Angie." His speech was clipped and sharp. "You know I've got to do this. My job is to help the congregation get well as soon as possible. Helping catch the killer is what I have to do now." Angus was lost. *How do I make her trust me,* he thought.

A tear welled in Angelica's eye. Angus reached over and wiped the tear away as it rolled down her check. They hugged, then kissed each other lightly on the lips.

Michael and Jessica came to the campfire with arms full of wood and began building up the fire. They talked about what Angelica and Angus had been discussing. Michael, too, was worried for his dad, but thought it was cool he was in the middle of a murder investigation.

THEY ENJOYED the meal, especially the wine. After lunch they walked the beach and up country a little way. It was mostly scrub oak, cactus, and brush. They saw a jackrabbit dart out from one bush and scamper into the woods. They kept their eyes peeled for rattlers at Angelica's insistence, but never came across one. They came back to the lunch spot, packed up their things, and put out the fire. They loaded up the canoes and shoved off for the last hour of their lazy journey down the Pedernales, this river they called home.

ANGUS STARTED to get uneasy as they rounded the river bend, near the end of their journey. As they got closer to the place Michael had left the Jeep, he saw why. Another car had joined the Jeep. It was a police car with City of Shoestring Police painted on the side in light blue letters. Hector Chavez stood next to it, waving at them as they came into view.

Hector's face was shaded in dappled sunlight as he stood under a huge live oak. Angus thought he looked much older than when he'd first met him just a few days ago. *Murder will do that to a man,* he thought. *I wonder if my looks have changed?*

"How was the float?" Hector asked, as he pulled Angus' canoe ashore.

"Fine," said Angus. "But what are you doing here? Is something wrong?"

"As a matter of fact," Hector's smile vanished, "there is. There's been another development, and I thought you needed to hear it from me. Your secretary told me where I could find you, so I thought I'd take a drive out here to get you 'up to speed' on what's been happening."

"What's happened?" Angus asked.

As they unloaded the canoes, putting the contents into the Jeep, Hector told him about the call to Beth. "Actually, this is a good thing, because the killer's revealing a little of himself," Hector explained.

"That's just awful," said Angelica.

"Beth's okay but could use a call from you, Angus."

Angus said, "I'll call her right away."

As Hector and Angus were loading one of the canoes on top of the Jeep, Angus slipped and lost his grip. The canoe twisted out of his hands, and Hector fought to hang on, but also was forced to let go. The canoe fell to the ground with a thud.

Angus looked at his hands that were now shaped in the form of claws, and screamed, "Bloody Hell!" The sound of his voice echoed through the woods. Angelica looked at him, aching for the pain of her husband.

Hector, at first startled by Angus' outburst, assisted Michael in retrieving the canoe. Hector said goodbye and headed back to Shoestring.

Angus and his family drove home in silence. Angus thought, *What more can happen to this church, to this town, to me?* He was about to find out.

Chapter Ten: A Pregnant Angel

BEN IRWIN needed help. Shoestring was growing, and there was some talk of a Shell station or Tiger Mart coming to town. But for now, he was the only game in town. He could no longer keep up the hours needed to make money and still have a life beyond the pump and the oil changes that were the backbone of his business. He'd thought about hiring a mechanic for a long time, but resisted until now. Hiring a high school kid with mechanical ability might be just the thing. He could mold him into someone who did things just the way he wanted them done. The kid would grow into the job, and Ben's life would be so much easier, with a little time to himself.

But he feared putting an ad in the paper because he wasn't sure who he'd get. Most of the people moving in were illegals, and just thinking about them made him angry. *Nobody has a right to live and work here if they don't play by the rules,* he thought. So he continued to do the work himself, and to make dumb mistakes that landed him in the emergency room.

Right now, he was working on a '96 Honda needing new plugs and tires. He really did love the work and was reluctant to give it up. It challenged him to figure out what went wrong. With patience and persistence he could find the problem and actually fix it. He feared nothing else would replace the sense of satisfaction he got doing this work.

The rest of his life was a total mystery. His marriage ended abruptly after forty years and her bout with breast cancer. Ruthie provided wonderful companionship, but she introduced feelings he hadn't had in years which confused him. He didn't think he could take another heartache if it ended.

He had no relationship with his children to speak of. This haunted him, but he seemed powerless to do anything about it. His daughter, Priscilla, the oldest, worked in a bookstore in Dallas. He supposed she had a husband and kids, but wasn't sure. He had sent a private investigator after her, but he was little help.

He hadn't heard from the youngest, since he stopped paying for college after Bill spent it all on parties. For all he knew, Bill was homeless or on the road.

He didn't blame them for anything though. After his wife died, he thought his life had ended, and his kids paid the price. He still loved them; he just couldn't be around them without remembering what he had lost. The more he saw of Ruthie, the more he thought about reconnecting with his children. He feared he was too late, and it would be too difficult to bridge those gaps.

And this murder thing. He couldn't get it out of his mind. Just then a man in a black suit flashed in his mind. He shook his head. *Where did he come from?* he wondered. He couldn't make out anything but the suit and the bright sun. He stared off into space for a moment, trying to see anything else. *Where was the black-suited man now? What was he doing?*

It was no use. It was gone. He bent to his work, concentrating on turning the nut on the tire. He tried to give his mind entirely to the task and succeeded–mostly.

AS SOON as the canoes and other gear were unloaded from the Jeep, and the dogs, barking and jealous at being left behind, were looked after, Angus called Beth. He found her at home after trying several places.

"I guess Hector told you about my gentleman caller," she joked nervously.

"He drove all the way out here just to tell me about it. Apparently, he's pretty worried about you, and so am I. Whoever is doing this has an axe to grind with the church, and anyone connected to it is in danger."

"But the other woman who died, what was her name?"

"Maureen Sullivan. We don't know much about her. She tried to warn..."

"She wasn't a member of the church," she interrupted. "I didn't know her."

Angus detected the anxiety mounting in her voice, but feeling he did not know her well enough to bring real comfort, replied, "Aye, well, that does complicate things, Lass. There's got to be a connection somewhere. Sooner or later we'll find out what it is. But for now, Beth, I'd like to get you out of there. Maybe take a sabbatical?"

"Angus, I can't. Besides, anyone else who comes here will also be in danger. The congregation needs me. They're in shock. If I leave, there's no telling how long it would take for them to heal. I need to be here for them, if not for me. I can't run from this."

"No, you can't, of course not. And I wouldn't expect you to. But I'm going to be with you as much as I can. I want to catch this guy as much as Hector does. We will, Beth. I promise."

"I know we will. And thanks, Angus."

"We'll work this out."

ANGUS TOOK a glass of wine with him into the bathroom. He would take a shower, get in his "pj's," and settle down with a good book. Angus loved John Grisham. His stories moved with such pace and suspense, it took no effort to read them. He also enjoyed C. S. Lewis. He was reading *Surprised by Joy*, the story of Lewis' early life, and how he lost and found his faith. But he could not concentrate on the page.

He couldn't get Maureen Sullivan out of his mind. She had been treated violently. She died without peace or dignity. The thought made Angus angry. She died trying to warn others of the present danger. He thought of the early church and how many died believing in something forbidden by the state.

The missing shoes and cat also troubled him. Maybe he'd call Hector on Monday. Why would anyone go to the trouble of removing any trace of a cat? And what would the shoes tell them that they didn't already know?

Angus lay there looking up at the ceiling, thinking, waiting for Angelica to come to bed. The book he had been reading lay on his lap. Then Adam jumped on the bed. He came from the foot of the bed up to the pillow, and bumped his head against Angus in an attempt to be petted. Adam got on Angus' stomach kneading him with his front paws. He stretched himself and turned around once and settled on top of Angus' book. Angus chuckled.

"You always want to be the center of my world, don't you, Adam?" he said, rubbing behind Adam's ears. The gray cat moved his head around to get the full effect. Angus kept it up for several minutes.

As he stroked Adam's fur, he heard the inevitable purring that filled the room with a peaceful hum. Angus thought about what Hector said about the cat in the window at the woman's house. The cat must have been comfortable in his surroundings. The killer may have known the cat; otherwise, why is there no trace of the cat? A cat can be gone for days and come back as if nothing was wrong. But the killer left the murder weapon behind and took the pains to remove all evidence of the cat. Obviously, the killer didn't want the authorities to know that a cat had been there. Angus thought, *The cat has a clue about who did this and must be found.*

At that moment Eve came bounding into the room and barked several times at Adam. She scared them both out of their reverie.

HECTOR WONDERED why he hadn't heard from Bill Person. It had been a whole week since they had been at the crime scene.

He had known Bill for twelve years and trusted him instinctively. They watched out for each other on several of the cases they had worked together, almost like brothers. Hector sensed something was wrong; it wasn't like Bill not to contact him. He decided to call him.

A man's voice answered. "County Sheriff's office, Sergeant Hudson speaking. How may I help you?"

"Is the Sheriff in?" Hector asked. "This is Hector Chavez –"

"Yes, yes, Chief," the sergeant's tone brightened. "I will see if he is; just a minute." After a few minutes Hudson came back on the line. "I'm sorry, Chief, he's in court. Will be all day."

"It's about the Sullivan woman. I hadn't heard anything, and I was just wondering..."

"Well..." A long silence settled over the phone like the notes in a funeral dirge. "I'm a little confused. He told me he talked to you about it yesterday. We've had the autopsy for a week. I looked at the log book, and there was a call to you on it."

"He never called me, Sergeant." Hector was just as confused as the man on the other end. "Maybe he talked to the front desk when I was out. Maybe they just forgot to tell me."

"Yeah, right. Is there anything else I can help you with?"

"Would you have him call me, first thing in the morning?"

"It sounds like you should have a talk with Max." Max was Hector's desk sergeant. Hector knew he and Hudson had some bad blood between them. He suspected some professional jealousy, but never took the time to figure it out. And he didn't want to take the time now, not with two murders on his plate. Besides, Max was too good to forget something so important.

Hector hung up the phone perplexed. *What in the world's going on?* he thought. *It's not like Bill to forget to follow up. Could there be something in the autopsy he didn't want me to see? And why would he write in the log he had talked to me when clearly he hadn't?* He scratched his head and looked out the window. He saw people going about their business—running errands, kids riding bicycles; but they did it in slow motion, as if it wasn't really happening. The more he struggled to understand, the more confused he became.

Hector's impatience got the better of him, and he decided to take a little drive to see Bill in court. First he went to find the desk sergeant to let him know of his plans.

SERGEANT MAX Brown was a life-long resident of Shoestring. He'd been with the force for four years. A big man with a soft heart, he had been an All State guard on the football team and had wanted to go to college. But his family needed him to make money, so he worked part time at Wal-Mart until he got criminal justice training at the local junior college.

They chatted about family and about little league

baseball. Then Hector asked, "Did I get a call from Sheriff Person a few days ago?"

"Not that I recall, Chief," said Max. "Did you check the log?" The phone rang, and it was Angus.

"Hello," said Hector.

"Chie – uh – Hector, I have a hunch about the case."

"And what could ..."

"It's the cat!"

"What about the cat?" Hector scratched his head.

"Ms. Sullivan's cat. Remember the cat you found, and then it turned up missing. I think the cat had something to do with the murder."

"So you still believe there was a cat?"

"Does that surprise you?"

"Well, yes, it does. What do you think the cat has to do with it?"

"Well, it's only a hunch really, but why leave the murder weapon behind and then remove all evidence of the cat if the cat wasn't somehow important to the case?"

"That's good, Angus. I hadn't thought of that. I have a call in to the sheriff over in Lockhart. He may shed some light on this thing for us, I hope."

"I know this cat business is such a small thing, but I just thought I'd touch base with you about it. Besides, I'm very worried about Beth."

"I'm glad you did. Sometimes these criminals are so clever, only the smallest details separate guilt from innocence. We can can have her watched to make sure nothing happens."

"That sounds like the best thing to do." Angus felt relieved, like a father sending his daughter to a prom dressed in a suit of armor. But he also knew Hector could only do so much. He wanted to be there for Beth if she needed him.

SHE LOVED her office. Angels and pictures of angels were everywhere. She loved everything about angels—their strength, their protection, and the way they communicated with humans by watching over them and helping in times of trouble. She wouldn't talk about it with her colleagues for fear of being ridiculed, but reruns of *Touched by an Angel* were her favorites.

She felt an angel had come to her in college in the guise of a young pregnant girl. The girl was lost and confused. The father of the baby had left as soon as she told him she was pregnant. She couldn't tell her parents because they would make her get an abortion. She did not think she could do such a thing, so she went to Beth for advice.

One college girl talking to another. Beth had not thought about seminary; in fact, she was leaning toward a career in elementary education.

But the conversation Beth had with the trembling girl helped her understand that a deeper dimension, a spiritual dimension, was a part of every decision. She realized then her life would not be the same.

Beth felt drained after their conversation. She had given her all to help the confused, lonely young woman. Beth saw herself in those weepy, bloodshot eyes, feeling the same fear, the same loneliness. And yet a strange calm came over her, as if she had discovered a central truth to her life, having helped a fellow traveler. She felt affirmed by how totally she had identified with her friend. This was a gift she had received and freely gave.

BETH FELT so confused about her calling in the early days. She went to talk to her pastor about the emotions swirling inside her. "On good days," he told her, "I would gladly do this job for free." Then he bowed his head and looked at her over his rimless reading glasses. "But on bad days, they can't pay me enough money to do this job. The important thing is, like everything we do, you have to feel *called* to do it."

She asked him what it meant to be *called*. He said it was like falling in love. When it comes, you'll know. Then he told the story of the call of Samuel.

Samuel was Hannah's only child. She was a barren woman who had prayed constantly for a child. Finally God gave her a son and, as a result, she promised he would be dedicated to serve the Lord. He went to work for an old priest named Eli.

One night, God called Samuel saying, "Samuel, Samuel." Samuel thought Eli had called him, so he went to Eli to see what he wanted. This happened two more times until Eli finally figured out God was calling the boy.

Eli told him, "When the voice calls again, say, 'Speak Lord, for your servant is listening.'"

The boy went back to sleep. The voice called to Samuel again, and he responded as Eli had instructed him. The Lord told him he would anoint a king, and Eli and his sons would die. Samuel did not want to tell Eli this, but Eli insisted. Samuel finally told him, and Eli reminded him that whatever might come, he should always tell the truth because he was speaking God's word.

The old pastor took his glasses off and scratched his nose. "That," he said, "is what it means to be called."

AND NOW she was the next intended victim of this lunatic, let loose on the church. Was this a part of her calling? Surely not.

She had, for the most part, enjoyed her job. The hours were terrible, and the pay, lousy. But she knew she had made a difference. She liked working with youth. She remembered how difficult and awkward her teen years had been, and she knew the world these kids were inheriting was a lot tougher than what she remembered. She wanted to do what she could to help them set a solid course for their future.

Now she could not spend as much time with them because she had to do Pete's work too. It meant preaching every week. Just the thought of it sent shivers up her spine. She never had thought preaching was very effective; there never seemed to be any tangible results. She'd much rather work one on one with someone. Presbyterians weren't like Baptists who would count the number of souls saved by how many came forward for the "altar call."

"Beth, are you in there?" said the voice behind the opening door. "It's pretty dark in here."

"I'm praying."

"Oh, I'm sorry. I can come back some other time. Louise said it was all right to come in."

"Yes, yes, of course, Tom. Please turn on the light. Come in, please."

Tom Branch was the clerk of session—thin with graying temples, in his mid-forties. Not a hair out of place.

"Beth, I've been worried about you."

"You don't know the half of it, Tom."

"What do you mean?"

She thought about telling him about the recent phone call, then thought better of it. Tom and Linda Branch had befriended Beth from the first moment she arrived. She didn't want to be a burden, and there was nothing they could do about it anyway.

"Never mind." There was a slight pause. "What's up, Tom? It's not like the busy city manager to wander out of city hall. You're not lost are you?"

"No, Beth, I just came from the Chamber breakfast..."

"The Chamber breakfast! Oh, my gosh! What could I have been thinking? Where is my head?"

"Don't worry, Beth, it's okay."

"Okay? How can it be okay? I'm supposed to give the prayer at something that happens once a month. Oh, I wouldn't blame you if you fired me."

"Don't worry. You did tell Louise you had to be there though, didn't you?"

"Please don't blame her. It's my responsibility, it's my fault."

"We just had the Baptist preacher, Brother Watkins, do it. I made some excuse about your being ill. No one is the wiser. And no one minds."

"But it's just so embarrassing. I don't know what to say."

"Say you'll come to our house for dinner tonight. I'm doing a brisket in the smoker. It should be pretty good, if I don't screw it up. Besides, Linda's been dying...I mean, she's really wanted to see you since all this stuff started happening."

"Okay, okay. It sounds good. I'll come. What time?"

"We'll eat about seven. That's not too late, is it?"

"No, no, that'll be fine."

"TOM, WHAT do you think of all this?" asked Beth, as the smoke swirled around Tom's backyard like a snake in a basket. It was difficult to see or to read Tom's reddened eyes.

With spatula in hand, he waved at the smoke with the intensity of a sword fighter. "Well, I certainly hope it's nobody at church. It would be devastating to the whole church if it was. But Hector is a good man, and he'll find whoever did this. I'm sure he will."

"But what if it is somebody from the church? What then?"

"But nothing!" Tom almost shouted. Beth took a step back, surprised by the rage in his up to now calm demeanor. "It's no different from the last police chief resigning in disgrace over taking bribes. Hector came in, cleaned house, and the public trust was restored in no time. Besides, Pastor Pete was beginning to wear out his welcome anyway."

"How do you mean, Tom?" Beth said with surprise and curiosity. "I thought everyone loved him."

"Well, obviously, someone didn't. No, I'm just saying, the thrift shop idea, and the rumors about him and the secretary. That in itself was just too much."

"Too much for what?" asked Beth.

"For common decency, for God's sake," Tom said, waving his spatula again. "We don't want to be the laughing stock of the whole town."

"You mean we were, Tom?"

"No, but we could have been, and I—we—don't need that."

"I can see that you feel strongly about this, and of course, you're right. The church is not immune from evil, and in fact, it seems to be a magnet for it."

"That's interesting, I've never thought about it."

Chapter Eleven: Chased by a Dream

HECTOR DROVE over to Lockhart to see what was up with Bill Person. He arrived at the courthouse about 3:00 and went into the only courtroom and sat in the back. Bill Person sat in the witness chair, and the young, pimple-faced lawyer asked him about a traffic stop he made, and the nature of the ticket he gave. The driver of the car was charged with drunk driving. Luckily, no one was hurt. Sheriff Person testified he saw the car weave back and forth, which is why he stopped the woman driver.

The judge believed his testimony, suspended her license, and ordered her to go to traffic school, with ten hours of community service. She also had to pay court costs and a fine.

Sheriff Person was excused from the witness stand as the judge lowered her gavel to announce the case was closed. He spotted Hector, smiled broadly, and went over to shake his hand. They stepped out of the courtroom together.

"How the heck are you, buddy?" asked Bill, reaching out and shaking Hector's hand vigorously. "What are you doing here?"

"I came to see how a real law man handles himself in court."

"Well, I'm flattered, but we both know you're lying," said Bill, clasping him on the shoulder. "Let's go across the street to get a cup of coffee. What are you doing here?"

"Well, I hadn't heard from you about the Sullivan woman. I called your office, and the sergeant said the log book recorded a call to our office. But I never heard from you."

"I called you, but you weren't there. Buddy, take it easy. Ask your sergeant if I called. He just forgot to tell you."

"I asked Max before I came. That's why I'm here. I don't get it, Bill. Help me understand."

"There's nothing to understand," said Bill. "I just forgot."

"But then why the log entry saying you called? It just doesn't add up."

"Look, I got the autopsy, and I'm willing to share it with you. Let that be enough, okay?"

Hector was like a terrier on a letter carrier; he couldn't let go. "Are you trying to hide something from me, Bill? Because if you are, I'll find out, and neither one of us would like what happens next."

Suddenly, Bill exploded, "Look, I was going to call you, wrote down that I did, but something came up and I forgot. Is that all right with you, your Majesty? Can Billy go out and play now, Mommy?" People were beginning to stare at the two law men as they circled like Sumo wrestlers. "Get off my ass, you son of a bitch. I don't answer to you anyway. What difference is it to you what I do?"

Bill took a step or two into Hector, pushing him after each sentence. Hector had always remembered his training. "Always use your opponent's anger against him," his sergeant would always tell him. And so he backed up with each push, defusing the force of Bill's anger, step by step.

Finally, Bill's frustration boiled over, and he took a swing at Hector. For a big man, Hector moved quickly. He missed the punch and swung around in time to deliver a counterpunch to Bill's midsection. Bill doubled over in pain, and the echo of it rang out through the huge rotunda. Sweat dripped off Bill's nose like a melting icicle, splashing on the cold marble floor. They moved out of the main corridor of the courthouse, as a few people watched. These two law officers panted, bent over from the exertion, and helped each other find a bench. As they sat down, their two huge sighs reverberated through the immense space.

Bill straightened up with a pained expression and a maroon face. He was breathing easier. The wild look was gone from his eyes. Hector's friend was back in control of the demon that temporarily had taken possession of him.

"I'm sorry, man. Of course you can see the autopsy," Bill sighed. "I guess I just lost myself for a moment there. I thought you were accusing me of doing something I shouldn't have."

"Billy, you surprise me. You and I go back to our academy days. We went through boot camp together. Anybody who'd put up with that crap would be friends for life. I just want to understand. I can't think you had anything to do with this. The stress of this sheriff business must be getting to you." They both laughed, knowing in this business, any day may be your last.

"Follow me over to my office, and I'll show you the autopsy. The one thing I remember jumping out at me was the cat scratches on Ms. Sullivan, on her neck. I thought it odd her own cat would have scratched her."

"Yeah, that is strange," said Hector, scratching his head.

ANGUS MADE it to work by nine o'clock on Wednesday morning. The hour-long commute from their riverside home was no problem for him. He could think about all this murder business, or listen to all the music his wife couldn't stand. Oddly, he was partial to all the American or British tunes from the sixties and seventies, particularly the Rolling Stones. To look at them now, these sixty-year old men prancing around trying to hold on to their youth, was just sad. *When I hear their music, it keeps me young,* he thought.

Francesca was there by eight, time enough to get the mail, make the coffee, and retrieve messages left overnight on the machine. She was at her desk when Angus came in. They began with the usual chit-chat about the weekend; and about those things Angus had missed since he had been so wrapped up in the occurrences in Shoestring.

Three or four churches always seemed to be in trouble. These took most of his time—if not in actual intervention, then in helping to figure out how to right the ship. Then there was the financial crisis. They always seemed to have enough to make it at the end of the year. It was the same in the two churches he served before he became an executive. Finances were always a problem, whether it was a perception or a reality.

He liked his job most when he helped start new churches. Everyone had great energy around the start up of a new church. But sadly, the majority of those don't make it. One did make it, and made it big. He loved to see when the church got it right. Just the right constellation of pastor and people and place and timing had to align in order for this faith venture to flourish.

But then it was Angus' turn to fill Francesca in on what he had been doing at Shoestring. She carried in a cup of coffee for him, and now all he could do, instead of protest, was to smile. She put the coffee on his desk.

"How is Beth holding up?" she asked. With only a handful of female pastors in the region, she was partial to them, and hated it whenever anything bad happened to one.

"About as well as she can right now. We need to get an

interim in there pretty quickly, to help start their healing process."

"Why don't you let Frank take that?" Frank Wellers was the Associate for Congregational Development. He had been on staff for only a year.

"Normally I would, but I can't give it to him just yet. The people know me, and besides, I feel kind of responsible."

"Please don't do that to yourself. There's nothing anyone else could have done for the Sullivan woman or Peter, for that matter. I know you; I know you're taking this personally. I'm afraid it's going to kill you."

"I know, I know, but I promised Beth I'd get to the bottom of this, and I will."

"But if you go talk to the session, you won't get home 'til after midnight again. You can't keep doing that."

"Well, I may just stay there through the next day. I'd like to talk to Hector, to see what he knows. I'd like to check on some things while I'm there. By then it will be the weekend again, and maybe Hector can take me fishing where he caught that lunker bass he had hanging on his office wall. I would enjoy the change. It wouldn't be work."

"And what will Angelica do all this time?"

"She could come with me. We can stay over at that bed and breakfast, and maybe we can get together later with Hector's wife...I never worry about her keeping busy. Besides, it's only a couple of days."

"Just as long as you're not neglecting your duties here."

"What letters do I need to write, or better yet, what phone calls do I need to make?" He often thought he spent most of his time on the telephone. He hated to talk on the thing. A disembodied voice confronted him on the other end of the line. He could tell inflection, and intuitively guess at the emotion of the caller, but it was so much easier to do in person.

Francesca handed him the list. Six letters and seven phone calls needed his immediate attention. In the next two days, he was scheduled to attend five meetings. He didn't know how he could do all that and still go to Shoestring. He would have to decide soon.

"You'll have me for two days before I go to Shoestring. We can get a lot of this done if nothing else comes up." The way things had been happening around here, that was a very big if.

Then the phone rang.

BEN IRWIN was changing the oil when he saw him. It was the man from his dream. He was thin with gray hair and a black suit. Ben just saw him out of the corner of his eye, but he knew he was the one. He let the oil drain from the car, drip by drip. He straightened up and watched as the man in the black suit walked across the street. Ben did not know him. That in itself was strange. Ben knew practically everyone in town. He decided he could leave this job for the time being and follow the man.

Black suit was unaware of being followed. In fact he walked with the confidence of a man who was in charge of his life. Once he crossed the street, he turned away from the gas station and walked by the Golden Fork. He stopped briefly to look at the banana cream pie that had made Ruthie's diner famous.

He walked down to the end of the block and turned left, down a tree-lined lane of residential houses. They were modest homes, but well kept. Most of Shoestring's residents were not wealthy, but were proud and hard working, mostly of German descent.

Black suit went to the end of the block and turned left again. About halfway down the block, he stopped and looked around. Ben froze behind a tree. Then black suit went down the alleyway, and Ben followed. After a few steps, black suit ducked into a fenced-in yard. Ben stayed some distance away, but kept watch for several minutes. Black suit never came out again. He was gone.

Ben wondered if black suit suspected he'd been followed. He walked up to the place where black suit had disappeared, his heart beating wildly in his throat. He saw a white fence and a garage, and garbage cans between them. Ben tried the garage door; it was locked.

Hearing a sound on the other side of the fence, Ben stood stock still. Just then a cat leaped to the top of the fence and crouched there for a few seconds, eyeing the frightened old man frozen in his tracks. The cat lifted his tail and jumped down on the other side and ran away.

Ben needed to get out of there, back to what he knew. He didn't know anything about murder, or surveillance, or what would happen if he had been caught too close to the person he'd been following. He knew about fixing cars and gas. He knew he was better off minding his own business. He knew what he had to do.

He also thought about Ruthie. In fact she was there with him the whole time. He had concentrated on watching where black suit went, and all the time he was wondering what Ruthie would do if she knew what he was up to. It felt good to have her with him during the scariest twenty minutes he'd experienced in years.

But Ben could not get the dream out of his head. He still saw the man in the black suit on the roof of the church. Then Ben was falling, falling. But by now he was able to figure it out. He had seen the man in the black suit murder the preacher. That was what the dream was trying to tell him. And seeing the man again brought it all into sharper focus.

But that was just the problem, he thought. *I know I saw the man who killed the preacher, but I didn't get a very good look at his face. I couldn't pick him out of a line-up.*

Why do I care what happens to that church? he thought. He hated the church and those phony preachers with their pasted-on piety. *If they want a woman preacher, then they deserve all the bad things that are happening to them. Maybe this was God's way of settling the score. They hired a wetback. He's probably 'illegal' too, which is another good reason for the preacher to have met his end. You just can't mess with these eternal truths and there not be consequences.*

He knew something else as well. He knew he could not hide. As long as he knew something, no matter how small, he had to help catch this killer. It's just the way he was wired. *As painful as it may be, I will tell the authorities what I know about 'black suit.'*

"I THINK we need a man who is a healer." Tom Branch, the chair of the interim pastor's search committee was the first to speak after the prayer and introductions. Angus, Angelica, and Hector sat in the shadows as they crowded around a small table in a dark basement. Seven men and women, lost and angry, were trying to find their way with only a foreigner to guide them.

"You want healing services in a Presbyterian Church?" Jim Williams, red in the face, had already worked up a head of steam. "That sounds awfully Pentecostal, don't you think? I don't want any of that speaking in tongues and rolling in the aisles in my church."

"You know what I mean," said Tom.

"Yes, Tom, I know what you mean," said Mary Blunt, a soft-spoken little woman. "We need someone who can bring us together after this terrible ordeal. We need a real shepherd."

"Look, we're all aware of Pete's flaws. After the organ was repaired, he lost some momentum. He got distracted.

We all knew it, but none of us would say anything about it. We didn't want to appear disloyal. This is perhaps not the time to say this, but I'm glad we have an opportunity to start over again. I think we needed new blood at the helm of this ship," Jim said.

"No one can replace Pastor Pete," Paula Snodgrass, a woman in her late thirties said, dabbing tears from her eyes with a handkerchief. "I don't know why we have to rush to get an interim. Beth can handle the duties well enough, and we can help her out more than any of us has so far. Let's just let her lead us for a time."

As Angus leaned forward, the light from the little lamp cast dark shadows across his face. "There is no reason to rush. This process could take a year or two. The length of the interim depends on how fast you get your pastor search committee up and running, but I would advise you to wait at least a year before you do. And it wouldn't hurt if we could solve the case and find out who did this. I'm sure most pastors wouldn't want a clergy killer on the loose. But who knows how long that will take?"

"If it ever will be solved..." Shane Edwards said.

"Well, now, there's a cheery thought," said Tom, shooting Shane an angry look.

"I'm just trying to be a realist. Who knows how long it will take? I'm sure the police have a lot of unsolved murders on their hands. More than we'd like to know."

"You know what's even scarier than how long it will take, is knowing it may be one of us who did it. That's the part that keeps me up at night," said Paula.

Angus saw this meeting unraveling faster than a ball of yarn chased by a kitten. "All of that is very interesting," he said. "But I think our time is better served by sticking to what we're here to do, which is help you get started looking for a suitable interim pastor in these unique circumstances."

AFTER THE MEETING, which ran longer than Angus would have liked, he asked several people to stay behind so that Hector could ask them some questions. Tom Branch, Paula Snodgrass, and Jim Williams all agreed. Angelica went to the car to wait for Angus who was allowed to sit in on the interviews.

Paula Snodgrass sat in the tiny room in a chair fit for a child. Angus thought she seemed even more uncomfortable than the chair made her look.

"Now, Ms. Snodgrass, you've stated you were seeing Pastor Pete in his capacity as a counselor, is that right?" asked Hector.

"Yes, that's right, Chief."

"I've had people tell me you were having an affair with Pastor Pete..."

"Why, that's absurd!" Paula straightened up. "Who told you such a thing?"

Hector and Angus looked at each other for a long second.

"So, it's not true?"

"No, it's not true." Paula seemed deflated.

"How did you feel about Pastor Pete?"

"I did love him. I can't hide that. But I knew I couldn't have him, and I knew it wasn't right to try."

"Had you heard about Louise and Pastor Pete?"

"Yes, I had. And the session was about to dismiss him for it...if..."

"He hadn't been killed?"

"Yes."

"Did you have anything to do with that, Paula?"

"Me? You have to be kidding! I loved him, Hector. I tried to warn him what would happen if he continued to see Louise, but he wouldn't listen to me. Maybe Louise is the one you should be talking to. Please, Hector, it's late. May I go now?"

"Just one more question. What were you doing at noon on Tuesday, March 25th?"

"I've already told you this. I was on my way from the bank where I work to the Rotary Club for lunch."

"Did you kill Pastor Peter or see anything that would indicate who did?"

"No. Now, I have cooperated. Please, can I go?"

"Okay, you may leave," said Hector.

As Paula was leaving and Jim Williams came in, Angus leaned over to Hector and asked, "Was any of that new information?"

Hector winked and said, "Almost all of it. Somebody's starting to feel some pressure. When they're tired, like now, we're more likely to catch them."

Jim Williams was a man of average height, but exceptional build. He had gray, short-cropped hair and a mustache to match. A retired Army colonel, he was used to being obeyed.

"You know, Hector, I resent being questioned at this time of night," Jim snapped.

"Well, Jim, I could come by your home in the morning with the sirens blaring and take you down to the station for questioning if you'd like."

"Very funny. Can we get on with this?"

"Very well. Where were you on Tuesday last at noon?"

"The wife and I had gone to the PX in San Antone to do some shopping. I believe we were having lunch in the mess. I think I can come up with a few witnesses who'll back me up."

"Had you heard how Pastor Pete was killed?"

"Yes, they said he was killed by the cross falling on him from the top of the church."

"Right, and its fall was aided by the use of explosives most easily obtained through the military."

"Oh, so you think because I'm retired Army I had the means to do this? But what about my motive? I had no reason to kill Pastor Pete. Oh, sure, we didn't see eye to eye on a lot of things, and spending all the money on the organ was just criminal, but I wouldn't kill him over it."

"People have died over a whole lot less," said Hector. "But what if I told you I knew you were blackmailing Pastor Pete about his affair with Louise. You confronted him about this, and he said to go ahead. He knew what he had done was wrong and was trying to make it right. And when that happened you just lost it, because you really did need the money. It's hard to make ends meet when you're trying to maintain two households, even on a retired Colonel's income, isn't it, Colonel?"

"Why, you son of a bitch! You have no proof. You have no motive, and my alibi is rock solid."

"How well will your alibi play if your two households come out in court?"

"I...I may have two homes, but I didn't murder that guy, and there's no way you can pin it on me. No way!"

"We'll see about that, Colonel. That's all for now, but remember not to leave town. We'll probably want to talk to you again sometime soon." Jim Williams left without shaking hands or looking at either Angus or Hector.

"Well, that went well," said Angus, and Hector laughed. "Pete was in the office the day before he died, asking about borrowing from his pension fund. Do you think that had something to do with the Colonel's scheme?"

Hector nodded. "Very likely, Angus. Very likely."

Just then the door swung open, and Tom Branch stomped into the room.

"What the heck is going on here, Hector?" he snarled. You don't scare me. It's late, and I want to go home. I've answered your questions before, isn't that enough? I've waited patiently. Let's do this and be done with it."

"All right, all right, Tom, keep your shirt on. Just a couple of things I want to clear up," replied Hector. Tom sat down, breathing heavily through his nose.

"You have no alibi for Tuesday noon of last week. Is that right?"

"Yes, that's right. I was out of town on business, by myself."

"That's too bad."

"Am I a suspect?"

"Not yet, but I'm looking for anything to eliminate people. As far as that goes, you have served in the military, haven't you?"

"Yes, I did a stint in the reserves. I served in Desert Storm. So far I have avoided the present mess."

"Were you trained in explosives while you were there?"

"Well, everybody gets introduced to them, but no, nothing special."

"Would you mind if an officer searched your house tomorrow?"

"Well, no. I've got nothing to hide. But it does mean you think I'm a suspect, doesn't it?"

"Not really. As I said, we want to eliminate people as well. Oh, speaking of motive, have you been having an affair with Connie Anderson?"

"Pete's wife? Are you crazy? Pete and I were friends. Why would I jeopardize my friendship like that?"

"I can't speak to the ways of the human heart, but I do know you've been seen meeting her on a couple of occasions at a motel outside of town."

"You've been following me? How dare you!"

"For someone with nothing to hide, it sounds like you're hiding some important things. I bet you'd like us to share this information with your wife, purely in the interest of 'nothing to hide'?"

"No, no, please don't. Yes, I've been seeing Connie. She knew about Louise, and sought someone to help her get through this. She didn't want to go to any of her family or other friends. She chose me."

"You could have said 'no.'"

Angus looked on as Hector and Tom went back and forth. The ugly red dragon of anger breathed fire in the back of his neck. And he was throwing water on it to no avail. Then the dark clouds rolled over his brain, and he slumped a little more in the uncomfortable folding chair. He identified the descending depression and understood he was feeling angry, with no good way to express it. He pictured himself on the golf course, hitting a perfect tee shot–long, straight and true.

Tom rose from his chair, breaking Angus' thought. Hector said, "You are free to go, just don't leave town." And they shook hands, which surprised Angus. As they were all leaving the church, Angus thought, *I'll have to call to get another tee time.*

Angus and Angelica headed over to the Colonel's Bed and Breakfast. He had talked to Jan Smith earlier and had explained he would be late. She had given him a key and told him where they would spend the night.

When they got there the porch light was on, but the house was dark. They found their room, and got ready for bed. The minute his head hit the pillow, he was asleep.

Chapter Twelve: He's All Right

THE COOL MORNING air smelled sweet, with a hint of coal dust from the nearby power plant. Several birds sang their praises to the brightness of the morning as the people below them began another day. Angelica and Angus had missed all this because they were comfortably snug in their king-sized bed with a down comforter. The first thing Angus knew of this brilliant new day was the sound of a sharp rap on the door.

He woke with a start, looked for his pj's and said, "Coming." He reached the door and opened it a crack to find Steve Smith standing there smiling.

He stuck his hand through the door. Angus shook it. "You remember me; I'm my wife's worse half, Steve? We run this B&B together along with a couple of other ventures. Anyway, you had asked for your breakfast to be served at eight."

Angus looked at the clock. "8:30! Bloody Hell! I am sorry."

"Last night must have gone longer than you thought. It's all right. You're our only guests, so you can eat whenever you like. We'll keep everything warm and serve it whenever you say."

"This has never happened to us. I am so sorry. We'll be down in two ticks. And could I get two cups of coffee right away, to kick start the day?"

"I'll bring it right up. And please don't rush."

"Thanks ever so."

They both dressed quickly, drank the cup of coffee Steve had fetched for them, splashed some water on their faces, and made it down for breakfast. Jan had prepared apple pancakes with apple cider syrup, fruit compote, and a soft-boiled egg presented in an egg cup, just the way his dad liked it so many years ago. They also served whole wheat toast with marmalade, juice, and hazelnut cream coffee. He didn't like marmalade, but Angelica did. He wanted to please her even if it was such a small thing. The breakfast was a memorable meal.

"So what are you in town for?" asked Steve after he had finished serving and sat down to have breakfast with them. Jan finished up in the kitchen and also sat down to eat.

"Oh, Steve, you don't need to be so nosy."

Angus raised his hand and said, "It's okay, Jan, we don't mind telling. We're in town to help the church that lost its pastor."

"We heard about that. It's such a sad thing. We came to Shoestring from Houston in hopes we could avoid the violence, but I guess it's just not meant to be," she said wistfully.

"So you've moved here from Houston. How long ago was that, and how do you like it here?" asked Angelica. Angus and Angelica exchanged a glance and a smile.

"We moved here five years ago. And we love it. Our kids seemed to make friends easily, and we settled in fairly well. Steve just got 'down-sized' at the power plant, but with the B&B and the *Century Shoppe*, I believe we'll be okay."

"It seems like a very nice—"

"So how are you helping the church?" Steve interrupted Angelica.

"I'm a minister here to help 'steady' the church and to find the killer," said Angus.

"Oh, I thought it was an accident," said Jan.

"No, there's too much evidence that indicates it was not an accident, although there's nothing solid yet," said Angus.

"Evidence, huh." Steve swayed back and forth.

"I can't say much more than that. I may have said too much already."

"No, no, that's fine. I'll just have to rethink this whole thing, now that they think it's murder. Makes me think of a question that's always bothered me, and you being a man of the cloth might have a good take on it."

"Well, you have me interested. What question is that?"

"Does evil exist, or is everything just cause and effect?"

"The short answer is yes, evil exists, and I believe what happened here was an act of evil. I believe there are no accidents. Everything happens for a reason."

"You'll have to pardon me, Angus. I had a minor in philosophy to go with an engineering degree. I don't get many people who like to talk about this stuff."

"No, this is fun for me too. But can I ask, do you go to church somewhere?"

"Oh, no," laughed Steve. "They're more worried about the color of the carpet than the existence of evil in the world."

"One of my favorite authors is C.S. Lewis. He wrote a book called *Mere Christianity*. He said a person moving in the right direction 'leads not only to peace but to knowledge. When a man is getting better, he understands more and more clearly the evil that is still left in him. When a man is getting worse, he understands his own badness less and less. A moderately bad man knows he is not very good; a thoroughly bad man thinks he's all right.'"

"So you think the guy who did this thinks he's all right?"

"You know, everyone in prison thinks they're there unjustly."

"True enough, but what is evil?" Steve leaned forward.

Angus looked at his watch. "I believe evil is the absence of God, or more precisely, turning one's back on the presence of God, and acting as if God does not matter."

Steve sat back smiling. "I want you to know this has been wonderful for me. I realize you have other things to do with your day, but you've made me very happy. Perhaps you can come back, and we can continue talking about this stuff?"

Angus stood up and shook Steve's hand. "I'd like that very much. Now if you don't mind, I'd like to settle our bill, get our bags, and be on our way."

AFTER LOADING the Jeep, Angus and Angelica waved to the Smiths and decided to walk to the police station. They walked hand in hand under the spring-scented, tree-lined lane, with shafts of sunlight beaming through at odd angles. They walked in silence for some minutes until Angelica cocked her head toward Angus. She smiled up at him said, "That was a fascinating breakfast, wasn't it?"

"Aye, and what was so fascinating about it to you?" asked Angus.

"The food was superb, and the conversation was odd, but stimulating."

"Well put."

"Would you like me to read up on C.S. Lewis so we can have conversations like that?"

Angus laughed. "Only if you want, only if you want, love. And it brings up something else I've been thinking about. The only people I see these days are 'church people.' There's a whole other world out there. Every time I run across a poor person, or a homeless person, or someone in jail, I think, 'Christ came to set them free.' And it should be my job to figure out a way to tell them so they'd understand. I can't do it behind a desk at the Presbytery office. This Steve guy intrigues me, and I'd like to get to know him and others like him better."

"So you're saying you want to go back to the parish? Take a cut in pay, possibly have to move, disrupt the family?"

"Wait a minute, Lass. I'm just thinking out loud. They seem to really need me here."

"You mean you'd want to come here! Wait a minute, '*Pancho*.' You'd want to come to a church that killed its last pastor? What are you thinking?"

"Well, so far there's no evidence to support that idea. And for another thing, we're just talking here. I suspect they'll have to have a long interim to aid in the healing process."

"And let's hope they find the killer before they call a new pastor. That ought to be written into the 'call.'"

"Yes, I'll see to it."

WHEN THEY made it to the police station, Hector was not there. Sergeant Brown said he was with Sheriff Person, following leads.

"The sheriff called Hector and told him his officers had combed Maureen's neighborhood, talking to anyone who might have seen something. They didn't come up with much," said Max, adjusting his glasses. "But they did find three people who knew a lot about her."

"That sounds promising," said Angus.

"Yes, I'd say so too." Max offered Angus and Angelica a cup of coffee, which they accepted gladly. "The sheriff said they discovered Maureen had worked in the local power plant as a secretary. They also found out she attended the local Baptist Church and was part of the singles ministry there. Going through her trash, they found out where she shopped and who her vet was."

"Well, they certainly sound like they've been very thorough."

The phone rang, and Max answered it. "Shoestring Police Department; this is Sergeant Brown, how can I help you? ...Yes, but who is this...Why yes, of course...A friend of Maureen's...Amy Holland, I see...Do you have an address for her...Great, shoot...1532 Oak Str—" Max moved the receiver away from his ear as he finished writing in the log book. "She hung up. I'll have to let Hector know about this soon."

Angus looked at Angelica. "Did the caller identify himself?"

"No, it was a 'she.' Just said she wanted to see justice done."

"If they want to see justice done, why don't they just tell us who did this awful thing," said Angelica.

"Yeah, that certainly would help," said Max.

"Thanks for the coffee, Max, and the information. We have to get going. We'll surely see you later." Angus grabbed Angelica by the elbow and practically pushed her in the direction of the door.

When they got outside, she said, "What's gotten into you? Why are you in such an all-fire hurry?"

"I'm sorry, I just want to see Amy Holland's place before Hector gets there. I just want to see what I can see."

"Are we trying to compete with the professionals now?"

"No, no, just curious, that's all."

"You know what curiosity did to the cat, don't you?"

"Oh, but our cat is too clever for that to happen, much too clever."

"I hope so."

They walked back to the Smith's house as quickly as they could, got in the car, and drove to the address he had overheard. A dark brown two-story brick house greeted them on their arrival. *That's an unusual house for Texas,* thought Angus. He pulled the Jeep in front, parked, went up to the front door, and rang the doorbell. He waited a minute or two and tried the bell again. No answer. There was no car in the carport, just a grease spot where a car had parked at some time. Angus looked inside the front window.

What he saw startled him. He pulled back from the window, his eyes wide, and his hands outstretched as if he were a blind man looking for the wall. He scratched his head and looked around to see if anyone was paying attention to the stranger in front of Ms. Holland's home. He looked again through the window. There on the top of the sofa, soaking up the morning sun, fast asleep, was a calico cat exactly like the one Hector had described having seen at Maureen's house.

What does this mean? thought Angus. *Is it a coincidence, or could this be Maureen's missing cat?*

Chapter Thirteen: The Death of the Party

THE FIRST STOP for Hector and Sheriff Person was Maureen's next-door neighbor. The house was in great disrepair compared to Maureen's. It desperately needed a coat of paint. The yard was overgrown, and a rusted freezer stood sentinel outside, waiting to be relieved of duty. The chain-link fence that separated the patchy, browning yard from the street had several gaps in it, and the carport was piled with junk.

Hector knocked on the purple door with peeling paint. The door crept open, and a large woman in a worn lime green nightgown peeked out from the darkness within. She moved slowly, squinting in the sun. Hector could see the inside was littered just as badly as the outside. The smell was practically unbearable, but Hector maintained an unaffected demeanor.

"Yes," she croaked, "what do you want?"

"Ma'am, I'm Sheriff Person, and this is Chief Chavez of the Shoestring Police." They both showed their badges. "We'd like to ask you a few questions about your neighbor, Ms. Sullivan, if you don't mind."

"I don't know nothing about that." She tried to shut the door, but Bill grabbed and held firm without shoving back.

"Ma'am, our officers said you had information that might be useful to our investigation. We'd appreciate your cooperation."

"I really don't want to get involved."

Hector leaned in, smiled, and said, "You want us to find who did this, don't you?"

She nodded sheepishly.

"And you'll do what you can to help us, won't you? We promise not to take too much of your time."

"Well, all right. I don't know if I can help you much."

"May we come in?" asked Bill.

"No, if it's all the same to you. If you're going to be as quick as you say you are, then there's no reason to bring you inside, now is there?"

"No, ma'am," said Bill.

"How long have you lived here, ma'am?" asked Hector.

"About fifteen years. My no-good husband knocked me up four times, and left me for the checkout girl at the grocer. That was ten years ago. I ..."

"I'm sorry to hear that, ma'am," interrupted Hector. "How long had Ms. Sullivan been your neighbor?"

"About four years."

"What can you tell us about her?" asked Bill.

"Not much. She was nice, as neighbors go. We would chat from time to time, but I was never in her house, nor she in mine."

"Do you know if she was seeing anyone, had a steady boyfriend? Or did she stay pretty much to herself?" asked Bill.

"I'm not one of those nosy neighbors." She lifted her hand to shield her eyes against the glare of the western sun. "I didn't see other cars over there very much. But it did seem there was one more than usual over there the week before she died."

"Now this is important, ma'am," said Hector. "Do you remember what kind of car it was, or the color? Anything."

"I don't know cars. Now, my boy does. He seen the car. He'd know. I'm sure he would."

"What about color, ma'am?" asked Bill.

"It was a brown car, fairly new, kinda' shiny."

"Did you ever get a look at the driver of the car?" asked Bill.

"No, not too much; I never paid much attention. He was average build, middle-aged. Nice looking, fancy suit."

"Thank you very much, ma'am," said Hector, tipping his hat. "We won't trouble you any more." They each gave their cards. "If you remember anything more, please give us a call."

"I will," she said, smiling for the first time through missing teeth. They said goodbye and were gone.

HECTOR'S BROW furrowed as he became more lost in thought about this impossible case. He called up an image of his grandmother looking at him when he was a kid, working on a puzzle at the kitchen table. "You're good at this, aren't you?" she said.

THEY WENT across the street to a pleasant place. The sign on the front door read, "Welcome to the White house." The house itself was white with green shutters, but Hector suspected the name also had to do with the occupants.

Bill rang the doorbell; there was no answer. A dog barked from inside the house. It was a small dog, jumping up and down with every ring. Just as they were about to get in their car, another car pulled up and swung into the driveway. It was a silver, older-model, well cared for Volvo. A middle- aged woman with a slender build and a worried look on her face got out of the car.

They introduced themselves and told her what they were doing there. "Any information you can give us, Mrs. White, would really help," said Bill.

"She was a very sweet person," she said, looking down beyond the ground to the center of the earth, the weight of the grocery sack making her feel like Atlas. "She kept to herself mostly. But on occasion she would baby-sit for us when we went out. She was very generous that way. She worked very hard. She would often come home from work at nine or ten o'clock."

"How do you know she was coming home late from work?" asked Bill, smiling. Hector frowned at him.

"We talked a couple of times about her work, and to hear her tell it, she practically ran the place. I think her family was from up north somewhere, so she had no one here to support her."

"Can you tell us anything unusual about the last week of her life, or about her associations?" asked Hector.

"No, not much. I know she loved her church, and especially the singles group. She had them over to her house about a month ago. They had a cookout in the back yard."

"How did they behave?" asked Bill.

"Oh, no problem. Just young people having a good time."

"Well, thank you, ma'am. You've been a great help," said Hector. They gave her their cards and turned toward the car.

"Officers! Officers!" Mrs. White shouted. "There's something else." As they retreated up the walk, the jonquils around the huge live oak waved a renewed hello.

"The night of the party, I remember one young man left kind of early, and in a huff. I remember because I was watering my plants and I heard squealing tires, and as I turned, I saw a car speed away in a cloud of rubber."

"Can you remember anything about the car?" asked Bill.

"It was dark, so I can't be sure, but I think is was purple, or maybe brown. I'm sorry."

Again they thanked her and got into their car.

"All we have to do is find a dark car, and we've got our man," said Bill.

Hector smiled, nodding.

HECTOR'S MIND wandered again to his grandma's kitchen table. Amber light streamed into the kitchen window, where a young Hector bent over a puzzle, and the smell of holiday tamales cooking on the stove permeated the whole house. This brown bundle of energy worked quickly and intently, matching the scene on the box with the pieces spread out before him. His grandma watched him more than the tamales, smiling a beatific grin.

"Mi hijo, you do love putting puzzles together."

"Gracias, abuelita, and I'm good at it too" said the boy, Hector.

It seemed that was preparation for what he did now. Hector smiled again at the memory, tilting his hat over his eyes for a little shut-eye, as they drove back to Shoestring.

"I DON'T see what the big deal is," Beth said, waving her hands wildly, as she had coffee with Angus and Angelica at the Golden Fork.

"Anytime one of my ministers gets a death threat," he said intently, "it's a big deal."

"Well, what can I do?" Her face clouded over like a dark thunderhead blackening the sky. "I will not take a sabbatical! Hector wants to put a guard on me. And for all I know, he's got people following me."

Angelica reached over the table and took Beth's hand in hers. "It's hard to know exactly what to do, isn't it?"

"Yes, it is."

"Please let us help you figure out what's best for you."

Beth shook her head, still frustrated.

"I have a hunch this poor bloke is going to try to scare you again. He's killed twice; there's nothing going to stop him from doing it again. But what we have to figure out is, why did he call you? He wouldn't threaten you if you hadn't seen something, or perhaps he thinks you know something that would expose him."

"Well, I'm the one who found the piece of cloth."

"But how would he know that?" asked Angus. "And besides, why is that so important? So we know whoever killed Pete probably wore black, but the cloth could have been there a long time, and there's no telling where it came from. The cloth itself proves nothing. It's the right combination of things that we need to catch him. You wouldn't be in danger just for a piece of cloth. I think he's afraid of something you know about him, not related to these murders."

"It could have been a crank," said Beth, trying to sound brave.

"Maybe, but I doubt it," said Angus, frowning. "You need to be safe. You're still in danger."

"If that's true, then it could be anyone," said Angelica.

Angus looked down at his coffee cup. Bubbles formed on the perimeter. It was called a "halo." He remembered a sermon he preached in seminary about a woman who had just gotten a divorce. She went to a coffee shop and saw the halo in her coffee cup, and took it as a sign of hope for her future. He couldn't remember anything else about the sermon. All he remembered was the hope. Sometimes hope is all there is.

He told this story to Beth. She laughed, and he could tell her mood brightened as a result. His pastor's heart warmed when she smiled again. He missed this kind of contact in his present job.

Presbytery Executives are a creation of a corporate culture. "Pencil pushers" and "desk jockeys" were the most apt descriptions of his work. Angus saw many people in trouble, mostly preachers. Some came because of self-inflicted wounds, many more because of the evil residing unchallenged in most congregations.

His principle battle was to confront this ruthless kind of power, let loose among unsuspecting, clueless people. The pastor most often battled it alone. Such struggles were usually less intense for Angus because they were not as personal. But being involved in this murder investigation made it all too personal, and gave him the feeling he was in a fight to the end.

Beth hugged Angus and Angelica, and they walked back across the street to the church. As they left, Ruthie said goodbye and waved to them.

As Angus and Angelica got into his Jeep, his cell phone rang. It was Hector.

"I'll be back in an hour and can see you then. I'm going out to where Maureen worked. You can come along if you want."

"I'd like that," said Angus. "Angelica played hooky from school today because I was going to be gone so long~"

"Say no more. I'll give you directions to my house, and I'll meet you there. I'll call Silvia to let her know to expect Angelica, and they can get into their own mischief."

"By the way, any chance we can go fishing this weekend?"

"I have it all planned. I know exactly where the big ones are. I want you to spend the night with us, and we'll hit it early in the morning."

"You're sure we're not imposing?"

"Of course not. We have plenty of room, and more than enough to eat, especially after tomorrow."

Hector gave him directions to their house and Silvia's cell phone number, in case they got lost. They drove around a little to give Hector time to check with the home front about the change in plans. Angus's phone rang again. It was Silvia, and she asked to speak with Angelica.

They exchanged greetings, then Silvia said, "How would you like to go horseback riding?"

"I'd love to."

"Then let's ride horses for awhile, come home and fix some margaritas, and put supper together by the time the fellas get home."

"That sounds wonderful. I can't wait to meet you."

"Me neither. We'll think about what to do tomorrow on the ride maybe."

Angus reckoned, *Are these the friends we've been waiting for?*

Chapter Fourteen:
"Who's to Blame for this Mess?"

THE POWER PLANT where Maureen had worked hung above the river like Damocles' sword. It had been built thirty years earlier, and at the time, was a state-of–the-art facility. The sad old building had broken windows, peeling paint, rotting wood, and crumbling brick which left the question in Angus' mind about whether the people inside it cared at all.

They came to a gate where a guard greeted them. Hector identified himself, and the guard raised the gate to let them into the parking lot. The razor wire around the chain-link fence gave the distinct feel of a prison.

Angus thought to himself, *How could anyone want to work out here?* He knew it was a ridiculous question. People go where the work is and can put up with a lot if it puts bread on the table. Besides, if where they work is "home," then they'll tolerate even more abuse.

HE FELT the same way about the home he and Angelica had made for their family. He thought about Scotland and his dear aunt who took him in after his mother died. He thought about calling her this weekend, and would plan a trip there with Angelica soon.

Angus remembered the hills where he lived. When he was not working in the mines, he would ride horses with his cousin across the glen. With the wind whipping through their hair, they would leap over logs, race down the hollow, and through the open fields. The memory made his heart race and his blood pump faster, reminding him of how intense life was when he was young.

They walked to the front door of the facility and pressed a button by the door. Hector talked to another guard who buzzed them into a narrow hallway. The guard behind glass asked who he wanted to see. Hector told him, and they were given directions to the director's office. "Down the hall, turn right, turn right again, last door at the end of the hall."

A young black woman behind another glass window greeted them. They told her who they were and what they wanted. She buzzed them into the waiting room. The room was institutional green with old, dark-green overstuffed chairs. They waited twenty minutes until the receptionist finally spoke to them.

"Mr. Waltrop will see you now," she said, directing them to an oak door with the name "Mel Waltrop, Director of Shoestring Power Plant" printed on it. She opened the door and ushered them inside. It was a large, pleasant room with light colors and a collection of African art on the walls.

Mr. Waltrop was sitting behind a massive oak desk, and as they came in, he rose to greet them. He was a big black man in a white shirt, unbuttoned at the collar, with a dark tie. He motioned for them to sit in the two black leather chairs facing the desk.

"How are you doing, Hector? It's been a long time since I've seen you," Mr. Waltrop said. "When was the last time?"

"At the Watermelon Festival last year," Hector smiled. "Remember, you beat me in the seed-spitting contest?"

Melvin laughed a laugh that came from deep within, seasoned by every experience of his long, fruitful life. "Yeah, I remember. Do you want a rematch?"

"You bet I'll be there! I'll make you pay." All three men laughed heartily.

Melvin's smile faded. "I understand that you're here about Maureen."

Hector said, "That's right, Mel. We're drawing mostly blanks on both these murders. Is there anything you can tell us that maybe slipped your mind the first time one of my men came to talk to you?"

"No, Hector, I didn't see her much. This is a large place. She worked in accounting which is at the other end of the plant."

"I've heard she practically ran the place."

Melvin laughed. "I was wondering who I could blame for this mess. This place is so big, it practically runs itself. I know she was a hard worker, and her supervisors had nothing but praise for her. We have a lot of employees, but we care about our people."

Angus couldn't help thinking Melvin was not telling the whole truth. He believed "Mel" knew Maureen more intimately than he was letting on. So he thought, *What is he trying to hide?*

"Who were her friends?" asked Hector. "Did she ever talk about her family? Did she belong to any associations?"

Melvin looked through the file on his desk. "Her parents lived in Nashville. She went up there twice a year. I don't know what brought her here. She had been married, I think, but got a divorce; I believe it was about three years ago. No kids, thank goodness. You know the kids are always the ones who suffer when a marriage goes bad." Melvin flicked with a distracted wave at a fly buzzing his face.

"Do you have an address for the parents?" Hector asked.

Melvin wrote it out and gave it to Hector.

What about the ex-husband?" Angus ventured. Hector looked at him, expressionless.

"I don't have an address, but I do have a name. His name is Harry. Mr. Harry Sullivan. I suppose he stayed in the area. He shouldn't be too hard to find."

"So she kept his name?" asked Hector.

"Yeah."

"Well, Mel, you've been a lot of help." Hector stood, extending his hand, and Angus followed. Melvin smiled broadly at both men. "I wonder if we could talk to her supervisor? I'd like to know who her friends were."

"Sure can. I'll arrange it right now." He pressed the intercom on his desk. "Sandy, can you get Bert for me? The Chief wants to talk with him about Maureen."

"Yes, sir," she said.

Five minutes later, Mr. Waltrop's phone rang. "Sir, this is Bert. You have some people for me to see?"

"Yes, Bert, Chief Chavez and a friend want to talk to you about Maureen."

"Sure I can see them; send them down."

Mel gave them directions, said goodbye, and shook hands again.

"At the Watermelon Festival," said Hector, pointing at him.

"You're on. I can't wait," Melvin said with a wave.

BERT PAVLICK was a short man with a wiry build, in his late thirties. He shook hands with the strength of ten men, and didn't know when to quit. Angus was not sure his arm was still in its socket, but he had a clear hunch that Bert was insecure.

Bert's office was half the size of Melvin's and all business. Diplomas decorated the wall, and one framed family photo stood on the desk. It was a picture of Bert and a pretty young woman with short, blond hair, and a towheaded little girl between them.

"Nice family," said Hector. He'd always found it easier to get information from someone if they first talked about themselves.

"Thanks," said Bert. "Mr. Waltrop said you wanted to know about Maureen."

This guy's all business, thought Hector. "Yes, friends, associates, and any odd coincidences you can remember."

"Amy Holland was her best friend here at the plant."

Hector and Angus looked at each other.

"What?" Bert looked from one man to the other. "Is Amy in trouble?"

"As far as we know, she's fine," said Hector. "It's just that we've wanted to talk to her and have been unable to locate her."

"Well, you can talk to her as soon as we're done here. She's working today."

"That would be great," said Hector. Angus looked at Hector again and smiled.

Bert talked about Maureen in glowing terms. It was as if Melvin and he were reading off the same cue cards. He talked about her sterling character and wonderful work habits. She was promoted to shift supervisor just two months ago.

Something's missing here. Nobody wants to tell us Maureen's faults, thought Angus. *Either she's perfect, or they're hiding things from us.*

"You mentioned she was good friends with Amy Holland. Can we talk with her now?" asked Hector.

"Sure, no problem." He rang his secretary and asked

her to get Amy. "She'll be here in five minutes. You can use the conference room at the end of the hall."

The secretary directed them to a place where they waited. A tall, thin brunette walked into the conference room.

"Hello," she said, extending her hand to Hector. "I'm Amy Holland."

"I am Chief Hector Chavez from Shoestring. This is Angus McPherson. Please have a seat. I have a few questions for you."

Amy sat down, with Angus and Hector on either side of her.

"So you knew Ms. Sullivan?" asked Hector. "How long had you known her?"

"She came here in 1990; started working here in ninety-three. I met her that year. I've worked here for ten years. The people are good, the pay is decent, and the benefits are great."

"Can you tell us anything about –?"

Angus broke in. "I'm sorry, Chief, but I've just got to ask her about the cat. Ms. Sullivan's cat. How did you end up with that cat?"

"What cat?"

"Ms. Sullivan had a cat. When I went to your house, I saw the exact same cat lying on the back of the sofa."

"Mister, I'm allergic to cats. I never went to Maureen's house because of that damn cat. Besides, I think they're smelly."

"Do you live at 1532 Oak Street?" he asked, looking at his notes.

"No, I live at 510 Center Street, Apartment B."

"You live in an apartment, not a house?"

"That's right."

Angus sat back hard, defeated and confused.

Hector spoke up. "Thank you, Ms. Holland. You've been very helpful to us today. We may want to talk with you again. Could we have your phone number as well? Here's my card, if you think of anything else that might help."

She wrote her phone number down and handed it to Hector. Then they stood up and shook hands. Amy stared dagger-eyes at Angus as she left.

Hector motioned for Angus to sit back down.

"What in the world were you trying to prove?" Hector exploded. "I let you come along as a courtesy. I didn't expect you to blow the interview."

"I'm sorry, Chief." Angus hung his head. "I really am. I was just so curious about how she ended up with that cat. Now the mystery is–Who lives in that house? And whoever called the station, why did they give us the wrong address?"

"And you're not going to find out, are you? You're going to let us do that, aren't you?" he said, nodding his head, smiling.

Angus smiled. "Aye, sir. You're in charge."

"Now, I have to find time to come back here again to talk to her about Maureen, thanks to you."

"I'm sorry, Chief. Thanks for letting me tag along."

"If you pull another stunt like that, it will be the last time. Now come on, let's go, Rookie."

"In spite of my enthusiasm, that talk with Amy was pretty strange, don't you think? I mean, we had the right girl, but the wrong address. What could that mean?"

"It means that your source got it wrong...or lied."

"But then what about the cat?"

"We'll find out. Don't worry."

As they pulled out of the parking lot, the dark car followed them at some distance.

"Where's your favorite fishin' hole?" asked Angus.

"I'll show you someday. It's on Old Man Weaver's place. It's his tank, but he lets me use it. He stocked it years ago. But tomorrow, we're headed for Canyon Lake, with my boy, Jorge."

HECTOR AND ANGUS drove by the station on their way out of town. Sergeant Brown greeted them and told Hector someone was waiting for him, a Mr. Ben Irwin.

"Hi, Ben, how are you? You know I need to bring the squad car by for an oil change and a tune up."

"I'll be happy to take care of ya', Chief, but that's not why I'm here."

"Then what's bugging you, Ben?"

He told him about the dream, about the dark suit, and about following him.

"Did you remember where you saw him last?"

"I think it was on Center Street."

"I'm glad you came in and told me about it. If you saw the guy again, would you be able to identify him?"

There was a long pause.

"I'm not sure, Chief. I didn't get a real good look. The only thing I really saw was a dark suit and gray hair."

"Would you want to look at mug shots? We need all the help we can get, and a little time on your part might help a lot. The guy might have a record." Hector's look reminded Ben of a bloodhound he had when he was boy. The sad, tired eyes drew him to the dog, but his uncanny ability to locate animals to hunt was what earned Ben's undying respect.

"If you think it would help."

Hector introduced him to Sergeant Brown, who got a collection of mug shot books. They directed him to an interview room and got him a cup of very black, very old coffee.

Hector wanted to offer up a silent prayer, but thought better of it. *Prayer isn't what's needed,* he thought. *What we need is diligence and patience.* Hector was running short of both.

Chapter Fifteen: Going Fishing

HECTOR'S HOME WAS a fiesta for the senses of color and aromas and scrumptious food for Angelica and Angus. Silvia and Angelica had thoroughly enjoyed their afternoon of horseback riding and hot tubbing. Angus and Hector told the women some of what they had encountered at the power plant. And everyone enjoyed the fajitas and margaritas Silvia and Angelica had prepared.

They discussed the plan for the next morning. Angelica, Silvia, and Maria would go to San Antonio to the Mercado, and Angus and Hector would go fishing with Hector's son, Jorge. Silvia showed Angus and Angelica where they would be sleeping. Angus, Jorge, and Hector prepared the fishing equipment and the boat for a ride on Canyon Lake in the morning. Hector and Angus had lost themselves in their preparation for the following day, and Angus came to bed hours after Angelica had fallen asleep.

The morning came early for Angus when Hector knocked on their bedroom door to awaken him. Angus dressed in the dark, kissed Angelica goodbye, and met Hector in the kitchen. They packed the car with fresh coffee and snacks prepared the night before, gathered up a sleeping

Jorge, and were on their way to Canyon Lake, a half hour from Hector's house. They drove in silence, sipping their coffee, while Jorge slept in the back seat.

Once they arrived, the two men were a flurry of activity. Hector's boat was nothing fancy with its green chipped paint and worn letters. It was a boat strictly used for fishing, but it took the same effort to get it in the water as boats costing thousands more. They loaded all the gear and finally woke Jorge from a sound sleep. Once he saw the boat in the water and his pole with the others, his excitement helped launch the new adventure.

Jorge decided he wanted to go crappie fishing, so they did. Hector knew just where to go, and the cool morning air slapped them all awake. By the time they arrived at the spot, the sun had announced its presence as the clouds on the horizon began to lighten and change color.

Hector was in the stern to mess with the ancient Mercury motor. Angus was in the middle, and Jorge was in the bow. Angus helped Jorge bait his hook with a night crawler. His was the first line in the water. When all three had prepared their hooks and cast their lines in, they studied their bobbers with intense concentration.

After a while Angus whispered, "Boy, is it quiet." The birds and insects were still asleep. Angus drank in the silence. He felt his body relax for the first time in weeks. All his anxiety, anger, worry, and fear seemed to melt away in the calm stillness of the shimmering lake.

Jorge's bobber trembled in the water, sending ripples out from it. Then there was a violent jerk as the bobber plunged beneath the water. Jorge yanked his pole upward with a strong thrust, making sure to keep the tip up. The line twitched and zigzagged through the water. Angus noticed Jorge had been taught well, even as both the men shouted instructions and encouragement. He reeled in and let the line out, until he was at last able to bring the good-sized crappie on board. Both Hector and Angus applauded his accomplishment as Angus took the fish off the hook and put it on the stringer. Angus then helped Jorge put another worm on his hook.

Angus' line jerked violently, and he almost lost rod and reel overboard, as it had been resting lightly on his lap. He quickly stopped helping Jorge and pulled at his own pole. After several minutes Angus added to the number a nice-sized fish.

Angus watched as Jorge finished dressing his hook. Then he attended to his own.

"You're a priest, aren't you?" asked Jorge as he was cleaning up.

"Kind of…yes. But we're allowed to be married," said Angus.

"Well, I've been thinking. This guy who's been doing all this stuff, all this killing. Are we supposed to forgive him?"

Angus turned to Hector and mouthed the word "Wow!" as Hector beamed.

"You know, Jorge, that's about the most important question anyone can ever ask at a time like this. What would it mean to you if you were to forgive this guy?"

"I hate what he's done, but I can't let that hate rule me. That would be two wrongs then."

"That's a great answer, Jorge. Forgiving this guy means his hate can't control you."

After some minutes in which each of them caught another fish, Angus asked Hector, "I've been thinking about the kind of person who could do the things he's done and wanted to check it out with you, if that's okay?"

"That's fine, but let's remember our only job out here is to relax."

"Sure, sure, but you'll indulge me this once."

"Yeah, sure. What are you thinking?"

"Well, this guy must be very meticulous, the way he drilled holes in the cross. He also had some training with explosives because he couldn't practice. He had to know just how much C-4 to use, and how to set the charges, and rig the remote detonation device. He has to be something of an engineer, the way he timed the cross to fall at the exact moment Pastor Pete came out of the door. Plus he's got to be major-league loony to even try a stunt like that."

"Yeah," said Hector. "That about covers it. The thing I've been thinking about lately is, 'What if he got the wrong person?' What if he was aiming for Louise or Beth to start with and just got his timing wrong? We looked all over the church neighborhood for the location where he must have hid when he pressed the button. Maybe he didn't have a real good view. There's one thing missing from your profile."

"What's that?"

"What motive did he have?"

AFTER SEVERAL hours and many more fish, they finally had reached their limit and decided to call it a day. They brought the boat back in, loaded it on the carrier, and started their journey home.

Hector phoned Silvia to find out where they were. They too were on their way home, but the men were closer. They would clean the fish and start to fry them for a late lunch. By the time the women got home, the table was set, the drinks poured, and the fish were ready to eat. Hector and Silvia again enjoyed a festive meal with their new friends.

Finally, Angus said, "I'm afraid it's time for us to head for home. This has been a delightful weekend and wonderful break from the gruesome business of the past two weeks. Thank you both very much."

Hector and Silvia protested that they should stay an extra day, but Angus and Angelica needed to get back to their lives. They bid them goodbye and were on their way.

IT BEGAN to rain. There was no telling in South Texas about the rain. It could last five minutes or all morning. It was unusual for her to be out this early. Usually she'd have so much work to do she wouldn't have a chance to look up. But she had to see him, had to touch him, smell him. She had to have him. He was like a drug, and she had become addicted. Besides, she told herself, *I've been working very hard lately. I need a break.*

They met in a run-down motel on the outskirts of Lockhart. They registered as Mr. and Mrs. Mike Jones and went to their room. They brought no overnight bag, no toiletries. This was all for the moment. For the sake of passion. There was nothing more. She fed off the excitement of the clandestine nature of it. Besides, she liked him. She liked the affection, knowing he thought she was the missing ingredient in his life.

Beth knew if anyone found out about it, it would jeopardize her career. She would have to leave the church. She didn't think she'd have to give up being a pastor, but she knew this thing with Charlie could not go on forever. It would have to end soon, but not now, not today.

They met when Charlie Cosslett came to the church as the choir director three years ago. He came from Austin straight out of the UT music and choral directing program. Beth liked being with a younger man, although she was not so old herself.

At least neither of them was married. Outside the church, such a relationship was their business. But in the church, things were held to a higher standard. In other circles, such a standard would be called oppressive. In the church, it was called orthodoxy.

As they settled into their moveable love nest, a dark car pulled into the parking lot. The intermittent beating of the windshield wipers kept time with the chirping of the crickets as it kept watch all night.

ANGUS STOPPED by Ben Irwin's place to get gas for the ride home. Ben was pumping gas for a large woman with dark features and glasses. She stood in the station's doorway out of the rain. She wore a light beige dress with large printed sunflowers that clung to her for dear life.

Angus pulled up to the pump opposite hers and got out.

"Be right with ya', Reverend." Angus knew Ben would be insulted if he offered to pump his own gas, a practice that was expected in the big city. He joined the woman under the awning.

"Take your time, Ben."

"Rev. McPherson, is that you?" asked the woman.

"Aye, it is." He was good with faces, but names often escaped him. He had worked on it off and on in his lifetime, buying several books, even a tape course from TV with a "money back offer!" It didn't work. He could not remember names, even sometimes his own.

"It's Paula, Reverend. Paula Snodgrass."

"Aye," he said. "You're on the interim pastor search committee, aren't you?"

"Yes, that's right. I'm so glad you're helping us. It's all so difficult for us to take in. It's such a confusing time."

"I'm sure it is." An awkward silence passed between them, thick as a fog, but not as visible. "How long had you known Pastor Pete?"

"I was born and raised here; been a member for twenty years. We started out Baptist, but Daddy didn't like the preacher—too much fire and brimstone, so we left. Presbyterians don't check their brains at the door, and I like that. Peter is one the best pastors we've had...He was, I mean...I just can't believe it." She bowed her head and turned away.

"He obviously meant a lot to you..."

"He certainly did...Please don't tell this to anyone, will you?"

"My car is your confessional." Angus smiled.

Paula looked over at Ben who was ringing up the sale. "I had been going to Pastor for counseling. I've been depressed lately, and he was helping me."

"I'm glad to hear it." He thought how that sounded, then said, "That Pete was helping you, not that you were depressed."

Paula smiled for the first time. "That's how I understood it, Reverend. Now if you'll excuse me, I have to get home. I have a sick husband."

"Call me Angus, please," he said. "Nothing serious, I hope?"

"No, not too. The fool broke his leg falling off a ladder trying to be helpful. He's like a little baby. Men are such wimps when it comes to pain. Sorry, Rev...Angus."

"No need to apologize, guilty as charged."

Paula got in, started the car, and waved at them both as she drove away.

"I went to the police," said Ben, rain dripping off his hat.

"I know, I saw you there yesterday. You wanted to look at mug shots. Why?"

"I witnessed the preacher's murder."

"You what?"

"I saw some guy in a black suit messing with something on the roof of the church. I didn't see his face, but I saw all the rest."

"Well, that's good news!" Angus was excited. He had almost given up hope.

"I spent the afternoon looking at mug shots, but nobody looked familiar."

"It may just mean he doesn't have a record."

"Of course that's what it means, but I was hoping we could nail him."

Ben told him about following black suit and ending up on Center Street. Angus thought about the mystery of the cat and the mixed up address for Maureen's friend, Amy Holland. Center Street played a role in all this.

ANGUS INVITED Angelica to get a piece of pie at the Golden Fork before heading home. The restaurant was practically empty at three o'clock in the afternoon. Ruthie was still there. Angus had come to see her as well as try the delicious pie.

He asked her to recommend their best pie, she said the banana cream pie, and he and Angelica ordered two pieces and two coffees.

"I've seen you in here a couple times," said Ruthie, pointing to Angus. "Are you new in town?"

"I'm with the Presbyterian Church, trying to help clear up this awful mess." Angus took a bite of the pie and fell in love.

"I didn't know him too well, but he was a nice tipper," she said with a wink. "I always liked seeing him come in. He wasn't like the Baptist preacher, so tight his knees rubbed together."

Angus laughed. It surprised Ruthie. She had never seen a preacher laugh. She thought maybe they weren't allowed, although how could you keep from it was something she'd like to know.

Angus had noticed he hadn't laughed since all this murder business had started, but the weekend with new friends and a morning on the lake had relieved him of much of his tension. He had tried never to let a day go by without laughter. He credited the success of his marriage to their ability to laugh and kid with each other. Angelica, in particular, was a master at breaking a tense moment between them by making him laugh.

The little laugh refocused him, and he decided to go fishing a little with Ruthie. "What have you heard about all this?"

"Oh, honey, what haven't I heard? I've heard it all. Some people are so out of it, they're talking aliens inhabiting somebody and doing this thing."

Then she leaned in again and almost whispered, "I've heard about the preacher and his secretary having a 'fling.'"

"But what about who might do this; anything there?"

"Everybody's saying it's somebody from the church, but that's all just talk. I did hear something about the city manager, Tom Branch."

"What did you hear?" asked Angus.

Ruthie leaned into him after looking to both sides. "I heard he hated Pete. I heard they really got into it at one of their meetings. Then I heard he stormed out, saying, 'You're dead, you're dead.'"

"Did you hear what they were arguing about? And where did you hear this?"

"Oh, no help there; these things have legs of their own."

"Yes, but legs are usually attached to a body."

Ruthie left to get them some more coffee and to tend to other customers who had just come in.

"We have to narrow the field of suspects, but how?"

"Well, you're not in this alone, Angus," said Angelica.

"Maybe you need to talk to Hector some more?"

"Yes, I suppose you're right. I just hoped we'd be closer to a possible solution than we are. Unless Hector isn't telling me everything he knows, and why should he? Half the people who have any information aren't bringing it forward without a heavy suggestion from me."

A BLACK fog rolled over Angus like a steam roller. He felt weightless and at the same time so heavy he couldn't move. He did not know what was happening and started to panic. He looked around, and all he saw was the thick, gray fog. He breathed deeply, and that seemed to relieve the grip of this awful uncertainty. Angelica reached over the table and took his hand, concern etched on her face.

"Angus, honey, are you all right?" she asked.

"I am now." He barely managed a smile.

Angus pulled his Jeep onto the wet highway and began the long road home.

"Is that Ben character one of the suspects?" asked Angelica.

Angus had a puzzled look. "Why?"

"Well, have you interviewed him, does he have an alibi, and might he have a motive?"

"I don't know because I haven't asked."

"Don't you think you should?"

"He came forward because he thought he saw someone connected to the murder. Does that sound like the activity of a guilty man to you?"

"Not necessarily, but maybe he did that to throw suspicion off him and onto someone else. If so, it seems to have worked."

"If that's true, then what about Ruthie? For all we know, Ruthie could have done it."

"That's highly unlikely. She's too nice to do something

like that."

Angus laughed. "And Ben's not nice, so he must have done it?"

"Yeah, something like that." Angelica smiled.

The black fog that followed Angus had lifted. For all the stress he felt, for all the pressure he was under to help Hector bring this killer to justice, he knew his beloved would always be there to support and care for him. He also felt responsible to do the same for her.

BETH KISSED Charlie goodbye, then got into her car. Charlie would follow a few minutes behind. They had done this a few times before, and it seemed innocent enough. But they were always as careful as they possibly could be. The beating of the rain on the hood matched the beating of her heart. In fact she couldn't tell them apart.

She would be home in about forty-five minutes. On a windy night like this with rain whipping the car, the twisting hilly road would be especially dangerous. She would have to take it easy. She played Paul Simon's "Graceland" on the CD. It made her feel alive, especially when she needed extra courage. She always played it when she was in a good mood. Nights like tonight helped restore her soul.

She got about halfway home when it happened. It was the darkest, hilliest, and tonight, the slickest part of the ride. She had taken a sharp corner a little too fast and applied the brakes. They did not respond. She swerved off the road, the tires churning up gravel with a roar. She turned the wheel hard, and the car made the curve, wavering like a snake in sand.

Her dad had taught her not to ride the brakes in the mountains, and always down shift coming down a steep incline. She did it now. The car responded with a lurch, but now there was a curve in the opposite direction. She swerved to the left, and the car did so with more control.

Beth saw the headlights of an approaching car in her rear-view mirror. She hoped it was Charlie. She wasn't sure there was anything he could do, but she relaxed thinking he was near, and might actually do something heroic to save her. She honked frantically hoping he would figure out what to do.

She soon discovered this nightmare was all too real. She felt her head jerk back and then heard the crash. The car behind her was slamming into her bumper! He wasn't there to help, he wanted her dead! The car behind her crashed into her again, more violently than at first. She could do no more than try to keep her car on the road.

Another sharp corner and both cars went off the road, fishtailing in the gravel on the shoulder. She tried the brakes again, thinking they might simply be wet, but again they didn't respond. She began to panic. As they were coming out of the last curve, she saw the headlights of a semi-tractor-trailer bearing down on her. She whispered through clenched teeth, "Oh, God!"

As Beth came out of the turn, she could not keep her car from entering the on-coming lane. The semi was coming too fast; it was headed right for her with its horn blaring! She turned away from the impact onto the shoulder of the road and smashed into a huge boulder.

Chapter Sixteen: Dead Man's Rock

CHARLIE DROVE UP as the trucker got out of his semi and headed toward Beth's mangled, upturned car. He approached Charlie with a scowl and clenched fist.

"Do you know who was driving that car?"

"Why yes, she is a good friend. We were on our way home when–"

The trucker's face turned red with rage as he leaned into Charlie. "That crazy bitch almost got us both killed. She's lucky I was able to stop."

"From what I saw, it looked like you were driving too fast for this rain..."

The trucker took a step back and straightened up. They walked in silence to Beth's car.

Charlie could see no movement. What he did see was a tangled wreck of an automobile and steam rising from underneath the crumpled hood. *Have we ruined our lives for one night of passion?* he thought. *Was there something else I could have done?* He felt like crying, but getting Beth out of the car was his first priority now.

He tried the door. It was almost too hot to touch, and besides it would not budge. Beth's head rested on the air bag, but she was turned the other way. Charlie beat on the window and yelled her name, but she didn't move. The trucker tried all the other doors, and found the back right would open with some great effort. Together they pulled with all their might to open the mangled door.

The trucker told Charlie to go sit down while he snaked his way to the front of Beth's car, unbuckled her seat belt, and slowly dragged her out to the side of the road. By that time the paramedics and state police had arrived, their flashing red and blue lights beacons of hope against the wet wind and darkness.

They detected a faint pulse, hooked up the oxygen, and gave her a shot. They put her on a gurney and placed her roughly inside the ambulance doors. They checked out Charlie who felt fine and insisted on riding along. Charlie thanked the trucker for his help, and he was gone.

HECTOR ARRIVED on the scene with the wrecker and the ambulance. The cars would be taken to the State Police impound lot. He spotted a trooper interviewing a man and asked who the supervisor on scene was. He pointed to a tall, thin man talking to another witness.

Hector introduced himself.

"Hello there, I'm Eugene Riley." They shook hands with the warmth of camaraderie.

"What happened here?" asked Hector.

Eugene told him what he had learned from Charlie and the trucker. "We're taking the cars to the impound lot."

"Why?" asked Hector.

"What do you mean, 'Why?'" retorted Riley.

"If you believe Charlie's story, then there may be some tampering. Brakes don't usually just go out. Why don't you have someone from forensics take a look? Just in case he's telling the truth."

"I suppose we could do that," Riley said coldly.

"Do you know which hospital they were sent to?" asked Hector. Riley told him, and then Hector asked him if he could look in on the patient. Riley agreed and asked for Hector's card to keep in touch.

"Here you go," he said, digging into his wallet and producing a card. "I may stop by the hospital on my way home."

"It's a free country."

Oh, indeed it is, thought Hector. *You have no idea.* They shook hands, smiled faintly, and parted.

ANGUS PULLED up the winding gravel drive. The shadow of a jack rabbit darted in and out of the light, and then it was gone. He felt an instant kinship, slowing the Jeep and peering into the darkness for another glimpse of the magnificent animal. But it had disappeared. His life was darting in and out of darkness. He was afraid for the first time in a long time. The more he sought the truth about these murders, the more deeply involved he got. He couldn't stop thinking about it. This was now more than the death of a friend. This was death itself; something he'd been running from his whole life. He was afraid it would catch up to him and to his family. This fear was new to him, and it made him very uncomfortable.

As he drove up to the house, the lights passed over the barking mouth of their golden lab, Eve. Angus and Angelica had loved Mark Twain's *The Diary of Adam and Eve* and named their puppy and cat accordingly.

The other dog was a mutt named Calvin. He was old and moved slowly as Angus got out of the car. Angus bent down and looked deep into Calvin's wet, brown eyes. He had great affection for the dog and the man for whom he was named. The dog had been with them since they were first married. The man, Calvin, had fascinated him in seminary. Angus devoured the "*Institutes,*" marveling at the way he laid out his arguments with such logic and precision.

Angie retired, and both dogs marched with Angus into the kitchen in hopes that he would give them a snack, which he always did. The kitchen was one of the biggest rooms in the house and one of the reasons they were so drawn to it. It was the place where everyone gathered in the morning before departing for their day. It was the last place they gathered to share with each other how the day had gone.

He got a glass of merlot and some Ritz crackers and sat down at the center island to read. He had just finished *Moby Dick* and wanted something light. He chose a Grisham novel and settled down for some happy reading. He was glad he had these little escapes, especially now in the middle of this grisly business. After reading for a half hour, he got up, turned off his cell, and unplugged the house phones. For one day, nothing was going to bother them, no matter what.

Angus thought if it was a nice day tomorrow, they might take the horses for a ride. It would be one of the roughest rides of his life.

ANGUS AWOKE the next morning, fixed the coffee, and picked up the paper. The sun began to rise with all the promise of the first day of the world. Angus knew sunrises were a good deal more subtle than sunsets, yet for some reason they filled him with awe. As he saw the soft, fluid pastels emerge, he thought of the first day of the world, "*In the beginning...*" Those words never failed to stir him, no matter how many times he had heard or read them. This was a new day. He meditated in an old rocker handed down to Angelica by her Mexican ancestors.

He was meditating on Psalm 139, his mother's favorite. "*O Lord, you search me and know me...I praise you because I am fearfully and wonderfully made...Search me, O God, and know my heart, test me and know my thoughts...*" It was a psalm about identity, about knowing who you are and whose you are. It's about seeing this sunrise and knowing who to thank.

Every time Angus sat down, Adam, their gray short-hair cat, took it as an invitation to lie on his lap. It's as if Adam knew that Angus belonged to him, and Adam's fate lay in Angus' lap.

Even though he was trying to concentrate, Angus let Adam up and petted him. There was something so soothing, so calming about the sound of Adam's loud purr. Angus could feel his blood pressure go down with every stroke of Adam's fur.

HECTOR HADN'T been out fishing twice in one week in years. But he had such a good time with Angus and Jorge, he decided to see if Jorge would go with him to the tank on their neighbor's land. It would give them a chance to catch up. At least that was Hector's hope. Jorge was growing up, and before long he would be a teenager.

Hector needed to warn him about the changes happening to him. His body, mind, and emotions would go through all kinds of new changes. It might be a bumpy ride, but one thing Hector wanted Jorge to know was how much he and his mother loved him. Armed only with that knowledge, he would be okay.

"Warning!" Hector had almost forgotten. He would have to warn Angus about Beth. He had gone to the hospital. She was very bruised up, but would be all right with rest. They would not know about the car for a week. She had been very lucky. He tried to call Angus, but the phone had been disconnected. He would call the Driftwood Police to get someone over to see Angus and tell him all that had been happening.

Hector and Jorge packed up the car and drove to the tank near their home. They didn't take the boat this time. The sun and a slight breeze met together on the plain, mingling like two lovers in a soft embrace. Hector caught two good-sized bass, and Jorge caught one huge catfish. They took pictures to remember the moment and would have a family feast later to celebrate their *buena fortuna*, their good fortune.

But no matter how hard he tried, he couldn't get these cases off his mind. The clues were many: a piece of black cloth, plastic gloves, a suspect list, Maureen's death, and a missing cat. He had been so distracted by the second murder that he had lost sight of the first. And the fight with Bill Person felt so strange. *Was he the same guy I went to the academy with?* he wondered.

He was sure the second murder was more of a spur-of-the-moment thing than the first. *Therefore, it's more likely that whoever did this might have slipped up somehow on the second one, assuming they are related,* he concluded. *Was it a crime of passion? Were the killer and Maureen involved, and she said 'no' which cost her life?*

Hector was operating on the assumption that the second murder was done to cover up the first. And if there was foul play involved in Beth's accident, then her life must be safeguarded. But if Beth were to die, what would that mean in relation to the other two? Does this killer just not like preachers, and Maureen simply got in the way?

Regardless of where the answers would come from, Hector knew he must protect Beth. Hector called Max to have him send someone to watch Ms. McKinley around the clock.

Meanwhile he would try to forget all this, and celebrate this manhood moment with his son. When they got home, he gave his wife a squeeze as he beamed at Jorge and his joy.

ANGUS HEARD the crunch of tires on the gravel drive. He parted the curtains and saw the green and white squad car of the police department. It was their only car. The dogs barked to announce the arrival of Hank Morehouse, police chief of Driftwood.

It must be pretty important to get Hank out this early on a Saturday, thought Angus. Hank was in his mid-fifties with bushy gray hair and evidence of a few too many beers and too little exercise. His uniform was starched, but his personality was not. They had known each other for the ten years that Angus and Angelica had lived out here. They met at a town meeting and had been good friends ever since, occasionally playing golf together.

Angus invited Adam to get off his lap. He had found you can tell a dog what to do, but not a cat. Adam had to be convinced that whatever you were asking of him was in his best interests. He did so now.

Angus got up and went to the back door. Everyone knew to come to the back door. The only people who used the front door were sales people, tax men, and undertakers.

He was struggling with himself as he walked slowly down the back stairs, through the den to the kitchen. A sense of foreboding came over him. He remembered Hector meeting his family on the river with the news about the threats to Beth's life. *This can't be good news*, he thought.

On the other hand, he struggled with the anger welling up within. *I deliberately am trying to arrange some time alone with my wife*, he thought. *Why can't they leave me alone?*

ANGUS KNEW Presbyterians did not venerate saints the way Catholics do. But he had his own anyway. Jacob, the patriarch of Israel, was his saint. Jacob came out of his mother's womb, grabbing the heel of his brother, Esau.

Jacob later tricked Esau out of his birthright for a mess of porridge, and so he was a clever fellow and also a jerk.

What Angus admired most was when Jacob wrestled with the angel at night. It changed his life. Jacob could not let go until the angel had blessed him. He walked with a limp after the angel wounded him, but he was a blessed man.

Angus was a wrestler. Right now he was wrestling with whether to open the back door or not. He knew he would, but he didn't want to. His civic duty fought with his need for some rest, some peace and quiet from this whole mess. He knew he could not run, and the fact that he called this man a friend meant that he would at least listen to what he had to say. He owed Hank that much.

He sighed deeply and opened the door as Hank came up the steps. Angus welcomed him in, and poured him a cup of coffee, black, 'the way God intended,' as Hank would say. They sat on the deck to watch the rest of the sunrise.

"You're out early on a Saturday, Hank," said Angus.

"You know I wouldn't be here if it weren't important, Angus," Hank said. "Hector Chavez from Shoestring has been trying to get hold of you. It seems another minister has been hurt."

Beads of sweat glistened on Angus' forehead in the morning sun as Jacob's wrestling angel body-slammed him onto the porch. Angus replayed that move over and over in his mind. He felt the ache of it all over his body.

"Oh, my God," he said finally. "Not Beth."

"Yes, I'm afraid it is," said Hank. He looked at his notes. "Beth McKinley."

BAM! HIS body ached, emphasizing each one of his sixty-three years. He winced as he got up and went to the railing, looking out as the last remaining pinks and grays of the soft sunrise turned slowly into the sharp blues and whites of a glaring mid-morning sun. But he really couldn't see it.

"She's all right, isn't she?" Angus said, pleading.

"Well, she's in the hospital," Hank said.

Bam! Bam!

"But they think she'll be okay," said Hank, referring to his notes. "The clerk of session, Tom Branch, also wants you to lead worship for them tomorrow if you're able. Here's his number."

"Tomorrow? But...that's fine. I've got his number," said Angus.

"Was it foul play?" asked Angus, as Hank got up to leave.

"They don't know yet. The state boys are looking into that. I don't think they'll know for a day or two."

"How's Charlie?"

"Who?"

"Charlie, Charlie Cosslett."

Hank searched his notes. "I don't think there was any mention–Oh, yeah. Charlie Cosslett was at the scene. But we don't know what his involvement was. How'd you know about him?"

"Where Beth is, Charlie is sure to follow," Angus said smiling.

They shook hands and said their goodbyes. Angus walked absently to a deck chair and sat down hard, exhausted and spent. *Jacob did not let go of the angel until he blessed him.* Angus could see no blessing here. He sat there for several minutes with his head in his hands. Then an idea began to creep into his head, like the dawn.

"Oh, my God," he whispered out loud.

He thought about Jacob and the wrestling and the blessing. He hadn't searched for it, it just came to him. The blessing was to remind him why he left the parish and went into the kind of work he did now. He wanted to be a pastor to pastors. Being a pastor is an impossible job, and they need someone who understands what they go through every day.

The problem is the job had gotten in the way. There were budgets to balance, conflicts to mediate, new churches to start, along with an endless, mind-numbing array of meetings to attend, phone calls to return, and letters to write. This whole business with first, Pete, and now Beth had shown him what was important. Up to now, precious little of his time was devoted to the support and nurture of "the folks in the trenches," as a pastor friend once called them. That was going to change.

Enough time wasted, Angus thought. *I've got to get busy.*

Chapter Seventeen: Guilt Offering

HECTOR WAS HAVING a bad day. These murders had dogged him and left him frustrated. He decided he would try to push things along a little bit. He decided to see Tom Branch. He stopped by City Hall to see if the city manager was in. He was led to Tom's office on the second floor of the courthouse. Tall ceilings and big windows greeted Hector who had never been in here before.

Tom stood up from behind his desk and shook Hector's hand firmly.

"To what do I owe the honor of this visit?" asked Tom, leaning back in his black leather chair, with his hands folded behind his head.

"Well, Tom, as clerk of session for the church, you must know a lot about how it runs," Hector paused, "or doesn't."

"So this is about the mess at church?"

"I'm afraid so, yes. Until we find this guy, I know I can't rest."

"I've already spoken with your deputy, Max. I was nowhere near the church the day Pete was killed, and I didn't know Ms. Sullivan."

"No one's accusing you of anything, Tom. I just want to go over some things you might have forgotten to tell Max."

"Like what?"

"Like what you were doing that day? Where were you?"

"I had gotten away for a quiet lunch in Gruene. I maybe can remember the waitress if I need to."

"Did you get along with Pastor Pete?"

"I thought he was a good minister and man. I respected what he stood for and bought into his vision."

"Did you ever disagree about anything?"

"Not that I can think of," Tom said, scratching his chin.

"Did you two meet to talk about something on the day before he was murdered? And did you argue then?" asked Hector. "Louise Lassitor is prepared to testify that you did."

"Yes, yes, we met. I don't know if you would call it an argument, but I guess we did raise our voices."

"Ms. Lassitor said she could hear practically every word from behind a closed door. That sounds like an argument to me."

"Okay, we argued, but I didn't kill him." He looked around the empty office just in case someone was listening.

"Who said anything about murder?" Hector smiled.

"Hey, look buddy, I could get you fired."

Hector leaned into Tom so they were nose to nose. "I could get you put away for twenty to life." Hector could see a glimpse of genuine fear forming in Tom's eyes. He walked away.

After a pause, Hector asked, "What did you argue about?"

"Money. We had just spent thousands on the organ, and that was expected, but the general fund was running dry. I was worried."

"And so you argued?"

"Yeah, and I may have suggested cutting staff, and he took exception to that."

"Who did you suggest be cut?"

"Beth McKinley."

"But doesn't a church this size need at least two pastors?"

"It would be temporary, until we get a better financial footing."

"But Peter took exception to the suggestion?"

"And that's why we argued. B... but I didn't kill him."

"So you said."

ANGUS DECIDED to make breakfast. They would have Denver omelets, bagels and cream cheese, home fries, and a fruit salad. He loved to cook–again, like Jacob, he thought with a smile.

He loved bringing ingredients together for a pleasing result. There was something magical about the art of cooking. Also there was a beginning, middle, and end to it. He could see a finished product, which was rare in his work.

The same was true for him regarding this "murder business." No matter how painful or tragic the whole thing got, Angus knew in his gut, sooner or later the killer would expose himself and would be caught. His faith told him.

He would have to go back to Shoestring today. He would preach there tomorrow, though what he would say was a complete mystery to him. But for now, this moment, it was all about his wife. He hoped Angelica would go there with him. He knew she would be disappointed, and it made him feel bad that it could happen yet again. They would plan something next week, maybe this same outing. And nothing would stand in their way. He would promise it, but could he deliver?

He was beginning to doubt his own trustworthiness. This "inner Jacob" was beating Angus up pretty badly. He didn't know how much of this he could take.

Adam liked to help in the kitchen. That's the spin Angus put on it anyway. The dogs were bigger, the humans were more intelligent–perhaps–but Adam ruled the house. This was his place; the others were just guests. What Adam wanted were the tasty bits. Not the green peppers or onions, but the ham and cheese.

They even did a little dance together. Adam would get on top of the action as Angus chopped the ham and cheese. He would rub up against Angus' arm and purr so loudly it filled the whole house. But Angus wasn't fooled. He knew Adam wasn't doing it to be affectionate. He wanted FOOD, and even the One Who Ruled the House was not above a little flattery if it could get him some of those tasty bits.

Angus would take so much of this close scrutiny and then would toss Adam on the floor. Angus would not put him outside. He rather enjoyed the dance, and today he needed this cat ritual as much as the cat needed him.

His thoughts drifted to Shoestring and the grisly scene being played out there. *This killer is playing with us*, Angus thought. *To kill two people and attempt to kill another is simply maddening. But that's what he wants. When you're angry, you don't think straight. You just react.*

He rubbed Adam's glistening fur. As much as the death of Pastor Pete and the attempt on Beth bothered Angus, it was Maureen's death that troubled him most. He had figured the motive had something to do with anger at the church or someone in it. But Maureen wasn't connected to the church. What *was* the connection? Angus looked down and Adam was lying on the business section of the paper. What he could read of the headline said something about a utility rate hike. Angus smiled and said, "That's it!" out loud, and he kissed his cat.

He arranged the breakfast on a tray and got a red rose from the garden and placed it in a vase. He ascended the stairs, opened the bedroom door, and put the tray on the bedside table. Angelica was sound asleep.

Angus bent down and kissed her on the cheek. Her lashes twitched, and her eyes slowly opened. She blinked and stretched her shoulders slightly, mumbling something as she came into consciousness.

"Speaking in tongues so early in the morning. Very impressive," said Angus.

They both smiled. Angelica saw the breakfast tray and blinked again, then gave Angus a beatific grin.

"My Mona Lisa," he said, kissing her lips.

She wore a white cotton granny gown tight around her neck. To Angus there was no sexier sight in all of Christendom. She sat up and smiled again, and a strand of dark auburn hair fell across her face.

"I'm impressed, sweetie, thank you very much." She looked again at the breakfast. "Why did you go to all this trouble? I thought we might go out." It was her favorite thing to do on Saturday morning.

"Oh, I was up early and thought this would be a nice treat for a change," he said, placing the tray on her lap.

"Where's yours?"

"I'll get mine and join you in a minute."

He got his tray and climbed into bed next to her. They enjoyed this moment of grace, chatting happily about the meal, and the children and then...

"What are we going to do today?" Angelica asked. "You said something about horse..."

She stopped herself, her eyes narrowing into little slits, her brow furrowing with each angry thought.

"That's what this breakfast is about, isn't it?" she asked. "We're not going to have a day together, are we? You were trying to buy me off."

"No, no, no. It was a guilt offering to my goddess," he confessed.

Angelica interrupted, "Oh, that was good."

"Did you like that? It was just a sudden inspiration as I gazed at your beauty."

"Careful, don't lay it on too thick."

"Okay. I want you with me for two days. It just wouldn't be riding horses."

"Well, what is it?" She folded her arms across her chest, turned her head, and pursed her lips.

He told her about his early morning visitor and the news he brought. Finally she said, "Angus, of course, you must go do this. You know I support you 200 percent. But this keeps happening. It's always something, it always has been. It never stops."

"Aye, *mi hija,* I know. If I could make it up to you and the boys for all those years I missed, I would gladly. I'm sorrier than you'll ever know."

"That's what you always say, and oh, you try, but it keeps happening."

A pause hung heavy in the air between them. All the past disappointments and missed events in a lifetime of living, all the regret and anguish, and broken dreams hung like a thunderhead above them. It hovered on the ceiling ready to release the full fury of its rage.

"You know I have a life too. I've got papers to grade and the parent/teacher conferences to get ready for."

"I know that, sweetheart. I'm sorry about this. This has just come up, and it would mean a lot to me if you could come with me. I promise we'll be back no later than two o'clock."

"I'm the one who always has to drop whatever I'm doing and help you. Why don't you help me once in a while?"

"Well, when we get back, I'll help you grade your papers while you prepare for your conferences. When do they start?"

"Not until Wednesday."

"Well, see, you've got plenty of time. Please, baby. Pretty please, with syrup on top?"

Then she smiled, put the finished meal back on the bedside table, and flung the bedclothes off her side of the bed. The threatening perfect storm turned into a nourishing spring shower.

"When do you want to leave?"

After a pause, Angus said, "Thank you, mi hija."

"I would really appreciate it if you worked a little harder on learning to say 'No.' Maybe old dogs can learn new tricks."

"Aye, they can." Angus came to her, hugged her tightly, and kissed her passionately.

"I'D LIKE to speak to Beth McKinley, please." Angus gripped the phone like he wanted to choke it.

"I'm sorry, sir, but doctor's orders are for her to have no visitors or phone calls for twenty-four hours." The nurse's pleasant tone had an undercurrent of steel, and Angus could sense it.

"Please tell her that Angus McPherson called, and I'll be by to see her tomorrow."

"Are you family?" the nurse asked, as ice formed on the line.

"Excuse me?"

"Are you–?"

"No–"

"Only family is allowed–"

"I'm the only family she has, 'Lass.' I'm a minister as well, and I believe you give..."

"Why, yes, sir. I'm sorry, sir. I didn't know."

"I'm sorry too," said Angus. "I didn't mean to raise my voice. Please give her my message, won't you?"

"Yes, sir."

He hung up the phone and started punching in Tom Branch's number. He knew it was early, but he needed to let him know some things. When Tom answered the phone, Angus could tell he was agitated. He apologized and told him he had heard about Beth and that he thought it was not an accident. He also told Tom he would be coming in later today to see her and to preach in the morning. Tom thanked Angus and was quickly off the phone. Then Angus went out for a quick morning ride with Angie before they left.

He went out to the barn to saddle the horses. The dew on the grass and the slight haze in the air gave the place a pastel feel, like a Monet painting. *Now there is something I'd like to take up when I retire,* he thought to himself. In the back of his mind, he knew he had no gift for painting. He couldn't even draw flies. But just to capture a moment like this and freeze it to share with everyone, what a gift that would be!

He worried a lot out of earshot of Angelica about retirement. He didn't usually concern himself about finances, although the way the stock market was acting, he was beginning to worry. He had started saving for retirement when he was in seminary and had been ever since. And even though he started late in his life, he knew they would do just fine.

What worried him was what he would do with the time. He couldn't see himself chasing that little white ball around all the time. He'd need something a bit meatier than that. He had thought about getting back into preaching. Of all the things he had given up when he took the Presbytery job, he missed preaching the most. He enjoyed studying scripture. There was always some truth to rediscover, some new angle of interpretation to explore. He also found joy in sharing those insights with others.

He had never thought of it before, but interpretation was one of the central tasks of life. *How one looks at life is one's interpretation of events. And those interpretations go to make up how we see ourselves, what kind of people we become.* He adjusted Dixie's bridle.

Or maybe, if the economy continues to 'go south,' I'll be flipping burgers at McDonald's, he thought. *At least the guy had a proper name.* He smiled at the thought.

He worried because the church had been his life. There was nothing else. *I have no hobby, unless you count horses, and if I didn't have the money to eat, I certainly couldn't feed the horses.* That's why he had taken up golf now that he neared retirement. It would give him something to do, just in case.

At that moment he saw more clearly than he had ever seen. He remembered the story of St. Paul's conversion. He was on his way to Jerusalem, taking prisoners who claimed to be Christians to be jailed there. Just outside Damascus, a bright light blinded him, and out of that brilliance, Jesus asked a question that changed his life. *"Saul, Saul, why do you persecute me?"* Then he was taken—blinded—to Damascus where he stayed for several days. Then someone was directed by God to baptize Saul—who became Paul—and to tell him that he would be a missionary to the Gentiles. At his baptism, something like scales fell from his eyes, and Paul could see again.

Angus knew how Paul felt at that precise moment.

HE LOVED the smell of horses and hay. If it wasn't for his allergies, he could get addicted to it. There was something earthy and grounded about it; the memories, so many memories. He brushed down each horse, happily saddled Rex, and then he sneezed. He felt lighter than he'd felt since this stuff at Shoestring had begun. It felt good.

Chapter Eighteen: God's Half Brother

"YOU'RE QUITE a lucky young lady." Dr. Benson was a bent-over old man, but his sharp mind and keen eye made him a huge asset in the hospital. The reflexes weren't as quick as they once were, and his arthritis was quite literally a constant pain. But the eyes still twinkled, the same brilliant blue they were when he was a kid.

Beth laughed, then regretted the impulse with a painful moan.

"I'm serious. Your injuries would be much worse than they are if you hadn't had the air bag. I think you can put up with two black eyes in exchange for your life."

"When you put it that way," she whispered, "I see what you mean."

"Now, you lie still," he said. "Try to get some rest. We'll do some tests in the morning to make sure everything's where it's supposed to be. You should be able to go home in a day or two."

"That's good news, Doc," said Charlie. He hadn't left her side since the accident. They had wanted to keep their relationship a secret, but the time for secrets was over.

"You understand," Dr. Benson said to Charlie, "when

I say she can go home, I mean she has to rest. At least for a week before she can go back to work or anything."

"I got ya'," said Charlie, and he shook the old man's arthritic hand. The force of the handshake shot pain throughout the doctor's frail body.

"Hi, Beth." Angus stood in the doorway with Angelica, who held a bouquet of flowers. Beth saw the soft glow of the hall light shining on Angus and was hopeful for the first time since the accident. Charlie's face flushed as red as the roses in Angelica's arms.

"We're sorry to interrupt," said Angus.

"No, no, you're fine," said Dr. Benson. "I was just finishing up here. My name is Fred Benson. I'm one of the oldest 'sawbones' in these parts."

"I'm Angus McPherson and my wife Angelica. I'm a colleague of Beth's and would like to see her, if that's okay?"

"I think it would be fine, if you don't stay long." The old man scratched his thick mane of white hair as he left the room.

Angus and Angelica walked over to the bed and looked down at her. Angelica showed her the flowers. Then she took them and proceeded to find a vase and some water. Beth looked a mess with tousled hair, black, sunken eyes, and bruises everywhere.

"Hi, wee Lassie," he said.

"Hi, Angus," she whispered. "Thanks for coming. You don't know what this ..."

He put his finger to his lips. "Don't speak now. I'll come by after the service to see how you're getting along."

"What service?"

"Tomorrow's Sunday. You were planning to have worship tomorrow, weren't you? I know you're indispensable, but as they say in show business, 'The show must go on!' and so it shall."

"So you're preaching in the morning?"

"Don't look so shocked, Lassie. You know, I've done a fair bit of preaching in my day."

"Oh, but I'd love to hear you again. Maybe they'll let me..."

"You're right where you need to be. I don't even know what I'm going to say. It was one of those cases where my heart answered before my brain kicked in."

Beth smiled a crooked smile.

Angus looked at Charlie, and Beth followed his glance. "Angus, you remember Charlie Cosslett, the choir director at the church."

"Nice to see you again," said Angus, shaking his extended hand.

"Same here," said Charlie.

AT THAT moment, a man in a dark, late-model car pulled up into the hospital parking lot. The man in the shadows did not really know what he was doing there, or if there was anything he could do. He just parked his car and looked and waited and thought. He'd have to be patient. He certainly couldn't do anything in broad daylight. But whatever it was, it would have to be soon, and it would have to be fatal. *That bitch cannot live,* he thought. *She knows too much.*

ANGUS' CELL phone rang to the tune of the Bach fugue in D Minor. He still was a big fan of the organ. All the church growth people said 'lose the organ.' Only about six per cent of the public listened to it anyway. But Angus thought about baseball. Even with all the labor unrest and steroid scandals, baseball is still America's game. And even though they have state-of-the-art sound systems in each one of those parks, it's still the organ that excites them to cheer their team on to victory. Thousands listen and cheer to that music and so would he.

He excused himself and went into the hall. It was Hector. He said something that shook Angus to his knees.

"Listen, I just got off the phone with the State boys. There's something you need to know."

"What is it?" asked Angus.

"The brakes were tampered with."

There was a pause on the other line. Angus swallowed hard, not knowing what to say.

"Angus?" asked Hector.

"Yes, amigo; I'm still here. How? How do you know?"

"The brake lines were cut. There are definite knife marks on the tubing."

"I'm with Beth right now. Of course I won't tell her. I'm glad to see you have someone watching her."

"So, he's there? Good."

"He sure is. He wouldn't let me in because I wasn't 'family.'"

"I'm going to talk to Beth on Monday. I need to know what she knows that puts her life in jeopardy," Hector said.

"I'd like to know that too."

"I'll tell you what I find out. But promise me you won't do anything foolish."

"I promise." Angus hung up and went back into the room.

"Well, I've got to think of something to say tomorrow. We're staying at the B&B. Here's the number in case you need to talk. We'll drop by tomorrow on our way out of town. You take care of yourself, young lady. And please be careful."

"Don't worry, Angus. I'll be fine. Thanks so much for doing this tomorrow. It means a lot to me."

"Don't mention it, Lass. You just get well, and get back to work. That church needs you."

"I know it does. I'm so worried about this business. When are we going to catch this guy?"

"What's this 'we' stuff? You're going to get well, then we'll worry about what 'we're' going to do."

"Actually, I guess I should go too," said Charlie. "It's the fourth Sunday in Lent. We're doing one piece from *The Messiah* each week. If I don't get my rest, I won't be worth shooting in the morning." Charlie realized what he said, turned tomato red, and stammered an apology. Angus put a comforting hand on his shoulder, shaking his head.

"You sure you're going to be okay, Beth?" asked Angelica, bending down to kiss her on the forehead.

"I'm going to be fine. Now all you worry-warts clear out so a girl can get her beauty rest. By my looks, I really need it," said Beth.

THE DARK car sat empty in the dim light of the hospital parking lot, waiting for its owner, who had entered the hospital to look around. He got Beth's room number from the unattended information desk. The volunteer who sat there had gone home long ago, feeling satisfied she had done another good day of helping where she was needed. The only mistake she made was leaving the list of patients' room numbers on the desk. But after all, she would say later, what if a loved one came and wanted to know what their room number was? She was still good, even though she didn't feel quite so perfect.

He slithered his way carefully through side stairs and up empty passageways to the third floor, room 314. As he approached her room, he heard the sound of people talking. The nursing station was empty because of the shift change, so all were in the conference room going over the patients' needs. *After tonight, there would be one less to care for.* The scar over his lip turned into a second smile.

He also saw the guard at her door. *I guess they discovered the brake line,* he thought. *No matter, I'll take care of him too.*

He ducked into a supply closet, hoping the janitor hadn't started his shift.

He had no weapon and looked around for what he could use to subdue the guard. He found a rag and a broom, and a piece of twine. He took off his coat and his shirt and tied the rag around his head. He slipped on his gloves and brought out the mop and the bucket. He put the string in his pocket and started mopping the floor.

He saw the doctor and Angus, Angelica, and Charlie all leave. Each said goodnight to the guard, shook his hand, and left in the elevator.

The guard began to read. The man squinted to see what he was reading. It was the Bible. *Now isn't that quaint,* he thought. *His God won't protect him tonight. He won't protect that bitch either. I am God's half brother tonight,* he thought. *The fallen angel.*

No one can stop me from what I must do, not even God; maybe even especially God. The Bible portrays God as so strong, so capable... But he never had seen God that way. At one time he bought into what he called 'all the faith crap,' but soon he was disabused of it.

His father beat his mother to death, and God never lifted a finger to save her, even with all her faith. *That bastard played with my sister, and God was nowhere to be found, no matter how hard I prayed. And tonight, God's half brother, the avenging angel, will exact his revenge!*

He bent to his task, oddly at peace with himself. He started whistling as he mopped, partly as a cover, and partly because he felt so good. He knew what he had to do. His course was clear, and he was following it.

He got close to where the guard was stationed. They even nodded greetings to each other. And then, as though God was trying to make up for all he hadn't done for him and those he loved earlier in his life, there was a noise down the hall, and the guard looked in that direction. The mop-bucket man grasped the string in his pocket and wrapped it around the guard's neck. He put a knee between the guard's shoulder blades and pushed hard. The guard grasped at his neck, but the fight was over before it began. Mop-bucket man didn't want to kill him. He just wanted him out of the way for awhile. *But sometimes the innocent must die before the guilty can pay for their crimes,* he thought.

He placed the guard back in the chair. He looked like he was sleeping peacefully.

He entered the room where Beth was sleeping. He paused for a minute to adjust his eyes to the darkness. Beth, exhausted after a busy day of constant visitors, had soon fallen into a deep sleep. He knew he had to move quickly or someone would be in soon to check her vitals and wake her so she could go back to sleep. He shook his head at the silliness of institutions supposedly designed to help people and ended up only contributing to their harm. Like the church.

He was making this up as he went along. He did not bring a lot of stuff from home that could be traced. He found a pillow in the easy chair next to the bed. He'd seen it in dozens of movies, but never actually thought he'd be using it on someone he barely knew. But his course was clear. She had to be eliminated.

He took the pillow in both hands and quietly made his way toward the bed. The light from the street lamp shone through the partially opened blinds, making shadow and light dance across her face and around the room. It was as if God was present for the sacrifice.

He took a deep breath, and a wave of emotion overtook him. What he was about to do repulsed him. He could see the image of his mother imploring him not to do it. "Be a good boy, Peepers." That's what she called him because of his deep blue eyes. But he was driven. Other worldly forces compelled him, and he couldn't help himself. Besides, it would all soon be over.

Then God would be in heaven, and all would be right with the world. What he meant was—*God would stay in heaven and mind his own business! Then we could get on with life without the meddlesome interference from a judgmental freak like* God. He had to do this to balance the universe again.

He stepped forward. The moment of truth had arrived. He placed the pillow over her face and pressed down hard. Beth awoke, struggling for breath. She was disoriented coming so quickly out of a deep sleep, the best she'd had since the accident. She grabbed for his hands to push them away.

Realizing that she was too weak to budge her assailant, she got a sudden inspiration. She reached for the nurses' button and pressed it. She turned the TV on instead. She tried again, and this time hit it.

Then she went limp, and turned her head sideways. She stopped struggling. He appeared to notice this and stopped momentarily. He didn't think it could be that easy, but he wouldn't question it. Questions were a luxury for him right now. The nurses would be here soon to check on their charge. He turned off the TV and looked to make a quick exit.

He took the pillow and put it back on the chair. He took a deep, cleansing breath and smiled. Now all he had to do was get out and he would be home free, the sacrifice complete. He went to the door, looked down the hall to the nurses' station, and saw no one. He looked back toward the exit to confirm the guard was still out. He took the rag off his head and threw it away, and then walked hastily toward the stairs and escaped without any witnesses.

Except one. The custodian, Willie Harris. As Willie entered the building, he noticed a stranger leaving. It was a small hospital; still there were a lot of people in and out, and he couldn't possibly know everyone. But this late at night, whether this stranger was a doctor or a visitor, it seemed pretty odd.

Chapter Nineteen: The Deception Begins

THE CHARGE CONFERENCE was breaking up; the nurses picked up the charts and went first to their stations. Patrick Lawton, a tall young man with good features, looked at the blinking light on the main console.

You've got to be kidding me, he thought. *Who would be up at this hour?* He saw the room number, 314. It was one of his. Beth McKinley was there. She would be released in a day or two. Oh, well, better check it out.

The guard was sleeping which seemed odd to Pat. Bob Abel was just as his name implied, a very capable, conscientious young man. They had gotten to know one another well in the few days he had been here. There wasn't much to do on the night shift, and so they talked.

He touched Bob's shoulder and shook him gently. "Bob, Bob..." he whispered. He shook more vigorously, speaking his name out loud. Pat checked his neck for a pulse. It was there, but weak. Then he saw the rope burns, faint but distinct. He called for help. Orderlies came and roused Bob with smelling salts.

As the nurse ministered to Bob, Pat stepped into Beth's room. It was quiet, but *too quiet*, thought Pat. He came to the side of her bed and looked at her sleeping. She was sleeping, wasn't she? He checked her neck for a pulse too. It was there but faint, too faint even for sleep. He checked her breath; there was none.

"CODE BLUE!" Pat shouted. One of the nurses attending to Bob jerked her head to attention and ran for the cart. The loud speaker announced the emergency, and the other nurses, an orderly and two doctors came running.

Meanwhile, Pat climbed onto the bed and applied CPR to Beth's limp body. As he gave her the breath of life, the others crowded around ready to apply other means if that didn't work.

After a few minutes work, Beth's eyes blinked hard once, and then she began to cough. Everyone in the room applauded. What a gift life is, especially if someone had tried to cut it short, and now it's been given back.

Pat got off the bed and smiled at Beth, as though he had been given his life back too. *It's moments like these that make my job worthwhile*, he thought.

"Beth, Beth," he whispered.

She turned her head toward him.

"You're going to be fine." Pat took her hand. He checked her pulse again. It was much stronger.

"Man..." she whispered, "tr...kill."

Pat frowned. "Don't talk, Beth. We'll hook you up to an IV, get things going again. I'll call Hector."

Everyone left the room. Bob was taken to an empty bed to lie down where he could rest and recover. Pat was about to leave, but Beth grabbed his arm as he turned.

"Don't...leave...Can you...stay awhile?"

"Sure, I'll stay here until you wake up again. As long as you need. I'm here."

"Thank you...You saved...my life. What's...your...name?"

"My name is Pat, and don't mention it, Beth."

The nurse arrived with something to help Beth sleep, and Pat sat beside her for the rest of the night, while she slept peacefully.

HECTOR GOT the call from the hospital. He had been looking at the evidence from Pete's death. He studied the plastic gloves. He remembered reading a detective story about plastic gloves and how fingerprints were found inside the glove. He would call the state police and ask them about that. From what he knew about such things, it seemed highly unlikely. But first he had to speak with Beth. It was obvious to him she knew something that someone was trying to silence. He had to find out what it was.

He drove over to the hospital and went to her room. A male nurse, dressed in white with red sneakers, was in the chair next to her bed, half dozing and unaware. He was sitting on the pillow that the man in the shadows had used to snuff out her life.

"Oh..." Pat whispered, rousing. "Hi, I'm Pat Lawton."

"Hector Chavez, police chief." They shook hands. "Can I talk to her?" Hector asked.

"Can't it wait, sir? She'd been through a rough time. I know you need to talk to her, but she needs her rest."

"Well, yeah, it can wait. I got the call and thought you wanted me to come over."

"Yes, I'm sorry. The guard, Bob, is resting here too. He probably can help you. Maybe he saw the guy."

"You think? That'd be good news," he said.

Beth stirred and blinked hard, then saw Hector standing there. "Hector," she said, attempting a smile.

"Hi, Beth," Hector whispered. "How you feeling?"

"I'm...fine..."

"Listen, I'll come back tomorrow, and we'll talk. Right now you get some rest. I'll talk to Angus, but for now I have some ideas about how to flush this guy out. I'll look around while things are fresh. I know it doesn't do any good to say, but don't worry. We'll get him."

They looked at each other for a long moment, and for a second, Beth reminded him of his baby sister. They had been so close growing up, but then she moved away, and they lost touch. The reminder made him want to reach out to her at the earliest moment.

He motioned for Pat to come with him to the door of the room. "My idea, Pat," Hector whispered, "is for Beth to stay 'dead.' We'll arrange everything. Please don't tell anyone, not even Beth. Except the nurses, of course. We need a doctor to sign a death certificate. And we need someone to call the paper. I'll take care of the doctor if you take care of the paper?"

"I can do that. In fact nothing would make me happier to help in any way I can."

Then Hector asked, "What did you see of the struggle, anything?"

"No, I saw the call button flashing and came to see what she wanted. I saw the guard down, and determined he was still breathing. Then I went in and found Beth barely alive. I performed CPR on her, and she revived."

"So you were just starting your shift?"

"That's right," said Pat. "We had just gotten out of the charge conference when I noticed the light."

"Did you notice anything like a possible weapon? Or was there anything out of place?"

"Not that I can think of. Bob had rope burns on his neck, but I didn't notice any marks on Beth at all. She did say something about a pillow though, now that I think about it."

"Is this the pillow, you think? Can I take this with me?"

"It could be. And yes, you can take it."

Hector said goodbye again and found Bob's room. He opened the door. The hall light penetrated the darkness, casting shadows on the bed and on Bob, who lay sleeping soundly.

He didn't want to wake him, so he closed the door. He felt certain there would not be a second attempt, but Hector would feel better if someone was over here watching. Rather than get anyone else out here in the middle of the night, he decided to stay himself. He found the chair Bob had occupied and sat down. It wouldn't be long until morning, and he could rest easier knowing that everything was all right.

He called Max to let him know what he was doing and to tell him that Beth had died. *The deception begins*, thought Hector.

Chapter Twenty: Holy Ground

ANGUS SLEPT fitfully through the night. The B&B where they stayed was pleasant enough, but Angus never slept well the first night away from home.

But Angelica loved it. New places, new faces, and new experiences gave her renewed energy. Angus loved to watch Angelica sleep. *The virgin in repose*, he thought. Catholics venerated Mary so much because women were not a part of the power structure. Protestants paid little attention to Mary because they did not honor her part in God's plan.

Angus thought of his mother and the fact that they would plan a trip to Scotland soon. Even though both his parents were dead, he could see his sister, and remember what life was like there. He could show Angelica where he grew up, the land he loved. He recognized he was starting to get homesick, which felt odd.

He got up quietly and went looking for a cup of coffee in the kitchen. It was right where Jan said it would be. *She must have gotten up at four o'clock to make that*, he thought. Then he noticed the coffeemaker was equipped with a self-starting feature.

He wanted to talk to her about Pastor Pete's plans for a thrift store next to her *Century Shoppe*. He didn't have a chance yesterday. He would have to make an opportunity today.

He felt nervous about his role in church today. This was the least prepared he had ever felt to step into the pulpit and share the word from God. He had skimmed the lectionary for an idea, but nothing struck him. He decided to go to *the Revelation of John*, though God only knew why he felt drawn there. He could count on one hand the number of times he had preached from it, but now it seemed oddly appropriate.

He turned to the sixth chapter. In this part the seven seals are broken by the angels. The fifth seal is what intrigued him. He repeated the words: "When he opened the fifth seal, I saw under the altar the souls of those who had been slaughtered for the word of God and for the testimony they had given."

This is what the people need to hear, he thought. He scribbled some notes on a piece of paper and then prayed. *What 'testimony' did Maureen give? Pete testified as a faithful witness to the word of God. But Maureen's seemed more like the death of the innocent than anything else.* There just seemed to be no connection between them. Angus knew Hector was worried about this too.

He knew that the cataclysm of the seventh seal was yet to come, but he assured himself if they remembered Pete and Maureen in the right way, they would bear witness to a loving, gracious God. That, as they say, will preach.

He had no idea what calamity yet lay ahead for him and for this church. But for this day, this time, they were all gathered under the altar of God's protection. That would have to do for now.

HE WENT back downstairs. It was still early, but Jan was up now, preparing for breakfast. Angus and Angelica were the only guests.

"We're having omelets and fruit compote with muffins and your choice of meat," Jan said, as she began to clang around the kitchen.

"That sounds wonderful," said Angus. "I'll take ham, if you've got it?"

"We have country ham if you like it."

"Aye, that would be a real treat."

"And your wife?"

"Bacon, I'd imagine."

There was silence as she bent to her tasks. Then they talked about the choice of ingredients for their omelets. Angus preferred a Denver, and Angelica would go for a ham and cheese.

"Mrs. S–, Jan, can you help me with a little puzzle I've been working on?"

"Oh, I love puzzles. My husband loves old movies, but I am the puzzle nut in the family."

"Well, it's not that kind of puzzle."

"What kind is it?" She sounded very interested.

"I'm curious about your relationship with Pete Anderson. How did you feel about him? I understood you didn't much care for his plans to put a thrift store next to your shop, is that right?"

"We had no opinion one way or the other. They owned that property and could do with it as they pleased." Jan's nose took a decided turn upward.

"So you or your husband didn't argue with Pete about his plans for that vacant store next to yours?"

Jan stopped cooking and turned toward him. "We most certainly did not! And for you to insinuate anything else is totally absurd." She put her spatula down and looked at the floor. "Yes, we did want something a bit more 'up-scale' to go in there to help our store, not hurt it. But we didn't do anything to harm anyone over a piece of property."

"People have done much worse for less."

"Are you talking about me?" Steve said as he came down and began helping Jan get breakfast on the table.

Jan laughed nervously. "No, darling, we were just discussing our talks with Reverend Anderson about the property they bought next to our shop."

"It's too bad what happened to him, but we certainly didn't have anything to do with it, if that's what you're implying," said Steve.

"Oh, I'm not implying anything. I was just curious," responded Angus.

Angelica came downstairs dressed for church. She wore a black dress with a pleated skirt and white pearls. Angus thought about skipping church and going right to that fancy restaurant in town. But that would have to wait.

As soon as Jan saw Angelica, she said, "I'd better get busy here." She prepared the rest of the food and served it with Steve's help, in a timely manner.

After a delightful breakfast, Angus finished dressing and paid the bill. It was a pleasant morning; the Texas heat was a promise yet to be delivered. But for now, it felt more like Scotland, cool and damp, and so they decided to walk. They had several hours before the service, but Angus liked to get to church early to get his spirit prepared. Still they had time to sip coffee on the front porch, read the San Antonio paper, and watch the cars go by.

The walk to church did them good. The earth was just awakening from a short winter's nap. *Here in Texas, they don't know what winter can do,* Angus thought. *Just as the heat here gave rise to the siesta, winter made us strong. We need something to battle, something to strike against, to see what we're made of.* For now, in this moment, he was comforted by the new color shooting to life.

"Lawns can get quite ragged this time of year because

people let their wildflowers bloom. They bloom like weeds, wherever they please," said Angelica.

"It reminds me of the parable of the wheat and the weeds," said Angus.

"What do you mean?" asked Angelica.

"A farmer got the best seed he could buy and did everything he could for the soil before he planted it. But in the night, an enemy came and planted weeds among the wheat. Sometime later, the man's servants came and told him what happened.

"At first the servants were mad at him, as though he had for some reason done it intentionally. When the farmer told them an enemy had done it, they were quick to want to pull up the weeds.

"Then he said, 'Leave them alone. Wait until harvest. Then we'll harvest both the weeds and the wheat. The wheat goes into the barn, the weeds we'll use for fuel.'"

"But what does that have to do with mowing around wildflowers?" asked Angelica.

"They bloom where they want. You can't control them. They're beautiful, but on their own terms."

"Kind of like me, huh?" She smiled.

Angus laughed. *But it was really so much more than that. Having the weeds and wheat together means we have to take the good with the bad. We have to hold them both together, sometimes for a lifetime. We have to be patient, be the best 'wheat' we can be, and let the 'weeds' get what they deserve.*

"Kind of like you." He smiled, nodding. They hugged each other.

THEY ARRIVED at the door of the church, and Jesús was there to let him in.

"*Hola, Jesús, buenos días,*" said Angus. His Spanish was peppered with a Scottish accent. Angelica insisted that he learn her language, and he studied nights at a local Junior College.

"*Buenos días, Señor, Señora,*" said Jesús with a gap-toothed grin. He bowed to them.

Angelica and Jesús launched into a conversation in Spanish. Angus could tell that she was happy talking to someone without having to slow down to be understood. It filled Angus with joy just to witness it. Jesús was animated, smiling and energized by the exchange.

"Let me get the lights," he said in Spanish.

As they waited for the lights to come on, Angelica leaned into Angus. "He really likes coming here on Sunday mornings, being the first one here. He loves opening up the church. Call me crazy, but I get the distinct impression he is anxious about keeping his job."

"Unless he actually did it." Angus smiled.

Angelica smiled and hit him on the arm. Angus flinched.

"I'm serious," she said.

"I know, I know," he said. "I'm sorry; I just couldn't resist. Maybe we'll, I mean you'll, have a chance to talk to him later."

"While you get ready, maybe I can talk to him some more now. Just see if my hunch was right."

THEY FOUND Jesús again and asked for a key to Pete's office.

"You mean Beth's office, don't you?" he asked with a sheepish grin.

"No," said Angus, tilting his head, "I mean Pete's."

"I can't do that, *Señor,*" he said, looking down. "They told me not to let anyone in there until we get a new pastor."

"Does that include the police?"

"Well, they were in there the day he died, but after that, no one."

Angus stared at Jesús for a long moment, then at Angelica, and back to Jesús. When someone kept you from seeing something, it generally meant that person was hiding something. What was this church trying to hide? And who specifically was trying to hide it?

Angus really didn't have time to argue further, so he accepted the invitation to enter Beth's office. He draped his robe over her couch and sat behind the desk in her big comfortable chair.

He prayed for several minutes about the service he was about to lead. He prayed about the sermon he was ill prepared to deliver. Then he remembered a dream—a recurring one he hadn't had in quite a while. He was in the sanctuary at his home church in Scotland. It was a massive Gothic structure with gray stone ceilings, floors, and walls. A huge vaulted ceiling reached to the heavens like giant redwood trees, and ornate stained-glass windows covered the walls. The sanctuary was packed with people. His mother, father, brother, and two sisters were all there smiling up at him as he stood there naked in front of God and everybody. The memory was broken when he heard knocking and the door opening. Tom Branch, the clerk of session, stood in the doorway. Angus looked up from his sermon notes and smiled at him. He thought he might ask Tom about Pete's office being off limits, but decided that could wait.

"Hello, Angus," Tom said, stepping into the office. "Am I glad to see you!"

Angus rose and shook his hand. *I think he means it*, he thought.

"Are you okay in here? Is there anything I can do for you?"

"Aye, there is something. I tried to get into Pete's office, but Jesús said I couldn't."

"I was afraid of that. After the service, if you'd like, I'll let you in. It's no big deal. It's just a mess in there. Connie's boxing up his books and cleaning up. And besides, going in there has been tough on the members."

Angus didn't know if he believed his story, but there was something just as important. "So she's doing all this by herself?"

Tom looked down. "Good point. I will see if she needs any help."

"I'd suggest you help her whether she says she needs it or not. She needs you all right now, just as much as you need one another."

TOM LEFT Angus to collect his thoughts. Angus went to the sanctuary to get a feel for the space once again. As soon as he entered the room, the rose window shone upon him in all its brilliance. Its light was usually diffused throughout the room. But today, for this instant, the red and the blue-tinged light focused like a laser beam on Angus. It focused upon his heart. The force of the beam was so strong it knocked him to the floor.

"What the...?" whispered Angus, as he stayed on the floor for a brief moment, supported by two trembling arms.

"Angus," a voice spoke from the light.

"Excuse me?"

"Take off your shoes."

"Oh, come on. Who is this?"

"I said, Take off your shoes."

"Well, this is ridiculous," he said as he took off his shoes.

"The ground you're on is holy ground."

"Where have I heard that before?"

"I called Moses to lead an entire people. I want you to lead these people through this time."

"I'm doing the best I can. What more do you want?"

"I want more."

"Is this my choice or a command?"

"This is America, Angus. I can't command anyone here. They wouldn't listen even if I did."

"Good point." Angus struggled to his feet. "Will you help me find this killer?"

There was no answer. The piercing laser light was gone, replaced by the soft, diffused light that shed its benediction on all it touched.

Waves of emotion flowed through his body like electric shocks. He didn't know what to do so he just stood there hugging himself, shaking all over. To look at him, one would have thought the weather was twenty degrees below freezing, and him without a coat.

Chapter Twenty-One: In Search of Jesus

"*DIOS MIO*," said Jesús, crossing himself. His legs had been propped up on Louise's desk where he was sitting, reading the Sunday paper. But they quickly came off the desk and hit the floor with a crash. He stood, trembling.

"I am an 'illegal.' I came here to get a better life than the one I could have had in Mexico. Pastor Pete helped me, made all the arrangements. He helped bring my family here, knowing I was illegal. He gave us both this job so we could put food on the table. He even helped us find a place to stay."

Angus had come from the sanctuary back into the office. "Why are you telling me all this?" he asked.

"You are a messenger of God. To God, I tell the truth."

"What do you mean?"

"*Brilla... la cara....*"

Angus looked in the office window. He saw nothing. "So you came here illegally, and Pastor Pete helped you. Does anyone else know about this? Does the treasurer, or the clerk of session, Tom Branch?"

"I do not trust that man."

"Tom Branch? Why not?"

"When Pastor Pete died, he took over. More than once I saw him sitting at his desk, pretending to be this pious, spiritual man. All along he was an *amigo traidor*, a snake in the grass."

"What makes him an *amigo traidor*?" he asked.

"The way he locked up Pastor Pete's office. He took over even before Pastor Beth knew what was going on. When all the–how you say–evidence was collected, he was always there. The day of the murder, he was here all that morning. What he was doing, I don't know, but I know he has an important job with the city. What was he doing here all that time?

"What indeed?" Angus said.

"*Señor*, please don't tell them I told you this. It's hard to work here, but it is better than not working at all."

"Oh, don't worry, Jesús. It will be our little secret." He shook Jesús' hand.

"Well, I'll have to talk with Mr. Branch later."

ANGELICA WENT looking for Angus. She left the church office and went toward the sanctuary. She didn't see Angus in there, but came up behind him as he was talking with Jesús.

Immediately she noticed something different about him. His face and skin were shining, numinous. Angelica flashed on her childhood in Mexico City, the hours they had spent in Catholic school studying the saints. They all had that numinous glow about them. When she became a teenager, she dismissed it as so much mumbo jumbo, just about the time she dismissed the church and its teachings.

Then much later she met Angus. Suddenly religion returned to her life. She had to confront those parts she didn't like and remember what meant so much to her, like the lives of the saints. For the most part, she hadn't rejected her faith, she just preferred not being so tied to a set dogma, or to the local church with its bureaucracy and politics. She had very little role to play in Angus' leadership at Presbytery. She liked it that way.

As he approached, she didn't know quite what to make of him. She had never seen him like this in her life, although she thought she understood what it was. Angus had seen God.

As he came closer, the light surrounding him got weaker and steadily weaker, until it disappeared.

PEOPLE STARTED coming into the hall; Sunday school was about to begin. They began to mingle with the people, making introductions, although he was so well known to the congregation, introductions weren't really essential. Angus could have used the extra time to go over his sermon, but he decided to join the Senior Adult Sunday school class instead.

A large man with a full head of white hair led it. He was tanned and fit and looked like a tennis player, or perhaps ex-military. He lectured the class for forty-five minutes on the four-source theory of the writing of the Pentateuch. It was all Angus could do to keep his eyes open. The rest sat in rapt attention to one of the most boring lectures Angus had ever heard. *No wonder the church is dying,* he thought. *The good news is, at least he doesn't think Moses wrote all of the first five books of the Bible.* On that they could agree. He was just appalled at the lack of imagination most churches demonstrated about how to present this stuff.

After class they were walking out with an elderly woman, stooped and frail, supported by a cane. She looked uncomfortable, like a hermit whose skin crawled at the sight of other people. Her name was Myrtle Bigsby. Angus had learned that much. Her lips were pursed like a balloon about to pop.

Angus leaned down to her. “Ms. Bigsby,” he said, “are you all right? You seem very agitated about something.”

She looked both ways like she was afraid to cross the street. Then she shoved Angus with her cane into a corner with such force it surprised him and nearly toppled him over.

“Ms. Bigsby!” he gasped. “I didn’t know you had it in you.”

“Sorry, my boy,” she said. “I’ve been anxious to tell someone what I know.”

“About what?”

“About Pastor Peter’s death, that’s what!”

“What about it?

“That Beth woman.”

“What about her?”

“She’s the one you want.”

“How can that be? She’s dead. Someone killed her.”

“She’s what? Beth is dead?...That’s awful...serves her right though! She’s just trying to throw suspicion onto someone else. She didn’t belong in the pulpit. She was jealous of Pastor Pete. She thought with him out of the way she could take over.”

What do I say to her? thought Angus. *If I call her crazy, she’ll resent me. If I humor her, she’ll go on spreading rumors about the pastors in my care.*

“Thank you for your information, Ms. Bigsby. I’ll certainly look into the things you are saying. However, with Beth dead, such allegations are meaningless.”

She huffed a little and said, “Well, anyway, mark my words. She was the one that started this whole thing.” She tottled off, bent over and frail once again, while Ed Kramer, the church treasurer, approached Angus.

“Hello, Ed, how are you?”

“I’m fine. I see Myrtle got her hooks into you. She’s harmless in a raspy sort of way.”

"That's well put. That's exactly how I would describe her. She thinks Beth had something to do with Peter's demise."

"Even though Beth is dead? That's weird."

"She said Beth was trying to throw suspicion off her and onto someone else. Excuse me, what did you say?"

"When?"

"Just now, about Beth. Did you say she was dead?"

"Yes, I suppose I did. What of it?"

"I haven't told anyone about that. How did you know?"

"Well, well, I don't know. Maybe I overheard you telling Mrs. Bigsby. You did say Beth was dead, didn't you?"

"Yes, I suppose I did. But you hadn't arrived by then."

"So I'm a suspect, am I?"

"I didn't say that. I could have sworn you couldn't have heard me say that to that woman."

"Well, for the record, I had nothing against Pastor Pete. He spent too much on stuff I thought didn't matter, but he was a good man."

"WHEN IS the funeral?" asked Angelica, trying to change the subject. "Let me guess. The funeral is Tuesday, and you've been asked to preside over it?"

"My, you're uncanny," said Angus. "That's exactly right, on both counts."

"Will you announce that this morning?" asked Ed.

"Aye, aye, I'd be happy to. Do you have a pen? If I don't make a note about it, I'm liable to forget."

Ed produced the pen. "I suppose we'll have the service here?"

"Aye, that's the plan." Angus made the note and handed Ed back his pen.

HECTOR HAD told Angus about Beth and what he had planned for Tuesday. She had been taken to a vacant rental property Hector owned. They didn't even tell Charlie, the choir director, what they were doing.

Angus looked at his watch. It was 10:30. The service would start in fifteen minutes.

"I've got to go," he said, and darted back to Beth's office. He took off his blue suit coat and placed it on the desk chair. He unzipped the garment bag and took out his robe. It had three strips of red and black cloth, symbolic of his doctorate degree. He put the microphone on. The last thing was a cross he placed around his neck. Not surprisingly, it was a Celtic cross, given to him by his mother before she died. She knew he would one day become a minister, and he had treasured the cross for years before he was ordained.

It was a bitter-sweet memory because his dad would not hear of any of it. He did not fancy any McPherson a "preacher," and he certainly didn't think any son of his should be. Somehow his mother managed to give him the cross without his father's knowledge.

After he dressed, he grabbed his Bible and his notes, stopped and took a deep breath, then let it out slowly. He said a short prayer about the service and about his words making sense. It was the same prayer he always prayed.

As he backed out of the office, he turned quickly around and bumped into someone. Angus' Bible and notes went flying as they both tumbled to the floor. When they straightened up, they both laughed, rubbing their foreheads.

"Hi, Angus," Tom Branch said, still smiling. "It's a good thing we ran into each other. I'm your worship leader this morning."

Angus noticed his shoes. They were patent leather, certainly the most expensive shoes he had seen in some time. Worn by a man, no less.

"Look," Tom said. "There's no time for a prayer with

the choir. Why don't we take our place in the chancel? It's right this way."

He led Angus downstairs to the first floor, down the hall beside the sanctuary to the door, and up three steps. It was dark back there. Tom was about to open the door when Angus stopped him.

"Let's pray, shall we?" he asked. Tom nodded, and Angus took his hand like he was going to shake it, and he prayed that God would continue to bless the church today and always.

Then they walked into the chancel. The place was packed again. The balcony was full, which hadn't happened since Pete's funeral. Angus took his place in the seat by the pulpit. It was a huge, kingly chair made of dark oak and maroon leather. He spotted Angelica sitting next to Connie Anderson, Peter's widow, in the front row with the rest of the family. Angus smiled at his bride, and she smiled back.

The organ music swelled to a deafening crescendo and then vanished like a puff of smoke. Tom stood to greet the people at the stroke of 10:45. He said something about being pleased to have the Presbytery Executive leading them in worship, and the whole place erupted in enthusiastic applause. Angus smiled, and his face flushed crimson. Angus was from the old school when it comes to applause in worship. *Our focus should be on God, not humans*, he often said. When you applaud, it's too easy to confuse the issue. Are you applauding the person or performance, or are you praising God? Angus thought it was too fine a line, and he didn't like crossing it. *But this is America, where casual is King*, he thought.

Tom went on with the rest of the announcements. Then the service began. Presbyterian worship has a flow like an hourglass. Worship begins in torrents of praise with words of wonder at God's majesty, and accompanied by cascading music. Glory fills the space like the prophet Isaiah, as he witnessed angels greeting God and singing, "Holy, Holy, Holy is the Lord Almighty." Such outpouring of praise leads to the acknowledgement of how far humans have fallen from God's grace, and so the congregation whispers, "I am a man of unclean lips who lives among a people of unclean lips." But confession without forgiveness is not grace. Once cleansed, the worshipers are put right with God and ready to hear God's word. This is the narrow part of the hourglass. After the word, we offer prayer, and something tangible like money, and then the congregation is called to ministry for others; and the hourglass widens again.

Tom read from the Old Testament, and Angus read the passage he had chosen for the day.

> *When he opened the fifth seal, I saw under the altar the souls of those who had been slaughtered for the word of God and for the testimony they had given. They cried out with a loud voice, "Sovereign Lord, holy and true, how long will it be before you judge and avenge our blood on the inhabitants of the Earth?" They were each given a white robe and told to rest a little longer, until the number would be complete, both of their fellow servants and of their sisters and brothers who were soon to be killed as they themselves had been killed.*
>
> *-Revelation 6:9-11*

Angus looked up and moved from behind the pulpit. He bowed his head in silence and prayed for himself and the people, that they would hear the word of God today. Then he said "Amen" out loud and looked up and smiled at Connie again. She smiled back.

"I didn't have much time to prepare this morning's message since I only responded to the need yesterday. As you know, Beth was in an accident that landed her in the hospital. What you may not know is that someone made a second attempt, and this time succeeded. She died last night. This is indeed a very sad day for this church, the Presbytery, and for me personally because I counted her among my friends. The funeral will be Tuesday; the other arrangements will be passed along as soon as we know more. Let us please stand and remember her with a moment of silence."

The congregation stood as one. Angus looked from face to face. Many of the women were in tears. Some of the men shook their heads. Some of the children tugged at their parents' sleeves, asking what this meant.

He bowed his head and prayed silently, hoping that what he was about to do would work. He saw the prayer go up like the smoke of incense, a sweet perfume curling into the heavens. He said "Amen" out loud and motioned them all to take their seats.

The congregation sat down, and Angus went behind the dark oak pulpit. "The fifth seal is the most important part of this enigmatic revelation by John from the island of Patmos. It doesn't matter about the devastation soon to be wrought on the earth. It doesn't even matter about who's next to die. What matters is that God has not forgotten. God has a place for us. And it is under the altar.

"Presbyterians don't have altars. We have communion tables. Altars are from the Old Testament. They are for sacrifices. We don't have altars because we believe Jesus Christ made the last, best, most complete sacrifice. Altars are no longer needed because Jesus altered our need for and understanding of sacrifice.

"This congregation has suffered much. You have lost two of your leaders, and another woman has died, a beloved member of this community. This fifth seal is there to remind us that God has not forgotten. We all have a place with God. God is with us and will bring us through this to hope and wholeness.

"God has not forgotten Peter Anderson. He has a place where he belongs, in the bosom of the Almighty Father. He was not perfect, but he was your shepherd. His life was given to you to remind you who God is, and what grace looks like. He belongs under the Altar, protected by the loving grace of a compassionate God.

"God has not forgotten Beth McKinley. She was a good woman with the heart of a pastor. Children were her passion. She ministered to them and helped them become ministers in their own right. Beth has found a place for herself, in the bosom of our Redeeming Lord. Beth has found a place under the Altar of God's redeeming grace, and so can we.

"But before that happens, we have to make right what has gone horribly wrong. We shall make the wrong done to them right, not by vengeance, nor by the violence of a mob, but by justice, God's justice."

Angus paused and looked out at the entire congregation. All eyes were on him as he smiled and then continued.

"With her dying breath, Beth may have helped us find God's justice. She was able to name the person who did this to her."

Again Angus paused. Murmurs went up from the shocked congregation. He decided to push a little further. *Was Hector ever going to forgive him?* he thought. *Was God going to forgive him for telling lies from the pulpit? Please forgive me, God,* he prayed to himself.

"The authorities are getting a search warrant ready to check out her story. Soon justice will be served; the dead have not died in vain. We will work to keep the memories of Pastor Peter and Beth alive. They have found a place better than under the Altar. They have found a place with God. And if we do the right thing, we can too."

Silence. Silence as still as death clung to the ceiling of the venerable old building. It was a gathering silence, like the pause before a young wife becomes a mother, as she gathers her strength for one final push, and the chaos of creation begins.

The service continued to its inevitable conclusion. Angus got up to pronounce the benediction. As he stood there, he smiled at each of the faces in the room. Some smiled back. Others frowned, their arms folded tightly across their chests. A few had tears in their eyes. They stood together as a people God had remembered.

Angus lifted both arms, his hands holding up three fingers, the symbol of the Trinity–Father, Son, and Holy Spirit, and recited the Aaronic benediction from Numbers.

The Lord bless you and keep you;
The Lord be kind and gracious to you;
The Lord look upon you with favor,
And give you peace, both now and forever. Amen

Angus and Tom walked to the back of the sanctuary followed by the choir. Then the congregation sang the seven-fold "Amen." It sent a shiver up Angus' spine. Never had he heard it sung more beautifully. Never had he been so touched by the rush of grace brought by a people. They sang it "a cappella." And the sound of it filled the sanctuary, filled Angus' heart, and the heavens with the sweet fragrance of a people who had been given hope for the living of a new day.

Chapter Twenty-Two: No Rest for the Wicked

I'VE DONE what you asked," said Pat, Beth's nurse.

"Good," said Hector. "I'm putting the finishing touches on her 'obituary' now." He was sitting at his desk, and the light from the lamp shown full on his face, making it glow with an eerie light.

"Bob was released today. Were you able to question him?" asked Pat.

"Yeah, I talked to him and to Willie Harris, the custodian, yesterday. When Bob feels better he'll come down, and we'll get a police artist from Austin to get a sketch done."

"How is Beth, and where did you take her?"

"Beth is fine. She's getting stronger every day. My wife's caring for her. She's starting to get antsy. But as to *where* she is, I can't say. The fewer who know that, the better."

"Yeah, I agree. I just hoped I'd be one of the few since I saved her life."

"I know. Believe me," Hector said, "I'd tell you if I could. She asks about you; wonders how you're doing."

"Well, tell her I'm doing fine. I'm worried about her though."

"She's very grateful to you for what you did."

"Tell her she's most welcome. I'd save her life any time."

"I'll do that." They said goodbye, and Hector hung up the phone.

HECTOR WAS grateful too; grateful his wife talked him into being a landlord, in Lockhart no less. He was grateful now that he was between renters, and the house was empty. The place was fully furnished, so Beth would have a homey place to spend a few days.

It's funny, thought Hector, last month when the renters left and he had to drive all that way, back and forth to clean up the place, taking a week out of his life, he was anything but grateful. *Gratitude is like a smoked ham,* he thought. *It's only good if it hangs around awhile.*

HECTOR WENT to the evidence room and pulled out the box that held the secrets to this puzzle. He took it back to his desk. *If we could get a sketch of the guy Bob saw, it would be huge,* he thought.

He pulled the first item out of the box. It was a lab report about the blood from a cat's claw found at Maureen's house. It didn't match anyone's blood that he knew about, not even Maureen's. So the blood remained a mystery. There was a report about some of Maureen's neighbors seeing a dark green or brown car leaving her house on a couple of occasions.

They still hadn't found for certain what killed Maureen, other than a scarf near her body. The killer made sure of that. He made some mistakes with Pete and was learning how to cover his tracks. But then he got desperate, coming to the hospital, trying to finish off Beth.

The rubber gloves and the piece of cloth were in the bottom of the box. The bloody cross was in a place by itself. The burn marks on the cross were consistent with plastic explosives used by the military. He remembered the cartoon show called the *Simpson's,* his kid's favorite show. The introduction showed Homer coming home followed by Bart on a skateboard. Then Marge comes up the drive and nearly runs Homer over. He screams and jumps and starts running. He felt that way now, about to be run over by an on-coming car.

He sighed, and brought his hand down on the plastic gloves. He picked them up. He examined them closely. He turned them inside out, and started to inspect the inside of the glove. He got the report from the lab in Austin which didn't make him feel any better. There is no way they could get prints from a plastic glove. The only reason they kept the gloves is if they could prove they belonged to the killer somehow. And that would be a long shot.

"YOU MEAN Beth named her killer before she died?" Connie Anderson, Pastor Pete's widow, had circles of red around her soft blue eyes. They looked like bull's eyes going straight to her heart.

Angus and she were standing in Beth's office as he took off his robe, picked up the sport coat from the arm of the chair, and put it on.

"That's right," Angus lied. He was wrestling with himself more than he could ever recall, and it was exhausting. If there was anyone he wanted to take into his confidence, it was the woman who stood before him. He could tell she was grasping at the last strand of sanity she had. Any more information might just be too much. It was as though he was floating through time. He knew in order to play his part, he would have to be economical with the truth for a little while longer.

Throughout Angus' years of ministry, he always had a problem knowing who he could trust. He would size up one person as trustworthy only to be betrayed later on. However, one piece of advice he received had continuously seemed appropriate. It was given to him by one of the ministers who examined him for his ordination. After the exam was over, the old man with tousled white hair and soft brown eyes took him aside.

"Never trust the first people who offer to take you to dinner," he said. "They are the ones with the agenda and will bite you in the ass later on."

So that's how ministers really talk, he remembered thinking. As for the advice, it had been remarkably accurate.

Connie looked down, her sad eyes sinking into the earth from which they had come. Angus' instinct was to reach around and hug her, try to protect her from the pain she felt. But he knew that he could not. For all he knew, she was a suspect. While his instinct was to take care of hurting people, he also knew how to keep his distance, for his own protection if not for theirs.

"Who is it?" Her look changed. "Can't you see this thing is tearing me apart? I can't stand this constant sadness. I need some relief. I have to know. If I knew then I could finally get some rest."

She moved closer. Her eyes were now flashing, the red circles gone. They pierced his soul like a two-edged sword. Angus swore he could see fangs as she snapped at him.

"Connie, I don't know who it is. But even if I did know, I'm not sure it would do any good to tell you."

"Why not? I have a right to know who killed my husband. My children are deprived of their father. What can I tell them?"

"I'm truly sorry for your loss, Connie." Angus made a step toward her, and she moved away. "If I could undo what's happened, I would, but I can't. Knowing Beth's killer won't help you with your grief."

"Well, that's true enough." The lioness was gone, and

in her place was the sweet, vulnerable little girl, lost in a well of grief so high she couldn't get out.

They hugged each other. Connie stammered an apology for the outburst, and Angus reassured her. She left the office, dragging her heart behind her like a ball and chain.

I'M SURPRISED, thought Angus, shaking his head and straightening up the top of the desk. *I thought she was a stronger woman.* But then nothing much surprised him anymore. He got his notes and Bible and was about to leave when Angelica came bursting through the door and collapsed into his arms. She hugged him hard, as though her life depended on it. She started to cry.

"You are either the bravest or the most foolish man I have ever known."

"I know which one I'd prefer if I had a choice."

"Do you actually know who did all this? Are warrants being prepared as we speak?"

"You mean you didn't believe that part?"

"I mean, is it TRUE?"

The hall lights were turned off. The only light was from the small window at the end of the hall. It bathed the ancient space in gray and black. Shadows infested the dingy interior with doubt and disorder.

THEY WERE not alone. Angelica did not know what she could not see. The shadows shake hands with those who find comfort there. And so he went unnoticed and became one with the shadows surrounding him.

He heard the woman ask, "Is it TRUE?" and his head dropped. He shook it with a weight he had never felt before. *When will the killing end?* he thought. He was disgusted by the necessity of it. It seemed the only solution, time after time.

But he knew—sooner or later—the foreign preacher must also die and the chief of police as well. Then there would be an end.

His beef was primarily with the church. *It is such a vile place, and its leaders are the chief villains*, he thought. He believed he was doing society a service by ridding it of people who were on the surface so kind and loving, but underneath, so filthy—pure evil.

He had a sudden inspiration. He could take care of part of his problem today if he played his cards right. In fact he had come prepared for that very eventuality. He pulled out of his black overcoat a roll of very thin, strong wire that gleamed in the light from the window. He smiled. If it was going to happen now, he would have to hurry.

"WELL, NOT exactly," said Angus, trying to decide how to tell Angelica his predicament.

"What do you mean, 'not exactly?'"

"No warrants have been issued."

"But you got the name of the one who's doing this?"

"Not exactly."

"Will you quit that and be serious! Do you know who's doing this or not?"

"No."

"Not a clue?"

"Oh, we have plenty of clues, and plenty of suspects, but nothing solid. Not yet."

"Not one idea?"

"No."

"Then I have only one thing to say to you," Angelica said, her sobs turning to an angry stare. "What on earth were you thinking?" She hit him on his forehead with the palm of her hand. "You may have signed your own death warrant. You know you really are a fool. I had so much respect for you before, you know that. But now, I think you've gone off the deep end. You really are nuts, you know?"

She paced back and forth like a leopard frustrated by the bars that held her captive. Her anger pierced his heart.

"I had to do it, honey, don't you see?" He pleaded and moved toward her with his arms outstretched.

"Don't you 'honey' me, '*Bobo!*'"

"Don't you see I had to force his hand? Up to now he's always been a step ahead of us. I figured if he knew we were on to him, it would put a little panic in him, and he'd make a mistake."

"Yeah, and kill you."

"There's always that." Angus laughed.

"Don't joke with me now." She looked at him, her eyes squinting.

"Sorry," he smiled.

He approached her. She relaxed a bit, still folding her arms in front of her. He persisted, not letting go. Finally she dropped her arms, put them around Angus and received his hug, tenderly and without pretense.

THE BELL on the front door of the station rang, startling Hector. What surprised him too was that everyone knew nobody would be at the station on a Sunday. He put back everything he had taken from the evidence box and placed it back on the shelf.

Ed Kramer, a busy executive and the church treasurer, was standing by the front desk. He was still dressed for church; dark suit and red tie. He was a young man, trim and athletic, but with prematurely gray hair.

"I saw your squad car and took a chance you might still be here," he said.

"What can I do for you, Ed?"

"Oh, nothing, Hector. I was just wondering how it was going with Pete's murder. Are you getting any closer?"

"And you couldn't ask me that on Monday, seeing as how our offices are across the alley from each other."

"Sorry." Ed stepped back. "I was on my way home and saw your car. I hadn't talked to you in a while, so I thought I'd ask."

"That's okay. There has been only one other murder in this town in the last ten years. And in my first year as chief, we have three in a row. It's overwhelming."

"No doubt, no doubt." Ed's smile looked warm and caring.

"To answer your question, no, we're not closer to anyone. It's the damnedest thing. I'm thinking about calling the state boys or maybe the FBI in on this." Hector turned toward the sergeant's desk and put the key to the evidence locker in its rightful place.

"You're working odd hours, aren't you? I mean I never knew you to come in on Sunday before."

"You know what they always say, 'No rest for the wicked.'"

"You're not wicked, are you?" Ed laughed.

"Not necessarily. Not unless my youngest makes me crazy before I get him out of the house." He paused for a long moment. "I didn't mean me, really. I meant the guy we're chasing. There will be no rest for him until we get him."

Ed's face flushed red. Hector noticed it and filed it away. They said their awkward goodbyes, shook hands with cold indifference, and smiled smiles they didn't mean.

HECTOR STRAIGHTENED everything and locked up the station. As he turned out the lights, his soul went dark as well. On his way home he passed St. Catherine's Catholic Church, where his wife and kids went to mass every Sunday. He hadn't been since he won the election as police chief. It was a matter of integrity, or that's what he told himself.

He didn't want to use God to get public support. Never mind he was hired by the mayor and not elected by the people. A heavy oppressive feeling suppressed any thoughts of thankfulness for the many blessings Hector had received in his life.

He came to a stop sign, then a right turn toward home. In the middle of the turn, some instinct made him pull over and stop the car. He put the car in park and sat behind the wheel for some time.

'No rest for the wicked...no rest for the wicked...no rest for the wicked.' It was ringing in his ears. He couldn't stop it. *Who in the hell is wicked here?* he thought. *How can I say I am not? I hate all this stuff. I hate the guy who did this. But what's weird is I hate having to chase him. I don't know if I'm up to it. That's why I came to Shoestring, for a little peace and quiet. This isn't fair!*

He got out of the car and climbed the steps of the sandstone building. It was neoclassical in design, with Doric columns and wrought-iron railings. He opened the ancient doors that held huge wooden crosses on each. Inside it was all glitter and gold and statues. Hector stood in the hallway looking around for a few minutes.

The doors to the sanctuary were oak, each with a wood carving. On one was the crucifixion; on the other were the three crosses on a hill, empty, with a sun rising in the background. He opened the door with the sunrise and walked in.

He remembered having been here as a boy. He helped Father Hemple carry the cross in every Sunday at mass. He remembered how the old priest walked so slowly, and he and his friends wanted to race down the aisle.

"You mustn't rush," he wheezed. "Our faith comes slowly, like a caterpillar. But when the caterpillar becomes a butterfly, then you learn to fly."

Hector never learned to fly. He was too close to the earth. Things moved more slowly for him now, sometimes achingly so.

He remembered his parents talking with others in the church. Many people were upset with Father Hemple because he was so old, and they worried they weren't keeping up with the times. Some complained to the bishop, and he was replaced with a younger priest. Perhaps it was the right thing to do, but Hector had not been back since.

HE DIDN'T really know what he was doing there now except that he was looking for a little peace and quiet.

He moved gingerly into the sanctuary. On the walls were the Stations of the Cross. He remembered how Father Hemple would take the boys to each station and explain what each one meant. Father's face shone with a tranquility Hector had never seen before, nor understood. It fascinated him. He longed for the same thing to happen to him, to have the same peace. Maybe he was there looking for it now.

He sat in the back pew staring up at the stations and the stained glass. He remembered how the light danced. When Father Hemple preached, he would follow the light as it played on the heads of the congregants. It was all Hector could do to stay awake, and he knew he'd better if he didn't want his dad to take a belt to him when he got home.

He bowed his head to pray. He hadn't prayed in years. He prayed before meals at home because his wife, Silvia, insisted on it. It was for the sake of the children. But his heart wasn't in it. Now he knew he needed to put his whole heart into it.

Chapter Twenty-Three: Toward the Gathering Storm

HECTOR PRAYED for direction and guidance. He prayed for an ending to this pain, for him and for Shoestring. He wanted desperately to catch this murderer, to help return his peaceful little town to some semblance of the life he had known as a young child. He knew it was his responsibility, but he didn't know if he was equal to it. *I guess you only find that out in the doing of it*, he thought.

As he prayed, he began to sense a presence. He heard no sound nor saw any shadow, but someone was there. How do we become aware of something so mysterious? It was instinct. It was as if God were telling him, '*Trust your instincts*.' Affirmation washed through him like a tidal wave. He could feel the hairs on the back of his neck prickling.

He opened his eyes.

A man was standing in the doorway of the sanctuary. He was thin and balding with white hair and wore horn-rimmed glasses. He was dressed in black except for the white tab just below his Adam's apple. "Father Sanders," said Hector. He was the priest who took over for Father Hemple when Hector was just a boy.

"I see you remember my name," he said, smiling.

"Of course, I ..."

"I was just joking, Hector. I mean, when was the last time you came by to see me?"

"Quite a while."

"I guess." Hector was beginning to think this wasn't such a good idea. He thought about leaving, but something inside made him stay.

"I'm sorry to bother you. I just wanted to say 'hi,' and see if I could be of any help."

The dying light caught the red in the stained glass images so that it shown on the head and shoulders of Father Sanders. Hector remembered that thirty years ago, he was the one who started the school his children now attended. It was one of the best schools in the whole state.

"Father –"

"Please, Hector, I'd like you to call me Paul."

"Paul?" asked Hector. "Father Paul?"

"No, just Paul."

"Paul." Hector was more confused now than ever. "Father, there is a reason why I am here. I am stumped. I feel like I'm in over my head. There has been only one murder in Shoestring in the last ten years. Now there are three in the area in three weeks. I just don't think I'm up to this."

"Nobody ever said you couldn't get help. I'm sure you've talked to the authorities in Austin."

"Yes, but they're a long distance away. They have a full plate already. They don't need some small-town hick whining that he can't handle the pressure."

"You think you're whining when you ask for help?" Father Paul sat down in the pew behind Hector. Hector wondered if his sad blue eyes were the result of witnessing so much human misery, or was it Father's own sadness he saw? In the end, Hector guessed, it didn't matter.

Hector told him about the cross falling from the roof of the church, the torn cloth, and the plastic gloves from Peter's death. He talked about the phone call to Angus, Maureen's cat found in someone else's house, the scarf, and the dark car seen around her place. Hector told him about the man in a dark suit that Ben Irwin followed into the alley. Then he told him about Beth's two brushes with death and what they had decided to do with her.

"After all that, the frustrating thing is we're no closer to naming the killer than when we started."

"Well, I can see why you're frustrated," said Father Paul. "That's an awful lot to take in all at once. But it sounds like you're moving in the right direction. I bet you know more than you think you do, if you just spend more time with the evidence. Also, the 'funeral' tomorrow may be a very important time."

THEY ENTERED the hallway hand in hand.

"Oops, I forgot my Day-Timer," said Angus, feeling his breast pocket and his pants. "Here are the keys, honey; I'll just be a minute."

Angelica walked the dim hall slowly, slightly smiling to herself about the man she loved, had married, and had grown a family with as an expression of their love. She was truly afraid for him, but she was encouraged by his confidence. If he said things would be all right, she knew somehow they would be.

She was seeing their lives in a whole new light. But she didn't see the wire stretched across the top of the steps.

"I got it," called Angus, holding up the small leather booklet he laughingly called his 'brains.' It bulged with important messages, appointments, and addresses. She stopped while he caught up with her.

She took two steps toward the top of the staircase. She turned to go down the steps, Angus almost directly behind her. As she hit the wire, her hands went up, and her face contorted into a slow-motion scream. Her purse went flying as horror gripped her.

Angus tried to reach out to her but was not quick enough. He watched helplessly as she tumbled down the stairs, coming to rest in a heap in front of the huge oak doors at the bottom of the stairs.

He looked down, saw the wire, stepped over it, and reached his wife in two long bounds. Angelica lay motionless, as Angus turned her on her back. He felt for a pulse, and a faint thump responded to his touch. He leaned down and kissed her forehead, saying her name softly.

He heard an outside door thudding shut. Angus got out his cell phone and dialed 911. He told the operator where he was and what had happened. He asked for an ambulance and the police. He described Angelica's condition and said he was going to track down the intruder before he had a chance to get away.

He leaned down again to his wife and told her what he was going to do. He kissed her on the cheek. Angelica did not respond.

He went to the door and propped it open, and looked both ways as he went outside into the hot blue brightness. He ran to his left a short distance, to the corner where he could see around the church. He saw clouds in the distance darkening with the coming rain. He saw shops beginning to wake up on a lazy Sunday afternoon. He noticed Ruthie coming out of the Golden Fork to get the Sunday paper. But he saw no sign of anyone who looked remotely suspicious.

Ruthie saw Angus and waved, which Angus returned. He signaled for her to stop and he ran up to her, slightly out of breath.

"What are you running around for on a Sunday afternoon, Reverend?"

"We've had an accident, Ruthie. I was just wondering if you've seen anybody coming out of the church looking to be in a big hurry?"

Ruthie cradled the huge paper like a baby, and it reminded Angus of the Madonna and Child. He didn't know why he made that connection.

Ruthie brightened suddenly and said, "I saw Ed Kramer running past here a few minutes ago. And I thought, 'I wonder what he's in such an all-fire hurry about.' What hap–"

"Which way did he go?"

"That way," she said, pointing toward the gathering storm.

Angus thanked her and turned toward the storm. He saw an EMT truck and Hector racing up to the church while sirens blared and lights flashed, causing confusion and panic where moments before it was all order and serenity, with only a thunder storm approaching. He decided to go back inside the church. *Besides*, he thought, *I know how to get hold of Ed.*

Chapter Twenty-Four: Prime Suspect

BY THE TIME he got there, the EMTs were loading Angelica into the ambulance. He asked how she was, and one of them said she had a broken leg, but she would be fine. She was conscious, barely, with her eyes half open.

Angus said, "*Hola, mi hija.*"

Angelica smiled, listening to him speak Spanish in his brogue.

"I'm coming with you, sweetheart. They said you'll be fine; you have a broken leg." He kissed her tenderly on the lips. She received it with difficulty, but with deep affection.

On the way to the hospital, Angus told Angelica the story of how they first met. She loved to hear him tell it. "I was at a flea market in downtown San Antonio, and I saw you for the first time. You loved looking for bargains. I was there with a couple of friends I met when I came to Austin to go to school. We had heard about this huge flea market and thought it would be fun to do on a lazy Saturday afternoon.

"There was a table of figurines. We were both looking at a statue of St. Francis of Assisi, standing tall, thin, with a halo over his head and a bird on his shoulder.

"I had it in my hand and was about to pay for it when you spoke up and said, 'Sir, I can see you like the statue. Can we talk about this for just a minute? You see, St. Francis is my favorite saint, and I've been looking for this statue for quite some time. I'm willing to pay you twice what you're paying for it.'

"'You must be Catholic?' I said, and you said, 'How perceptive of you.' Well, I was struck dumb right there. It was as if Cupid had a steamroller and just flattened me with happiness. I said to myself, *'I've met my match, and I am going to make her mine.'* But I took your deal, didn't I? I let you pay twice what the dealer charged me. I was in love, but I wasn't stupid."

Angelica laughed weakly.

"I remember the vendor wasn't too happy about that transaction."

Angelica smiled as the ambulance turned into the emergency room entrance.

HECTOR KNEW there would not be much he could do now. He wished he had been able to talk to Angus before he went to the hospital. Now it would be hours before he learned what Angus had found out.

Since he became chief, his life had been a series of hurry up and wait scenarios. He liked the hurry up part, and tolerated waiting. Truth be told – life in Shoestring had been an adjustment for him. He came to get away from the crowds, but he sometimes missed the excitement he could find almost on a daily basis in the big city.

Hector turned up his fleece collar and took a leisurely look around the crime scene. He most enjoyed putting himself in the criminal's shoes. He analyzed what the criminal might have forgotten, or misplaced, or was in too much of a hurry to replace. Something usually turned up;

some scrap of evidence. It fascinated him how careless most criminals could be. He thought most of them wanted to get caught, and Hector was all too happy to oblige them.

He opened the thick oak doors, paying attention to use his handkerchief. He stopped at the landing on the other side of the doors, and crouched down as the big doors clanged shut. He opened the doors again and propped them open to emit more light. He crouched again on the landing and looked over everything carefully.

Hector knew from years of training and experience that the crime scene investigation began with keen observation. *Notice where things are in the room, if anything appears to be missing. Notice the smallest detail, the tiniest inconsistency*, he reminded himself.

He looked with the eyes of an eagle, confident he would not miss the quarry. He was wise enough to realize he would need forensic help and had solicited the team from Austin. In the meantime, he would try his hand at it and discover what he could.

That's the key to waiting, he thought. *You figure out what to do 'in the mean time' to make the wait more meaningful.*

His head bowed and his eyes on fire like a lighthouse piercing a dense fog, Hector searched. He noticed the dust accumulating in the corner, painted over by a steady build up of wax. He noticed the wire stretching across the second step and even where a piece of Angelica's stocking was left where she tripped. He knew the place would be dusted for prints, so he left the stocking remnant alone. He also knew such dusting would be futile because of the number of people who had just used the building. There were two things you did at a crime scene. The first was to observe; the second was to keep your hands to yourself.

After several times over the crime scene, Hector decided he had seen enough. His cell phone rang.

"Hello, Angus," said Hector.

"I'm at the hospital with Angie. The doctor says she's going to be fine. She broke her leg, but will fully recover."

"That's good news," said Hector. "Did you see anything at the church that would help us identify anybody?"

"Well, I heard the door slam shut shortly after Angie fell. I went to look as soon as I could, but I didn't see anything."

"Did you see anyone outside?"

"I saw Ruthie and asked her if she had seen anyone. Hector, would you please go talk to her about who she thinks she saw?"

"Angus, it would be a pleasure. Maybe now we're getting somewhere!" Hector hung up.

THE GOLDEN FORK shone like the city on the hill with the dark clouds behind, and the sun shining full upon it. It was made of the familiar South Texas rock, limestone, and mortar with a dark red tin roof. It had a glass front with blinds blocking the view into the interior. Hector could tell by the shadows moving on the blinds it was busy.

He opened the door and let two men with yellow hard hats, tee shirts, dusty jeans, and big boots face their day. Patrons were stacked up like a pile of steaming pancakes waiting to be devoured. The sound was deafening. Hector thought he would hold his hands over his ears, but as he listened, he noticed how welcome the sound was. If he closed his eyes, he could imagine the sound coming from a babbling brook on a great Montana trout stream.

He spotted Ruthie by a table filled with expectant folks with healthy appetites, waiting to be satisfied. She came with two armloads of plates. Hector marveled at how she did that, like a juggler balancing plates on sticks as they spun in mid air.

Ruthie saw Hector after she deposited her load and came over to him.

"What can I do for you, hon?" she asked with her hands on her hips.

"I'm looking for the guy Angus asked you about."

"You mean that Scottish fella'?"

"That's the one. Did you tell him something?"

"Sure did. He asked me if I'd seen anybody comin' out of the church earlier, and I told him I'd seen Ed Kramer."

Hector made a note of it. "You're sure that's who you saw?"

"As sure as you're standin' here."

ANGUS SHIFTED uneasily in the small chair beside his wife's hospital bed. The chaos of the morning was too much for them both, and they fell fast asleep. They had traveled to the hospital in the ambulance and finally, after suffering through hours of waiting, got her leg looked at by a first-year intern. He diagnosed the broken leg, set it, and placed it in a cast.

Angus marveled at the mischief so many people could get into on a Sunday morning in a small town. He had heard somewhere that most accidents in the home occur on Sunday. There were two children still in their pj's; one was suffering from a headache, the other from a stomachache. A young man had fallen off a ladder and hit his head, requiring stitches. An older woman had an accident with garden shears. Finally, after all these, they tended to Angelica, and so now they slept.

As they began to relax, Angus noticed a need he had neglected. His stomach began to growl, and so his sleep was fitful.

He dreamed of his home, his mother cooking on an old cast-iron wood stove. The smell of haggis filled the whole house with its comforting perfume. But he saw his mother falling, and he was powerless to do anything about it. He reached out to her, and he began to fall as well. He panicked and started screaming for his mother.

Angus was jolted awake by the whisper of an intruder. She was a big woman in a white skirt and pink blouse, with a stethoscope around her neck.

"Ms. McPherson, honey, we need to check your vitals." She did her job, said everything looked fine, and was gone.

Angelica looked at her husband with concern. "What were you dreaming?" she asked.

"It was nothing, Lass." He told her about the dream, and assured her it was about his concern for her, and her recent trauma. "What happens to you happens to me too, you know." He kissed her on the forehead.

ANGUS WAS still hungry. Angelica quickly went back to sleep. Hunger didn't drive her; healing was her main occupation now. Angus had a different agenda.

Angus went on the prowl for some food. He stopped first at a Coke and candy machine. He shuddered. He had an aversion to the sugary and salty snacks that stared back at him through the glass. He next stopped at the front desk and was told about a new "Whataburger" constructed about a block from the hospital, the talk of the town. He asked the nurse to keep an eye on Angelica while he satisfied his hunger. Actually, going to such a place made him sweat. He hated the idea of "fast" food. After he had been in America for a few years, he found himself giving in more and more like the rest of the country with their busy schedules. Lately he had tried more healthy alternatives, but now, under stress, he wanted something fast and satisfying, no matter the grease.

Before he left, he watched Angelica still sleeping peacefully, her dark hair arranged on the pillow like a fan.

He always liked watching her sleep. She seemed so serene, so childlike, so given to the moment. He wanted to touch her China rose cheek, but thought better of it. She needed to rest. He kissed her softly on the forehead and made his way out to the front door toward the new burger joint a block away.

He walked with purpose into the late afternoon heat. It seemed unusually hot for this time of year. Trees were beginning to show their leaves, budding gingerly, not confident that the spring rains would last. The heat wilted the new leaves, so it seemed like death came before life. *You would really have to be determined to survive in conditions like these,* thought Angus.

There's got to be an end to this, he thought, *and soon.* Before, Angus was trying to help a church in his charge. Now it was personal. He didn't want revenge; he just wanted to get this killer with every fiber of his being. He was angry. And he was going to stay angry until the murderer was caught.

It was obvious to Angus, the person doing all this had to be a member of the church. But how did Maureen fit into it? Maybe as she suggested over the phone, she knew something about the people who had done this and threatened to go to the police.

If Ed Kramer was behind all this, Hector would know soon enough. Angus couldn't imagine someone in such a responsible position doing something so dumb. But responsible positions don't insulate people from making stupid mistakes. In fact, it was Angus' experience that just the opposite was true.

The more responsible the position, the more tempting it was to abuse the power entrusted to their care. Richard Nixon came readily to mind. Of course, Angus was just a young man when the whole Watergate turmoil embroiled the world, and he was not in America at the time, but still the blatant abuse of power and the hubris that imagined Nixon was above the law was a textbook example of how power can make you dumb.

SO ED Kramer was his prime suspect. *But what would he gain by killing his pastor, then Maureen who probably knew too much, then Beth, he thought, and now me and mine?* It looks like the guy had it out for authority figures, and Maureen just got in the way. But Angus considered it was much more sinister than that. Beth had said she suspected Pete was having an affair with his secretary. Maybe someone was paying too much attention to his own wife, and he felt cheated. It was worth checking out.

A mockingbird flew across the street and landed on a branch just above Angus' head. He'd always been fascinated by this bird. He'd have never known what he was looking at if it hadn't been for Angelica's aunt Emma. She was an old woman who spent her life drinking in nature, with a particular love of birds. She had an impressive naturalist knowledge and what she didn't know she researched until she found it. The bird got its name because it can mimic any bird call it wants, thus fooling birds into thinking one of their own species is nearby. Angus didn't like feeling the fool. But he had played that role many times in his life, none more frustrating than the one he was playing now.

The mockingbird flew away, and Angus shook his head, lowering it again to the steady beat of his footfalls on the concrete. With each footstep, he became angrier. He reviewed the events of a few short hours ago.

He remembered the helpless feeling he had as he watched his wife fall, playing the jarring scene in slow motion over and over in his mind. He recalled how the adrenaline kicked in as he went chasing after whoever had slammed the church door. He was angry at himself for not reacting fast enough. He could have caught him and ended this nightmare, once and for all. Now the only thing left was the anger and the desire for revenge—here inside, together, simmering like molten lava ready to erupt at a moment's notice.

Angus knew thoughts of revenge would get him nowhere. Still he couldn't help himself. Where Angelica was concerned, there was no other option. His life with her now felt like Israel crossing the Jordan into the 'promised land.' Finding her and making a life together was the most important thing he'd ever done.

The sun played with the buds on the just awakening trees as Angus made his way back to the hospital with his burger, fries, and shake. He reached into the bag, pulled out one French fry, and ate it. He thought about a routine he saw on Saturday Night Live and said out loud, "I love this country," and smiled.

His thoughts drifted back to Ed. As an assistant in the City Manager's office, he, like Tom Branch, knew about deals being made to try to grow Shoestring. Maybe there was money involved? He was also the church treasurer. He knew Peter wanted to buy the vacant store next to the Century Shoppe for a thrift store. The session had been talking about it for months. Maybe Ed saw a way to make some money for himself and wanted Peter out of the way.

It was all speculation. Nothing was solid. His Scottish blood refused to settle for anything so flimsy. He'd have to have a talk with Hector in the morning to see if he'd found out anything new.

Oblivious to the rustling leaves, the bird singing, or to a squirrel scampering across a telephone wire, Angus walked back to his wife in silence. He was enveloped in the stillness of the moment. He couldn't believe what he was experiencing.

Suddenly, he felt transported back in time to his boyhood and the green treeless hills of his native Scotland. He remembered running down a hill dressed in the clothes of his childhood, smiling at the wind, when he suddenly tripped and tumbled down the hill the rest of the way, but he wasn't hurt. He was laughing.

He stopped, looked up and said, "Thank you," out loud.

Chapter Twenty-Five: In for Questioning

HECTOR PARKED THE squad car in front of Ed Kramer's red brick ranch house. It struck him that the house was so modest for one of the leading citizens of Shoestring. It had, however, the right address, just on the outskirts of the wealthiest section of this divided town.

He walked up to the massive oak double door and rang the doorbell. He waited a few minutes and rang it again. If it had indeed been Ed that Ruthie saw, surely he wouldn't be home. He tried again.

He got no answer and so decided to look around. The house had only a carport attached, and no car. A few cardboard boxes were stacked on the side, and several bikes were hanging on the wall. A workbench sat near all the tools, neatly arranged on the pegboard, waiting within easy reach. Hector allowed himself to be jealous of the order he saw, unlike his own workspace with its haphazard organization.

A chill went up his spine at what he spotted next. Two things were placed askew on the workbench, as though someone were in a hurry and had forgotten about neatness. A spool of wire and some needle-nose pliers had been thrown on the bench without much care. He wanted to take them with him, but knew he needed a warrant. He would have to wait.

The machinery of justice sometimes moves too slowly, he thought. *No wonder these parts were known for their vigilantes.* But he also knew justice in the hands of angry men was not justice. It was anarchy. Hector knew justice was elusive, while order—at least a semblance of it—could be the difference between mob rule and a safe society.

He knew Ed would be back any time, and if he were to look around, he'd have to do it quickly. He made a move to the back of the house, which was protected by a wooden fence.

He heard a low growl followed by a deep bark. Hector stepped back. He hated big dogs. When he was on the San Antonio police force, his partner was mauled by a pit bull. Although the academy trained them in how to deal with such beasts, the training did not always translate to actual situations. Hector had been late getting to the scene and saved his partner by shooting the dog.

Hector decided he had seen enough. He went to his car and called Max to have Ed's house watched. Then he would drive home to a messy garage, but the ordered love of his family.

The sun was a bright orange globe in the darkening sky. The clouds drifted in to diffuse the color and light across the horizon. As Hector reached Maywood Lane, his street, he thought about the day. He remembered Angus and Angelica, and called his wife on his cell phone to tell her he had one more stop to make before coming home. He turned his car around and headed for the hospital.

ANGUS SAT in the recliner next to the bed where his beloved slept peacefully. Remnants of the burger and fries still spread across the bedside table, he held his chocolate shake like a goblet from the round table at King Arthur's court.

He had grown up on the stories of Camelot. He loved to hear his mother tell the stories of King Arthur, Guinevere, and Lancelot. He knew he had found his Guinevere in Angelica, and the tragedy in that story would not happen to them. He was too much in love, too devoted. He even hated to admit he was too dependent on her to ever let something happen to their relationship.

Angus got up from the chair and went into the deserted hall. A nurse walked by and smiled. He smiled back. He turned and saw a big Hispanic man in a police uniform coming toward him.

The two men greeted each other and shook hands.

"How's Angelica?" Hector asked after a short silence.

"She'll be all right. The fall broke her leg in two places. We're going home tomorrow, or so we've been told."

Again silence.

"I went by Ed's place. He wasn't there, of course, but we're watching it."

"Good."

"I don't think it means anything, but I found a spool of wire and needle-nosed pliers on his workbench."

"Well, isn't that evidence?"

"Lots of people use wire and pliers for lots of different reasons. It doesn't mean a thing."

"What does it mean?"

"It means he's a suspect in a murder investigation, and he's innocent until proven guilty."

Angus calmed himself. "Can you tell me what we do have?"

And for the next half hour they went over the events of the past three weeks. They talked again about Pete's death and the evidence from the scene. There was the massive

Celtic cross that appeared to be the murder weapon, with burn marks at the base. Those burn marks, Hector found out, were consistent with plastic explosives, used only in the military. He had checked out the military records of some of the people involved. Four of them had some experience with it, and Ed Kramer was one.

"And there were the plastic gloves," said Hector. "We thought we saw fingerprints, but they were too smudged to get a good print."

"And what about Beth? What does she have to do with all this? We even faked her death–it's been almost a week, and nothing's happened. And what about Maureen? We haven't been able to draw any connection between her and the rest of this."

"Well, this creep is very smart, and very patient."

"Smart! How smart was it going after me on a bright Sunday afternoon in the middle of a church?"

Hector held up a hand to calm the cleric. "I just mean, until then, he was biding his time. If Ed Kramer is our man, we'll get him. If not, I think the key will be Beth."

"How do you mean?"

"I mean we said she told us who did this, and we made no arrest. Maybe if we arrest Kramer, maybe he did it, or maybe not. If not then that might put pressure on this guy to show more of his hand like he did today."

"Could I possibly go talk to Beth? I just feel there is something she may know that's escaped us."

"It's possible. I'll have to check with the folks in Lockhart. They're in charge of her for now." Hector's cell phone rang and he answered it. "Yeah?"

"It's Max. Kramer just showed up."

"Bring him in. I'll be right there." Hector hung up.

"They got Ed. Why don't you come? I'll let you watch."

Angus looked at Angelica sleeping the sleep of the innocent. "I wouldn't miss it."

ED SAT staring blankly ahead in a small, windowless room, with a two-way mirror. One other chair was opposite his, where he sat at a small table. Angus watched from behind the mirror with Max. Hector entered the room, looking only at Ed.

Ed did not wait to get started. "Hector, what the hell is this? My wife is scared out of her mind. You have a lot of explaining to do. If I were you, I wouldn't get too comfortable in this new job of yours."

"Now Ed, it seems to me, you're not the one to be making threats," Hector said calmly. "I just brought you in for questioning. Nobody's being arrested. If you cooperate, we'll have you out of here in no time. If not..." He let the sentence trail off like the vapor from a jet engine. "Would you like a cup of coffee?"

"I'm fine," he said, frowning, with arms folded. "I just want to get this over with."

"As a matter of fact, I do too," Hector smiled. "Let's get started."

Ed sat staring laser beams right through Hector's head.

"You were seen leaving the church shortly after Angelica McPherson fell down a flight of stairs. She tripped on a wire strung across those stairs."

"She did? How awful!" Ed looked genuinely surprised.

"Can you tell me what you were doing there?"

"I'm the church treasurer. I was counting the offering. I'm always the last to leave."

"You don't have anyone help you to make sure you're counting correctly?"

"The person who was supposed to help me was sick and in bed."

"And you couldn't get anyone else to help?"

"I didn't think about it. I didn't think it would matter just this once."

"Did you see anyone else about that time?"

"No, I don't think so...Jesús usually comes in about that time to clean up after Sunday services, but I don't recall seeing him."

"What did you think of the sermon this morning?"

"That's an odd question. Since when is it a crime to have an opinion about a sermon?"

Angus smiled.

"It's just that I understand Angus practically accused someone in the congregation of having done all this stuff and..."

"Well, I'm not your man." Ed stood up, and his chair crashed backwards. Angus and Max both jumped.

Hector stood. "Take it easy, Mr. Kramer. Sit down. It's just that we have an incident that's linked to all the killings, and you're seen leaving the scene shortly after it happened. You can see how suspicious we might be?"

"Yes, I can, but do you think I'd be fool enough to try to kill Angus, and then walk out of the building in broad daylight right afterward?"

"Well, as you say, you have a decent alibi. You're the treasurer of the church after all. Oh, one more thing. Who said anything about the attempt being on Angus?"

"Well, it stands to reason." Ed stammered, beads of sweat forming on his forehead. "Angus is the one who's been sniffing around looking for who did this, not his wife. This is a small town, Hector. Everyone knows..."

"Yes, yes, everyone knows. Ed, why don't you tell me what you were doing March 25th."

"The day Pastor Pete was killed?"

"Very good! The very same."

"I was on my way to the Rotary Club for lunch."

"Were there witnesses?"

"The Mayor went with me."

"How very convenient."

"Hey, I'm telling the truth."

Hector could tell he was. It was as if the veneer of adulthood had been scratched off by this scrape with the law, and Hector saw beneath the surface a man who was afraid. He was just an innocent, frightened child, lost and confused. But he needed to pursue it further just the same.

"Where were you the following week on April 2nd, when Maureen Sullivan was killed?"

"I was out of town, I think. I was in Austin trying to get some answers about bills we owed." Ed spoke without hesitation. His glare grew in intensity with each question.

"Any...?"

"...witnesses? How about the State's Attorney General? Besides I didn't even know this Sullivan girl."

"But you knew Beth. What about her?"

"What about her?" Ed shook his head. "Beth's death was an unfortunate accident; an accident I did not cause." Ed stood up. "Now, Hector, I have answered all your questions. I'll take a polygraph if you want me to, but I've done nothing you can hold me for. So let me go!"

"Yes, you're right, Ed. I had to be sure. If you can think of anything that can help us find the killer, please let me know. No hard feelings?" Hector reached out his hand. Ed looked hard at him and walked away.

"OH, HE'LL be all right," said Hector, as he joined the others in the hallway. "I'll buy him lunch this week, and he'll be fine. The question is, if he didn't do it, who did?"

"My money, if I were a betting man, was on him," said Angus.

He went back to the hospital. The nurse said Angelica was asleep, but the doctor had been there earlier and would release her in a day or two. Angus would get her mother to stay with them for a week or so, until Angelica could get stronger. The nurse told him Angelica was to have the cast off in six weeks.

Angus wondered briefly if he should get police protection for her, now that he knew that someone was out to get him. He'd call Hector in the morning and ask him what he thought about the idea. *Maybe something could be arranged with the Driftwood police?* he thought. Angus stretched his long body in the hard "easy" chair and slept fitfully during the night.

ANGUS WOKE the next morning with a crick in his neck. He stretched like a cat and blinked himself awake. Angelica still lay sleeping.

He had mixed feelings as he contemplated her homecoming. He would be glad to have her where she belonged and felt comfortable. He did not know what other responsibilities he would have to assume with her care. He felt guilty about her getting mixed up in all this mess, and he felt a rush of protective instinct as he thought about how vulnerable she would be at home, alone.

He thought about Beth. He knew he would have to see her while he was in Shoestring. He wrote a note to Angelica telling her where he was going and that he would be back by ten o'clock. The doctor wouldn't be by to release her before then anyway.

He called the Lockhart police. Hector had cleared his visit to Beth but he needed to stop by the police station to get the address.

Angus got in his Jeep and drove to Lockhart. The road was straight and flat. Bluebonnets expanded before him as he drove. Hawks circled in the sky.

Every time he saw one of these graceful birds circling in the intense blue of a Texas spring sky, he always thought of God's grace. Having a drunk for a father and an over-protective mother gave him a conflicted view of life. He knew he did not want to be like his father and that he would not grow if he stayed within the loving, protective gaze of his doting mother. Yet he couldn't help being like both.

It was God's grace that brought him to America. It was grace that led him to his wife, and to this calling, and gave him the gift of children. He owed God everything he held dear, and he wasn't going to let anything happen to any of it.

The flip side of God's grace, Angus also believed, was God's judgment. Regardless of how well Hector and he did in bringing this criminal to justice, he knew sooner or later, God would be the ultimate judge. *Where does that leave the idea of 'forgiveness?'* he thought, remembering Jorge's comment on their fishing trip.

Angus believed God gave order to the universe, and he would in this case as well. Perhaps people thought him naive. After all, it is in vogue to be cynical about our world and its prospects for survival.

Chapter Twenty Six: Apparition

WHEN HE GOT close to Lockhart, the first thing he saw was the courthouse. Built before the turn of the last century, it had been renovated before the turn of this century. The tall and massive structure, both formal and whimsical, was built of brilliant sandstone, with turrets and columns accented in gold and Tuscan red. It had a mansard roof with a clock tower that never kept the correct time, even though it had been worked on numerous times. Angus always got goose bumps when he saw it. *Besides,* he thought, *it kept perfect time at least twice a day.*

He knew the address, 1517 Blanco Street. He found the house and parked out in front. It was in a part of town known as Cocklebur, the poor black section. Hector bought the house probably because the price was right and he hoped the investment would pay for itself once he fixed it up.

The green siding was gray with age. The white shutters were off their hinges and heavy with mildew. The brown door was grimy from neglect. It was a simple ranch-style frame house with rotting wood on the porch. Angus worried he might fall through if he put his full weight on it.

He looked around to see if a dark, late-model car had followed him. He saw several fitting the description, but was not sure if indeed he had been followed. He knocked anyway.

The sentiment he'd often seen expressed on T-shirts flashed through his mind, "Kill them all and let God sort them out." He shook his head; he couldn't help it. His anger over this mess was never far beneath the surface. It surprised him anyway.

A woman answered the door. She was a short, well built redhead. Angus could tell when people described her, they probably used the word, "perky." He smiled at her and showed his driver's license. She smiled back at him.

"Yes, Reverend, I've been waiting for you. Come in, please." She spoke with a note of formality that was odd under the circumstances.

She led him into the "front room." There was no carpet on the floor, but Angus did notice it had been recently taken up and removed. A long roll of carpet lay on one side of the room, stationed just under the two windows that stood open to the slight morning breeze. Nearby were a folding chair and a well worn, stained over-stuffed easy chair.

Beth sat down with sunken, sad eyes. As soon as she saw Angus, her face lit up like the moon, shining brightly in the sun's reflected light.

"Hello, Beth," Angus said, leaning down.

The perky woman introduced herself as Clare, and invited Angus to sit next to Beth while she went to clean up the breakfast dishes. She asked him if he would like a cup of coffee which Angus gladly accepted.

As Clare went into the kitchen, Beth and Angus stared at each other for a long minute.

"How are you, Beth?" he asked finally.

"I'm fine. I'm homesick," she said, looking down. "I can't wait for this to be over. I don't think my being 'dead' will change anything."

Clare came in with the cup of coffee, smiled, touched Angus on the shoulder, and went back to the kitchen.

"Can you tell me anything about that night?" he asked.

"Just that Charlie saved my life."

"Do you remember anything before the accident? Did you take your car in to be serviced anywhere before the trip?"

It was like a light bulb going off in her head. "Of course I did. The police never asked me that one. But yes, I took it to Ben to change the oil and rotate the tires."

"When did you pick it up?"

"The next morning before I went to work."

"Who took you to get the car?"

"Charlie had to go home to get ready for the trip, so he couldn't do it. So I called Linda, my best friend at church."

"Linda?"

"Yes, Linda Branch, Tom's wife. She said it wasn't a problem. They were only a couple of blocks away. But when it came time for Linda to pick me up, Tom showed up instead."

"Her husband?"

"Yeah, I thought that was kind of odd." Beth tilted her head the way his cat did. It made Angus smile. "He said that Linda had called him and told him to pick me up because she had gotten tied up at work. But you want to know what's really funny? After the accident and I ended up here, Hector came by to tell me that one of my messages was from Linda. She said she had gotten tied up with a customer, but that she would be right there."

"So you think Tom was lying?"

"Well, he did say Linda was busy and couldn't get away. That part was true."

"Did you tell any of this to Hector?"

"No, it just now occurred to me."

"Which part?"

"What do you mean?"

"Well, the oddness of Tom showing up when you had called Linda. That would have occurred to me right away."

Beth looked at Angus suspiciously. She looked down and spoke softly. "This is the clearest my mind has been for weeks."

"Oh, of course." Angus touched her knee. "Of course, that's right."

Beth felt odd not trusting Angus. He had supported her through all this and was trying now to make things right. But still she fought to hold things back, as if by telling everything, it would all fall apart. She couldn't stand to let that happen.

After a long silence, Angus said with a smile, "Tomorrow is your funeral. I hope we'll know more by then, but we can't be sure. I've never planned a funeral for someone who was still alive."

"It's kind of strange," Beth said wistfully.

"And then I want to take Angie home and get her well."

"How is she?"

"Very tired. All she wants to do is rest...Can't say as I blame her. But I do blame myself."

"You blame yourself?"

"If I hadn't been snooping around, Angie wouldn't be in that hospital bed. And besides, we all know he wasn't aiming at her but at me. I feel guilty because of it all."

Angus was in obvious pain and although he was her superior, the pastor in her knew just to listen and let him talk. All she could say was, "guilty?"

"Yes, guilty." Water started to form in the corners of his reddened eyes. "It's odd, I'm angry, but I'm also starting to enjoy this pursuit far too much. In fact I have never had this much fun in my life. It makes me wonder what I've been doing all these years—if I've followed the right calling. Perhaps I should have been a police detective."

"You feel guilty because you're chasing a murderer, and that makes you feel alive?"

Angus smiled. "Yes, that's exactly how I feel. You're right. You have summarized it beautifully and made me see how it looks, counselor."

"I'm sorry, Angus, but I am curious about how it does look."

"Please don't apologize. I know it does sound kind of sick."

"What do you mean?"

"I'm not supposed to be getting pleasure out of other people's pain."

"But you are called to root out injustice, point out evil, and love life, which is what you are doing. It's all part of the same call. It's just never looked like that before. Just do me one favor?"

"What's that?"

"Don't quit your day job." They both laughed, and then a silence passed between them. "I can't tell you how wonderful I feel talking with you about all this. You have given me a great gift, and I thank you. Makes me sorry I can't be there for my funeral tomorrow."

They both laughed again.

THE CHURCH was packed the next day. Beth was well loved in the church and the community. The story was that she had been cremated, so there would be no casket. Just a black jar stood as solitary sentinel on the communion table. Judy played Beth's favorite piece, Bach's "Toccata and Fugue in E Minor" to start the service. She played it brilliantly. *Here are two great gifts this church has:* thought Angus, *this wonderful instrument and someone who loves to play it.*

The question from yesterday crossed his mind again. *How do you have a funeral for someone who isn't dead?* He had to pull off a "convincing" funeral in the hope that with Beth out of the way, the killer could relax and perhaps slip up somehow.

Angus stood at the conclusion of the music. He began the service with words of welcome, scripture, and a prayer. Several people had asked to say a few words. First was an old college friend who spoke about how Beth had experienced her call to ministry. *Funny*, Angus thought, *Beth had never told me the story.* Then came the chair of the Christian Education Committee, Marti Bellows, a petite woman in her sixties with salt and pepper hair. Then came Beth's brother, Andrew, just arrived on a late flight, who spoke of her love for children and her desire to have them one day. He broke down near the end.

Last to speak was Charlie Cosslett, the choir director. He started out by saying how much he loved her and wanted to marry her. He started to tell about the awful night of the accident and how he tried to save her. But he did not finish.

There in the choir loft, wearing a diaphanous white gown and bathed in light, was Beth McKinley. Almost as soon as she appeared, she was gone. Angus saw her, and his jaw dropped. Charlie also saw her and he stammered, cleared his throat and continued.

"I…I…visited her at the hospital the next day but there was no hope…She was gone, gone…" Charlie was caught once again in mid-sentence by the spectral image of Beth smiling in the light.

"Gone, but…not forgotten." He choked the words out.

Angus' mind was racing, and anger was rising in his throat. *What's going on here?* he thought. *Why is she doing this? If this is some kind of trick, why wasn't I told?*

Charlie looked at Angus. Charlie's face was a pale sheet

of bleached white. Angus thought, *This must be Hector's idea. But why Charlie? Of all the suspects, Charlie was the least likely.* He loved Beth and respected Peter. He told Angus as much on any number of occasions. No one had yet figured out a connection to Maureen, if there was one. The people in the congregation began talking to one another, looking around, trying to figure out what was going on. Beth was gone again.

Charlie began again, "I...I...remember Beth as one who cared...for others." He looked down as beads of sweat formed in his palms and on his forehead. "I worked with her, loved her, and wanted to marry her...and an accident cut short the life we would have had."

Beth appeared again, her white dress blown by some invisible wind because there was no breeze in the sanctuary.

"Noooooo!" Charlie screamed. He looked again at Angus with a mix of anguish and despair. He stammered, "I can't go on, I'm sorry." And he left.

Angus stood battling between chasing after Charlie and his responsibility to the gathered congregation. *What the blazes is going on here?* he thought. *Who set this up? Hector? Why didn't he tell me? And what the heck do I do now?*

"Uhm, Charlie is obviously distraught. We have people available to help him. If you will open your hymnals to page 280, 'Amazing Grace,' let us collect ourselves in song." *There's a new pastoral technique*, he thought, while at the same time taking a page from the psalms. '*When in doubt, sing.*' He made a mental note to pass this bit of wisdom on at the next new pastor's conference he would be leading in the fall.

WHEN THE service was over, people filled the narthex with questions and gossip. It sounded like bees buzzing around the hive. But there was no Charlie.

Angus pushed through the crowd, his look a mixture of anger and worry. "What the heck..." He started to get in

Hector's face. "I'll tell you later," said Hector, holding up a hand like a stop sign. "Right now we have to find him."

"You didn't get him?" Angus was beside himself with rage.

"No, but we know he's still in the building."

Tom Branch overheard them talking, and told them about a room off the sanctuary which led to the roof. Tom showed them the room, and the door to the roof was open.

Angus was the first to take the stairs. They were small and a tight fit for his big frame, but he bounded up the steps two at a time. Hector protested it would be dangerous and pleaded with him to let one of the uniformed officers go first, but Angus didn't hear him.

Angus approached the top door that looked more like the little cubbyhole entrance to "the other side" in *Alice in Wonderland*. It was shut and all the budging his body could muster would not open it. Hector ordered one of the uniforms with a gun to the front of the line to try to open it. The officer shot the door handle, and the bullet ricocheted off into the wall.

"You better not try that again," growled Angus.

Hector ordered some of the people off the crowded stairway, and asked for the battering ram to break in the door.

OUTSIDE, SERGEANT Max Brown was directing deputies to surround the building. He could see Charlie running on the roof, but the footing was slick and unstable. Max got a bull horn from his squad car and spoke into it.

"Charlie, give yourself up. The place is surrounded. You have no place to go."

Charlie did not respond. He kept running around the roof, hunched over, using his hands to help him hold on. He looked like a gargoyle in motion. He hoped in fact that he would soon turn to stone, and his pain would end.

All this was for the love of his life. Charlie had wanted Beth all to himself, but Pete was always in the way. If he couldn't have her, then nobody could. The pounding on the door interrupted the pounding of his heart.

Why is this happening to me? he thought. *I'm a good man. I've been a good choir director. I've worked hard at recruiting voices, just like in the army. What more do they want?*

"I'm a good man," he said out loud. "I'm a GOOD MAN!" He shouted down at the police who stared up at him with guns drawn, pointed at him. When he looked down again, he saw Beth standing next to Max.

"Beth!" cried Charlie. "What?... Who?..." He sat down, his hands between his knees, and heaved a huge sigh.

"I don't get it," said Charlie, now clearly exhausted, spent, defeated. "I thought you were dead."

"You thought you'd killed her, you mean," said Max.

"Are you crazy? I love her. I want to marry her."

The hammering stopped, the door shattered in an explosion of wood, an arm reached through and unlocked the door, and the police rushed through. They grabbed Charlie who went quietly.

Chapter Twenty-Seven: 'I Have to Find Out'

"I CAN'T BELIEVE IT," Ruthie said, shaking her head.

"What can't you believe?" asked Ben.

"I can't believe it was Charlie. I mean he came in here every day. I liked him. I tried to fix him up with my niece. I thought they'd be great together."

"You know the strange thing," said Ben Irwin, sipping his coffee with both hands around the mug. He made an ugly face and gave the mug back to Ruthie. "This is too cold now. You've talked so long, you went and made me neglect my coffee."

"I'll ignore that if you say 'please.'"

"Please," said Ben, smiling broadly.

"The strange thing is they still could."

"Could what?"

"Be right for each other."

CHARLIE WAS led into the station house in handcuffs, his blond hair a tousled mess, a worried look of dread printed on his face. Hector and a state trooper followed him. Angus and Beth were at the squad car—she, in it, he, standing next to her under the shade of a huge live oak tree. The group with Charlie in tow had been inside the station several minutes when Max Brown emerged again and headed in Angus' direction.

"Hector wants you to watch the interrogation," he said, "if you'd like."

"Yes, I would. Does Charlie have a lawyer?"

"He called someone; I assume it was a lawyer."

"Thanks, Max, I'll be right there." Max left and went back inside the station.

Angus crouched by the squad car so his tall frame was face to face with Beth.

"Are you going to be all right?" he asked.

"Yeah, well, I'm pretty shaken by all this."

"Of course, of course. Are you going home now that we caught the guy?"

"You mean I can go home?"

"Let me check with Hector, but yes, I think so. It appears to be all over now. You can relax."

"But Charlie?" Beth said, a furrow on her forehead planting only seeds of doubt. "Charlie couldn't hurt a fly."

"Sometimes it's the quiet ones. I know this has all been too much for you. Just go home and get some rest, and try to put all this behind you. I'll keep an eye on Charlie to make sure he's treated fairly."

She looked at him with tears in her eyes. "Thank you, Angus."

The squad car took off with the lights flashing.

"THAT WAS a crazy, sick stunt you pulled, Charlie," said Hector. "What were you thinking?"

"I wasn't thinking," said Charlie. "I just bolted. I saw Beth and I panicked. I couldn't believe it."

"That she was alive?"

"Yeah, I thought she was dead." Charlie's face was contorted in pain. "I mean we were having her funeral, for Christ's sake!"

"Did you have anything to do with her *accident*?"

"What kind of a stupid question is that? Of course I did. You were there. You saw our cars. They were both totaled."

"Well, actually, Charlie, Beth's was the only one totaled. You drove up after she had her accident. Don't you remember?"

"Oh, yeah, right. It's kind of vague."

"Did you try to kill her?" Hector leaned on the table almost touching him, nose to nose.

Charlie looked away, "Me? Heck no, I loved her. I was going to marry her. She was mine." There was a pause. "Where is my lawyer? You can't question me without my lawyer being present."

"Oh, that's okay, we're just getting started. We won't do anything really serious without him."

Angus stood with Max behind the two-way mirror. It seemed to him to be unbearably hot in the tiny room. His leg began to twitch, and his fingers started drumming the wall beside him. Max looked at him and cleared his throat, frowning. Angus stopped immediately.

Charlie was like a rare moth, the last of its kind. Flittering toward the flame, he was about to be burned. Both a pest and a rare creature would be lost forever.

Angus was in agony as he watched Charlie's last dance. He felt somehow responsible. After all, this church was his responsibility, so any failure was his failure. Any thought of failure reminded him of those encounters with his father. In his drunken rages, he would berate Angus and his mother without mercy. And even though he knew it was the booze talking, that this was not his father, it was sometimes hard to separate the two.

Intellectually, he knew his thinking was not logical, but it was certainly how he felt. But more than that, it was about Charlie, one more lost soul. Such a realization drove Angus to distraction, and he couldn't keep his body still.

Then a young man with a pock-marked face entered the interrogation room.

"Who are you?" asked Hector.

"I'm Randall Windham, and you have my client in custody. If you have questioned him without a lawyer present, there will be consequences."

"You're his lawyer?" Hector looked from Randall to Charlie and then to the two-way glass.

"Yes, I am. Do you have a problem with that?" Randall looked at the two-way glass as well.

"No, no. I'm just surprised is all. I didn't know they let high school students become lawyers."

"Don't be. And don't be surprised if we bring you up on charges for this illegal investigation."

"We haven't gotten anywhere."

"That doesn't matter. Can I have a minute to confer with my client?" Randall said, sitting next to Charlie.

"Of course, be my guest."

ANGUS MET Hector in the hall outside the interrogation room. "Why didn't you tell me what you were planning to do?" The veins on Angus' neck stood out like the Blue Danube.

His eyes fixed on Angus, Hector took a step back from the encounter. "Angus, I'm sorry, but I have more important things on my mind than telling you about a police operation."

"More important?" Angus bellowed. "You told Judy, otherwise she wouldn't have been able to play the organ."

"Yes, you're right. We told her, of course. But really Angus, can we talk about this later? I have to think about Charlie and how I'm going to get him."

"I'm sure you didn't mean that. I'm sure you're not out to get Charlie. You're out to find the truth, no matter where it leads."

"Yes, of course, that's right. And Angus, I am sorry we left you out of the loop. You should have been told, and I just didn't think of it. I wanted to tell you, but in the end, it worked out. We got our man."

"Did we?"

"Sure, he's practically confessed."

"Not from what I've seen, he hasn't. Besides, it just doesn't fit."

"What doesn't fit? Charlie killed Peter because he was jealous of his relationship to Beth. Maureen got killed because she saw something that tied him to Pete's murder. And he tried to kill Beth because he knew she wouldn't marry him. She's the one he wanted to do in all along."

"How do you know Beth didn't want to marry him? Did she tell you?" asked Angus.

"Yes," said Hector.

RANDALL POKED his head out of the interrogation room door. "We're ready to begin. But before we start, I want to say again, I may bring you up on charges, Hector. You asked my client if he had anything to do with Peter's death."

"No," said Hector calmly, "I asked him if he had anything to do with the attempt on Beth."

"It's still a violation of his civil rights, and you're going to pay. We'll see where this leads."

"Yes, we will," said Hector, and they both went back into the room together.

"OKAY, LET'S start at the beginning, shall we? Why did you kill Peter Anderson?" Randall had not taken a seat yet. He stood erect and said, "Evidence! Where's the evidence? You can't just accuse him of something like that without laying out the case against him."

"It's okay, Randy," Charlie said, as he sat down. "I did not kill anyone. I have nothing to hide."

"Okay, then," asked Hector, "where were you the morning of March 25th?"

"I was in my office going over the music for the next month."

"But didn't you do that with Pete first?"

"No, I would choose the music, and then we would meet and see how the pieces fit together. We were going to do that after lunch."

"But you weren't there that morning, Charlie. I checked. The secretary rang your office, and you never answered."

Randall shifted his weight in the gray folding chair, "That doesn't prove anything. Do you always answer your phone, Hector, when you don't want to be disturbed?"

"Take it easy, counselor, this is not a trial. I'm just trying to get at the truth."

Randall exploded out of his chair like a Tomahawk missile. "You wouldn't know the truth if it walked up to you right now and bit you on the ass! You have nothing on my client. No evidence at all! You're just fishing, Chief. Save that stuff for the river."

ANGUS SAT back in his chair, his eyes wide with surprise and frustration. Hector seemed on trial here as much as Charlie, and Angus wanted simultaneously to either shield or to expose him. But he most definitely wanted to deck Randy. This coming from one who was supposed to be a man of peace.

He breathed heavily. Max looked over at him with a slow smile. Angus smiled back, breathing a little easier now. He settled down again to watch the unfolding story, struggling to be told.

"Okay," said Hector, "you're working on your music and the phone rings which you don't answer. Then what?"

"What do you mean?"

"What happened next? You know, it's a simple question."

"I guess I went to lunch."

"You guess?" pressed Hector.

"Yeah, I guess. I don't know what I did. Do you remember what you did three weeks ago, at lunch?"

"Yes, Charlie, I remember very well. In fact, I'll never forget it. I was called to investigate an accident of a friend of mine, which turned into a murder, for which you have been charged, and are guilty!"

"I had nothing to do with any of this, and you know it!" shouted Charlie, slamming his fist on the table.

"I know nothing of the kind. All I know is you refuse to tell me what you were doing at that day and time. It looks pretty suspicious to me."

"Okay, I went to lunch." Charlie shook his head.

"Did you see anyone?"

"I don't think so."

"As a matter of fact, Charlie, someone saw you."

"Who?" Charlie asked with a mixture of surprise, curiosity, and anger.

"Beth did," said Hector. "She had been talking with Peter in her office when the three of you met in the hallway. Remember now, Charlie?"

Randall looked at his client in surprise, and Charlie looked down at the floor, slump-shouldered. His body seemed to age thirty years in one moment. The transformation was so complete, Angus couldn't believe what he was seeing. *Surely*, he thought, *Hector saw this too.*

"Yeah, I remember," old man Charlie said. "But so what. We'd met in the hallway dozens of times."

"But that's what makes this meeting so special, Charlie." Hector was up pacing behind Charlie's chair like a hawk ready to pounce. "You hated Peter because of his relationship with Beth. You loved her and wanted her all to yourself, isn't that right?"

"No, no, that's not right. They were colleagues, that's all they were. I knew that. I know that what Beth and I had was special. No one can take that away from me. Besides, 'Pastor Peter' was doing Louise."

"'Had,' Charlie? Is it over? You know Beth is still alive, even though you tried to kill her."

"I did not try to kill her!" It was Charlie's turn to explode, but to Angus it was not convincing. It was like the anticipated big bang of a firecracker, only to have it fizzle out—too weak and tired, too wet and old to explode, dying a painful death in the grass.

"That's okay, Charlie." Hector placed a reassuring hand on his shoulder, guiding him back down to the chair. "We'll get to that later."

ANGUS STARED at Charlie in disbelief. In a matter of minutes he had been reduced to an animal—a lame opossum, scruffy and ugly, yet beautiful in an odd sort of way. Angus felt sorry a fine musician, a wonderful young man, could be reduced to this so quickly.

Angus laughed to himself, and Max looked at him with a quizzical gaze. Love can make you do some crazy things. But he knew Charlie; he knew it just wasn't in him, all this plotting and violence and murder. Even though Hector made a good case against him, he knew Charlie, he knew his parents; they were friends. None of this made any sense. Charlie looked as limp as a noodle in boiling water.

Suddenly, Angus thought about his wife. In all the excitement, he had forgotten about her, still at the hospital, waiting for him to pick her up and take her home.

He excused himself—they seemed to be taking a break again—and went into the hallway to call his Angelica.

Staring at the phone and punching in the numbers, he thought about his strange odyssey with these machines. When he first came to this country, they were just starting to catch on. Now they were everywhere. He remembered laughing at how people were glued to them. He also remembered vowing he would never get one. "Never say never," they say. Then he was called to this ministry, and it was getting one of these or never keep up with 10,001 demands on his time.

He remembered he would have to call the office after he had called his wife.

Angelica answered the phone. Yes, she had been waiting, but there was no hurry, and she meant it. She was reading a book in the lobby and looking at the people, making up stories about why they were in the hospital, remembering how Angus and she loved to do that at the airport. Angus thanked her for her patience and explained what was happening. He told her he would be about another twenty minutes. Before they hung up, Angelica asked, "Do you think he's guilty, Angus?"

"No, I do not."

"Then who?"

"I don't know, but I have to find out."

Chapter Twenty-Eight: Settling the Score

"I DON'T CARE what you say, my client is innocent." Randy Windham was nose to nose with Hector as they came out into the hall, startling Angus. "And your trying to bully a confession out of him will not wash."

"The D.A. thinks we have a pretty solid case against him." Angus was impressed by Hector's calm demeanor.

"At this point, I don't care about the D.A. What I care about is being fair to my client."

"We have been more than fair, counselor, and if you impede this investigation any further, we will take steps to see that you don't."

"Don't you threaten me, Hector," Randy snarled.

"Don't threaten me, Randy."

Collectively they took a breath.

Windham said, "I have to go now, but I'll be back. If I hear of anything out of the ordinary, I'll have you up on charges so fast, it will make you go bald."

"Oh, Randy—quite the pit bull today, aren't we?"

Randy scowled and stormed out of the police station.

ANGUS' CELL phone rang again. It was Francesca.

"Just in case you've forgotten, you have a job to do back here. The budget is almost 150 thousand in the red, another minister ran off with the church secretary, and the PJC is bringing a pastor up on charges that he welcomed an atheist into church membership."

"My, aren't we in a good mood."

"It's 'we' nothing, Angus. If you don't get back here and start doing your job, you may have to find another assistant. And this time, I mean it."

"I know, I know," said Angus. "If you're trying to make me feel guilty, you're doing a great job."

"Well, at least that makes one of us."

"Very funny. I'm sorry I've left you holding the bag. Get hold of the new Associate Exec, Karen. She can help do some of that stuff. I'll be back tomorrow. I'll make it up to both of you. Angelica is coming home today."

"So she's doing better?"

"Yeah, she'll be fine, Franny. But I think we've got the wrong man. I don't think Charlie did it."

"Then who did?"

"If I knew that, Franny, then I could solve the budget deficit as well."

She laughed. "I'm sure finding the murderer is a whole lot easier than finding a hundred fifty thousand."

"You may be right. I'll see you tomorrow, I promise."

"I won't hold my breath."

They said goodbye, and Angus hung up.

THE INTERROGATION room door opened, and Hector led Charlie out with chains around his waist and ankles, like a pork roast trussed up and ready to bake.

"Angus, thank you," Charlie said weakly. "I didn't do this, you have to believe me."

Angus thought, *I'd rather face a deficit of one hundred and fifty million than let down one innocent person.* "I'll do what I can," he said, not knowing what that would be.

"Hurry," said Charlie, as Hector led him back to his cell.

Yeah, right, 'hurry,' he says. But where? Which direction? We haven't got a clue.

The clank and clatter of metal doors opening and shutting brought Angus out of his thoughts. He shuddered thinking of Charlie's chains and about his own as well. *Each one of us is in a prison of our own design, one which is inescapable and yet all too comfortable.*

Hector emerged from the jail proper with a scowl on his face.

"You know what, Hector? The boy is innocent."

"Let's go into my office." Hector walked like a convicted man on his way to the gallows.

Angus sat in one of the chairs facing the desk, looking at the bass he saw when he first met Hector. He remembered the time they went fishing and what a relief it had been to get away like that. It seemed so long ago now. He also recalled Jorge's question about forgiveness. *The hardest person to forgive is never your enemy*, thought Angus. *It's always yourself.*

"First of all," Hector looked tired and spent, "Charlie is not a boy. He's a grown man, and he knew what he was doing. Second, all the evidence points to him."

"What evidence? You've got the cement cross that killed Pete, but nothing linking it to anyone, except that it has to be someone from the military. Do you even know if Charlie was ever in the military? I didn't hear you ask him that today, or did I miss something? You've got the plastic gloves that have no fingerprints, and a witness who saw someone on the roof of the church at the time of the murder, but he's not sure who he saw. You've got Maureen Sullivan dead from strangulation. You've got the murder weapon but no prints. A witness said something about a cat attacking the killer, but no one, including Charlie, has turned up with a scratch anywhere, except Maureen.

Then there is the brake job on Beth's car which caused the accident that Charlie tried to prevent. So tell me how the evidence points to Charlie."

Hector leveled a stare at Angus. "He didn't show up later. He could have messed with the brake line any time. As for Peter, I have witnesses that say Charlie was jealous of his relationship with Beth. He couldn't stand to see them together."

"If the witness you're talking about is the secretary, Louise, she had her own agenda with Pete, and from what I hear, she didn't like Charlie too much."

Hector smiled, "'From what I hear,' eh? You've got your ear to the ground, I see."

"It's not hard to hear things in a small town." Angus blushed.

"No, no, it's not. I think you're beginning to like it here, Angus."

"Yeah, it does have a certain appeal. If you must know, Beth told me that Louise couldn't stand Charlie."

"This church is starting to sound like an episode of *Survivor*."

Angus smiled. "There was a bit of graffiti found in the sixteenth century about the church. It said the church is like Noah's ark. If it wasn't for the storm outside, you couldn't stand the stink inside. Whenever I tell that joke in church circles, they don't laugh."

But Hector did laugh. The walls lapped it up like a thirsty horse after a long, hot ride. The chief's office was such a serious place; there was little room for laughter. It fell on the place like rain on the desert.

"If it isn't Charlie, then who is it?" said Hector, scratching his head.

"It's got to be someone with an axe to grind against Peter. Maureen and Beth just got in the way."

"That's the way it appears."

"Are you saying you don't buy that?" asked Angus.

"What if Maureen was the intended target, and Peter and Beth were incidental?"

"But Pete's murder was so well planned and timed perfectly. There was nothing incidental about it."

"What if someone at the plant where she worked was 'cooking the books' or something like that? Maureen found out about it, but also let slip she had been seeing Peter for counseling. Wouldn't that fit?"

"But why kill Pete first?"

"Good question," said Hector.

"Maybe because he had to be more careful about Pete? He could get to Maureen anytime, if he also worked at the plant. Maybe he wanted to make a statement with Pete's murder."

"Make a statement?" asked Hector.

"Sure, you know, someone with a history of hostility against the church."

"Now there's an angle I hadn't thought of."

"That's what I'm here for," Angus smiled. "The church has few friends and many enemies."

"But who?"

They talked for a few minutes more about some of the possibilities, but resolved nothing. Angus said his goodbyes and headed back to the hospital. Angelica would be anxious to get home.

The hospital was in a particularly nice part of town with well kept homes, tree-lined lanes, and curbs with sidewalks. He pulled his yellow Cherokee through the streets slowly, methodically, as though he were thinking about finding a place to live. He startled himself with the notion. He loved where he lived, and wouldn't want to move anywhere else. But the boys were grown and gone, and they didn't need a lot of space, except that they were accustomed to it. The space had become as much a part of them as their children were. It would be difficult to leave.

"Who said anything about leaving?" Angus said out loud, as he turned into the hospital parking lot.

THE CLOUDS began to gather and darken. *Rain's coming, I'd best get her in the car quickly*, thought Angus. *I don't want my princess getting wet.* He smiled. He got out his cell phone and punched speed dial.

"Hi, Michael. I just wondered if you're home today. I'm bringing Mom home; I could use some help getting her upstairs...great...I'll see you in about an hour and a half... Good!...See ya' then."

When he got to the front door of the hospital, Angelica, widely grinning, was waiting for him in a wheelchair. She held on her lap a floral arrangement Francesca had sent.

"There's my bonny lass," said Angus with his arms wide open. They kissed as though it was their first. "I'm so incredibly lucky to be married to you, my sweet."

"Yes, you are, and don't you forget it," Angelica said with a frown, followed by a devilish smile.

They got into the car and started on their way back home. The storm had stalled over to the east, and the dark clouds grew higher and higher. An awkward silence descended upon them. They had been separated for so long, they had to readjust to each other's presence. Angelica wanted to talk about the weather or to find out any news from home. But the magnet of the swirling events of the last few weeks was just too much to resist.

"So, did Charlie do all this terrible stuff or what?" she asked.

"Hector seems to think so, but I don't. It just doesn't add up. If Charlie killed Pete, why go after Beth? It would mean he was a 'serial' killer, and Charlie doesn't fit the profile. Maureen is the key. If we can figure out why she was killed, we'll have a clear fix on the other murder and the attempts on me and Beth."

"Well?" Angelica smiled.

"Well what?"

"Well, aren't you going to tell me how Maureen fits into this?"

The dark clouds flattened some, moving swiftly toward the Jeep. Then the rains came in sheets as if nature had been collecting each drop of water for this moment. It was such a powerful force, it made driving difficult.

"We sure needed this rain, but I hope we make it home."

"Angus!"

"What?" He turned toward her, smiling. "Okay, it was something Beth said. She said Tom Branch took her to get her car from the garage the day she and Charlie were to take their trip. Tom worked some with Maureen at the Chamber of Commerce."

"So you think Tom did all this?"

"Could be, but I think someone else was involved. Someone who knew Beth and Pete well, someone who knew Pete was counseling with Maureen, and that Beth was best friends with a co-worker's wife. Someone who knew the financial condition at the plant. Someone who wants me out of the way and..." Angus' face darkened like the sky outside the car, his thoughts trailing off.

"What is it?"

"I don't know what I'm talking about. I haven't got a clue about any of this. I'm just glad you're okay and that we're going back home."

Angus' cell phone rang, lighting up the darkness. It was Tom Branch, the clerk of the session. He wanted to know if Angus could fill the pulpit for the Maundy Thursday Service, and then again on Easter. Tom said they could have chosen someone else, but the people had really appreciated Angus' presence during this tense time.

His eyes got really big as he held the phone away from him and mouthed the words, "It's Tom Branch!"

Angus thought about his conversation with Francesca and how he had neglected his duties at the office. But he couldn't let this church down, especially at a time like this. He said he would be happy to help them out for those two services.

He told his wife about the call and Angelica said, "I've always thought the name of the Thursday service funny, 'Maundy.' No one gets it. Nobody understands what it means."

"I know. That's why some call it Holy Thursday instead."

"I hope we don't. I like the name Maundy. I like the fact that no one knows it means 'new commandment' or where it comes from. I like having a secret that only those on the inside understand."

"So you can keep out the riffraff?" asked Angus, smiling.

"No, so we can include those who want to bother to know what it means. Faith is simple but not easy, and this is a symbol of it."

Angus thought about going back for the two services. Typically, both are communion services, which he preferred. He remembered the last time he had a 'service' at the church and how Charlie got arrested. He said a little prayer for Charlie's safe return home.

Maybe this time they could apprehend the real killer, but how? We'd have to set it up somehow, he thought. He'd talk to Hector in the morning.

The storm outside drove as hard as Angus did to get home. Michael met them at the Jeep as it pulled up to the house, and helped Angus with Angelica and her belongings. They hobbled together to the second floor, and when they were settled, they went out on the porch to watch the show.

It was a ritual every time a storm brewed. They shut off all the lights and watched the lightening flash in the distance. It was better than any fireworks display because there was no plan. It was completely random.

Angus was glad to get Angelica home, away from the madness at Shoestring. He worried though if even this place were safe from harm. *The sooner we catch this killer the better. It's personal now, not just an intellectual curiosity. Whoever has done this made an attempt on my life, but injured my wife instead. I will not rest until the score is settled,* he vowed, as he watched the natural fireworks explode in the sky.

Chapter Twenty-Nine: The Missing Piece

ANGUS WOKE EARLY the next day, fed the animals, and meditated. His practice was to pray his way through the Bible, reading and meditating on a portion of scripture every day.

Today he read from Revelation. He couldn't seem to get away from the last book of the Bible. It was from chapter sixteen and seventeen concerning the seven angels and the bowls of wrath God would pour out on the land. Such language repulsed him because it went so counter to his understanding of God's grace. But he could identify with God's wrath. He'd like to see some people flattened by an avenging God, but couldn't overtly acknowledge it.

He thought of his obligation to the Presbytery. He hadn't spoken to the Chair of the Finance Committee or to the Committee on Ministry. *It's as if that life is far behind me now. And frankly, I'd have to admit, I don't miss it much.* His job was almost purely politics and administration with very little spiritual nurture left to it. *I've experienced more excitement in Shoestring these past few weeks than in ten years at the Presbytery. Maybe that's why I've been so obsessed with it.*

It's funny, he thought, *but as one gets higher up in the church, the air gets thinner and thinner. The Spirit somehow gets lost up there,* or so it seemed. That's what he missed about parish ministry.

HIS GRAY cat, Adam, jumped past the lit candle and up to the sill. He looked intently out the window, joining in the morning ritual. As Angus sat meditating, Adam's tail began to twitch with excitement as he watched a squirrel. Soon Angus smelled something strange and opened his eyes to discover Adam's bushy tail was ablaze. He leaped up to put it out, and Adam never wavered or took his eyes off his prey.

Ignorance is bliss, thought Angus, shaking his head. *But I haven't been too blissful these last weeks as regards this murder spree. I still am, however, in ignorance.*

He made a proper English breakfast that morning of eggs, bacon, whole wheat toast, and for a little homeland treat, he got some haggis from the freezer. Actually, the breakfast was more therapy for him than nourishment for Angelica. He doubted she would eat much of it, but he never doubted how good it felt for him to fix it for her.

In fact, she never ate a bite. She was fast asleep and would sleep most of the day. And so he sat there in their bedroom eating her breakfast and watching her sleep. He felt more content than he had in a long, long time.

He finished breakfast and brought the dirty dishes downstairs to wash them. The smell of Adam's singed fur lingered. He suddenly thought about work and phoned Franny.

"Hello, stranger," she said. "What's it like being a man of leisure?"

"None of your sarcasm, please. What's going on?"

"You have ten messages which you'd know if you checked your e-mail, ever!"

"I did yesterday as a matter of fact."

"And did you see one from Brian Hendrix? He's the

one in trouble over money at the University."

"Yes, yes, I know Brian. I'll call him today. Oh, by the way, I got Angelica home, and she's doing very well, thank you."

"I'm sorry. Of course I was thinking of her. I'm glad to hear it." Her voice changed slightly, warmer.

He told her about the Maundy Thursday and Easter services he agreed to lead and about Charlie. Then he said, "I'll see you later today."

Silence on the other end. "Excuse me, did I hear that right? You'll be in later today?"

"Quit it," laughed Angus.

HE FED all the rest of the animals, wrestled with Eve, and patted Calvin, then showered and shaved, and dressed in the next bedroom. By the time he was ready to go, he peeked in on Angelica, who was still asleep. He kissed her lightly on the forehead, and her eyes blinked. She smiled sheepishly and rolled over, content in the knowledge she was safe at last.

The sun crept up on the horizon like a thief ready to take your breath away. The red and gold, orange, and yellow tinged with purple stopped Angus in his tracks. "Life is such a gift so worth protecting, every inch of it," he said out loud.

The morning mist hung gently in the air. He started his Jeep and turned on the lights almost automatically. Just as automatically, he had turned to go toward Shoestring, but Austin and office were in the opposite direction, so he turned around.

As he did, he thought of Beth. He knew it would be too early to call, but he thought he'd better do it while he was thinking about it or he might forget. He got out his cell phone and dialed the number. There was no answer. He tried several times, and it was always the same. It could mean she was so exhausted that she could sleep through anything. Or it could mean something more sinister. He tried not to think about that. Still he was worried, but there was little he could do. He called Hector and told him he had been trying to reach her but with no success. He was worried.

Hector said, "Don't worry. I'll check it out and let you know something just as soon as I do."

What Hector had not told Angus was that he had Beth tailed and was unable to reach the person tailing her. He decided to go check it out himself.

HECTOR PULLED up in front of Beth's house. It looked like a lonely child in a schoolyard, waiting to be picked up by her parents. The shrubs were overgrown, the grass out of control. *The house could use a coat of paint*, he thought.

He went to the door and knocked, thinking probably no one would answer. He was right. On the way to her house, he had tried to raise Max on the two-way with no results. He scanned the neighborhood looking for anything he could to help explain this mystery. He feared the worst, but hoped for the best. His mother taught him to be that way, and it had stood him in good stead over the years.

He went around the back of the house and found nothing out of place or out of the ordinary. He cursed under his breath. This case was too much. Nothing seemed to fit. One minute it seemed it was all coming together, and the next minute it all unraveled. Not only had he lost Beth, but now he didn't know where his deputy was.

He went to his car and tried again to raise Max on the two-way. Then he tried his cell phone. Both times he struck out.

He sat for a long time out in front of Beth's house thinking. *Where could Max be? I sent him to watch over Beth, so she must be in danger. But Max is too good a cop not to check in. To be out of reach is the cardinal sin of police work. I'm not normally a worrier, but I'm beginning to make an exception now.*

If he were never in charge of another murder case, it would be fine with him. He decided to go back to the station. Maybe Max had left some word for him there.

ANGUS SPENT a productive day catching up on all the things weighing down his desk. There was an intrinsic reward in what he did as well. He was doing some good that God had called him to do. Those two realizations made the work all the more worthwhile. *No matter what happens*, he thought, *do not despair.*

But despair often visited him like an unwelcome guest who overstays his time. His wife was so positive and his secretary so funny. Being away for the last several days, he had forgotten how much Franny brightened his life. She was pushing the upper boundaries of middle age with short, gray hair and wrinkles to prove it. But she was effervescent and full of energy, efficient and organized while at the same time playful without being a flirt. Despair did not stay long when he was in Francesca's presence.

Her husband was home now, retired military. She retired with him for a time, but got bored. She had been an executive secretary of a big oil company in Houston but wanted something where she didn't have to apologize for being a person of faith.

Angus spent the day on the run. He called an embattled pastor, tried to stop the red ink in the budget, and spent time planning the new pastors' orientation. Always in the back of his mind were the two sermons he had to write for Thursday and Sunday.

At the end of the long day, the sun resting comfortably on the horizon, Angus said goodbye to Franny and other staffers who were going home to their families. He had called Angelica to tell her he would be late and that he would pick up something to eat on his way home.

THE TEXTS for Maundy Thursday were always the same. The gospel was from John 13 about Jesus washing the disciples' feet. He'd always had a hard time with this, which is why he knew he had to preach from it. Most Presbyterians he knew would not stoop to wash one another's feet. Primitive Baptists and Catholics were the ones who did that kind of thing. He had tried it a time or two when he was in the parish, and was met with the same response, which he had heard were the seven last words of the church. "We have never done it that way."

Such reluctance was understandable to Angus who knew it was alien, if not threatening, for most people. Washing another's feet was an intimate act that required humility on the part of the washer and trust on the part of the receiver. Such a combination is hard to come by in this day and age. "Love one another as I have loved you," he remembered Jesus said.

Angus stopped and shook his head thinking, *How do you love one another with a murderer among you? It's difficult for ordinary sinners to love one another, let alone a murderer. What should I say? What is the role of forgiveness in this situation? Can you pursue a killer and still forgive him?* He was still haunted by what Hector's son said on their fishing trip. He puzzled it over for another two hours, thinking also of the equally difficult sermon to preach on Easter Sunday. Thoroughly exhausted, he began the long ride home.

HECTOR WENT back to the station, but there was no Max and no word of his whereabouts. He was baffled and frustrated. He was confused because Max and Beth were missing–both, his responsibility. He was frustrated because it felt to him as though he were shifting gears. He had been searching for a killer; now he had to worry about finding his friend and the person in his charge. This ball of emotion was building up to a bursting point. But maybe if he solved this little mystery, the big one would clear up some. Besides, he had given Angus his assurance Beth would be all right. He desperately wanted to make good on that promise.

He went back to Beth's house to see if he had missed anything. He walked around the house and looked in the garage. The car wasn't there. *There's got to be something Beth left behind,* he thought. There was no way to get into the house though; not legally anyway, unless he got a warrant. *But who would I give it to. Beth could be anywhere, doing anything. If I could find something suspicious, a judge would be more likely to grant me a warrant. But I can't find a thing.*

Hector worried most about Max. He knew if he found Max, he would probably find Beth. Max was nothing if not dedicated. Those who didn't know him well might call him stubborn. Working with him as a friend for the past ten years, Hector was at turns frustrated and admiring of this central quality of Max's dedication.

He had walked around the house in ever-widening concentric circles, just like he would with a group of deputies, exploring a wide area for evidence. Finally, a few yards from his car, in a bare patch in the yard next to the driveway, he saw a stick with the words 'FN14' written in the hard-packed earth.

Hector took out his notebook and carefully wrote down what he saw. Observation was such a key to what he did. He often found himself on his day off looking at people and trying to tell their story just by how they looked and how they carried themselves.

He got back in his car and tried to think about what it could mean. *Maybe it was part of a word or a number. But what starts* "*FN?*" It could be an abbreviation for "fun," "funeral," or "fundamentalist." *We get a lot of those down here*, he thought. None of those made ultimate sense, but nothing about any of this did.

Hector got out his cell phone and called Silvia, his wife. She was very good with word games. She could do the New York Times crossword puzzle in a few hours, in ink, which was her Sunday afternoon ritual.

Silvia worked for the state, and Hector hated to call her because she always had ten things going at once. But this was important. "What could 'FN' stand for?" Hector told her about Max and Beth and the message scratched in the hard earth.

She had a word search program on her computer and typed in the letters. All the words he had thought of came up as possible meanings. The word "fourteen" made no sense either.

"Unless it was a road sign?" said Sylvia, shooting in the dark.

"But there's no 'FN' anything," he protested.

"Hang on," she said, and was quiet for a few minutes. "I ran it through the map of Texas. There is no 'FN,' but there are a lot of 'FMs,' farm to market roads. There is no 'FM 14,' but there is one 'FM 144' just outside of Shoestring, on the way to San Antonio."

"Thanks, honey, that's good work. That's the old stagecoach road. Bandits used to stop the coach regularly looking for loot."

It was a dirt road with a mind of its own. It came and went. It would wind for a few miles and dead end into another road. It appeared several miles later for a few miles more. Hector wasn't sure, but he thought it crossed the state like that. One long interrupted line, clear across the state.

Before he found a section of it and began looking for Max and probably Beth, he started thinking about the people who lived out here on this road. The Mayor had a place out here, as did Bob Bradford, who owned a hardware store. Alice Foreman, a widow, also lived in a little bungalow. He seemed to recall there were a couple of vacant places as well. One was just a shack; the other had belonged to a successful real estate broker who died without heirs.

Hector thought he'd start at the shack first.

ANGUS DIDN'T have a meeting and so was at a loss as to what to do with himself. *I need to look at the Thursday and Sunday sermons I'm going to preach this weekend,* he thought. *I preach so little, and it feels strange to have two sermons in the same week. What if I had to do three a week like some Baptists do,* he thought. *It would just be too much.*

It was far easier just to watch TV. He hated himself for doing it, it was such a waste. He could see his dad kicking him out of the house to go to work, and it made him want to sit there all the more. Anger was never far from the surface.

Sometimes though, waste was full of grace. Like when the woman poured a costly bottle of ointment on Jesus' feet before the crucifixion. Angus tried to justify this waste as such a source of grace, but it was a hard sell. He had grown up without TV; they were too poor to afford one. And what passed for TV programs in Scotland was a far cry from what they had here in the States. Besides, he liked the idea of turning his brain off and coasting through a couple of hours, even though he knew it wasn't good for him. *A lot of the most enjoyable experiences in life were not good for you,* he mused.

This being Holy Week, the networks were pulling out all the stops. Tonight they ran the final installment of the *Ten Commandments.* The best part for Angus was watching the water separate, and the Israelites walking through on dry ground. Angus heard the bell he had given Angelica to ring in case she needed anything. He removed Adam from his lap, despite his protests, and went up to see what she needed.

He ascended the stairs with a lightness born of commitment and desire. He was more committed to her than to any other person on earth, including their children. He smiled halfway up the stairs. *When you're young,* he thought, *desire comes before commitment. When you get a little older, commitment shapes one's desire.*

He reached the door to their bedroom. When she saw him, she smiled and held out her arms for a hug, which Angus gladly accommodated. He kissed her lightly on the forehead.

"What is it, m' lady?" he said with a bow.

"What are you doing?" She smiled.

"I regret to inform you, I am watching TV."

"Would it be possible to watch it together?"

They never wanted a TV in their bedroom, but allowed the boys to have one in theirs. Angus shook his head at the irony, thinking back to all the talking they did with their children and between themselves about that decision. *I should have been firmer,* he thought, *like his dad was with him.*

After Angus hooked up the TV, he fixed popcorn, and they watched the rest of the *Ten Commandments* together. The missing piece for tomorrow night's message was now firmly in his mind.

Chapter Thirty: Just the One

AS THE WORLD was beginning to wake up, Angus continued to work on his message. This was his favorite time of the day. He was alone with his thoughts and Adam. Their cat was a constant companion for whatever Angus was doing. Cats had a reputation for being so inscrutable, but Angus almost always knew what Adam wanted or was thinking. Now he was perched on the windowsill seeing what the world –Angus called it "reading the paper"–was up to as Angus put the final touches to his Maundy Thursday message.

Angus nearly jumped out of his skin when he heard the phone ring. It always frightened him when the phone rang too early in the day or late at night. In the ministry, it could mean anything, and it usually wasn't good. Now that he was married and living in America, it could mean it was a call from his sister in Scotland, or his uncle here in the States. He tended to call late at night after they had gone to bed. Angus tried not to blame him because he had such a weird work schedule. Part of it was during the day, and the rest was at night. Half the time his uncle didn't know if he was coming or going. It wasn't his fault, but Angus had no problem blaming him.

He answered the phone as quickly as he could so as not to disturb Angelica. It was Hector. "I'm sorry to bother you, but I thought you might like to know we found Max."

"You what?"

"Yeah, I got a great clue from my deputy. He and Beth were tied up in an abandoned house off FM 144."

"Good God Almighty!"

"Calm down, Angus."

"How are they....did you find anything? Any evidence?"

"No, not much. Max was clubbed from behind, and Beth was drugged. She can't remember a thing and has a huge headache. Doctors say Max somehow escaped without concussion or serious brain trauma, thank God, but he's very weak and disoriented. We're trying to get a fix on tire tracks, but that will take awhile."

"Good Lord...I assume you have them someplace safe?"

"We do."

Angus thanked Hector for the call and hung up the phone. The anger that visited Angus this morning had nothing to do with his father, nothing to do with being raised in an abusive home, and everything to do with what happens to people he cares about, but is unable to do anything to protect. He wanted to smash something or someone, but couldn't, didn't. All he could manage was a silent prayer of thanks that Max and Beth were safe, and a vow that whoever did this would pay, must pay. *Maybe*, he thought, *I'm finally getting a handle on this anger thing.*

Later he made some other calls and left his place about noon. He thought he'd get lunch on the road and take in a little more of Shoestring. It was starting to feel more and more like home. He hadn't felt so at home since he found their old Victorian and could see it as a place worth living in instead of a ruin deserving the wrecking ball. He felt blessed to live out there, but he knew something was missing.

He was from a small town, and Shoestring had the same kind of feel he remembered growing up. But the memories filled him with mixed emotions because of his love for his mother and disdain for his dad. Oddly though, through all this turmoil, he had felt himself coming closer and closer to his father's side. That in itself felt strange and somehow reassuring, if both things could be true.

WHEN HE got to Shoestring, he went to the Golden Fork Café. He had gotten to know Ruthie a little and found her to be a font of information. The place played hard to get, not because it was full of people, but because it was full of smoke. Apparently the owners had not heard of a 'smoke-free environment.' But the smokers had heard of the Golden Fork. *It's as though all of Austin's smokers had found a home here in Shoestring*, he pondered.

Being an ex-smoker, Angus found it particularly hard. He hadn't smoked for years, but it wouldn't take much for him to go back to it. He knew the physical liabilities of being a constant smoker, but remembered the experience with too much fondness to trust himself to take it up again with any kind of control. His remaining vices, caffeine and chocolate, would stay around to see him through.

"What's new, Ruthie?" he asked, trying to be more familiar than he actually felt.

"Nothing at church as far as I know, Reverend," she said, pouring him a cup of coffee, that jolt he needed. He was one of those who could drink coffee late at night, and it didn't bother his sleep. "But I did hear that the couple who own the 'Century Shoppe' are splittin' up and that the preacher's wife is leaving town."

"Do you think they're connected?"

"I have no way of knowing."

"Ruthie, come on." He lightly punched her shoulder.

"Surely you have an opinion?"

"Well..." She looked around the café like a searchlight on a foggy night. "Philip and the preacher's wife have spent a lot of time together lately."

"Who's Philip?"

"Philip Barnes. Vice President at the bank."

"Very interesting." He paused, at a loss for where to go next. "Have you seen Hector lately?"

"He was here for breakfast. In fact he comes in for breakfast most mornings."

"Did you tell him what you told me?"

"Not today."

"Why not?"

"He didn't ask!"

Ruthie went on to other customers. Angus got out his cell phone and called Hector. He told him what Ruthie had said about Philip and Connie. He asked about Beth, and Hector told him she was doing fine, resting at his place for a few days.

Angus decided to go over to the church to see if everything was ready for tonight. Gray clouds hovered in the distance; the play of the dying light gave the horizon an eerie, other worldly feel.

The church steeple cast a long, gaunt shadow over the town square, with the torn-away cross the only blemish. Sadness fairly seeped from the building. Angus shuddered as he approached it, though he didn't know what made him do it. It was a reflex. *Everything feels so incomplete*, he thought.

He went inside the hallway of the church and saw Louise getting ready to leave, shutting off the lights and computers and coffee pots.

"Hello, Reverend," she said formally as she heard footsteps coming up the hall. "We have a worship leader assigned to assist you tonight. She knows where the bulletins are. She will be here early to go over the service with you. Her name is Paula Snodgrass; she's on the interim pastor search committee."

"Yes, we've met." There was a pause. "Can I ask you a question, Louise?"

"Of course."

"How long were you and Peter seeing each other?"

The color went completely out of her cheeks. She took a step back.

"I'm sorry, Louise, but this is a very important piece to this puzzle, and I have to ask you about all this again. Apparently it was a pretty open secret."

"Who–?"

"I don't recall now," Angus lied. "But I've heard it from more than one person."

"We'd been seeing each other for about a year." It was Louise's turn to lie. It had been more like three years. "Look, I told all this to Hector. I don't have to go over it again with you." She folded her arms across her chest.

"Louise, I'm really on your side. I want to help in any way I can."

"You have a funny way of showing it." Storm clouds cracked and crashed as she stormed out.

He turned his attention to the sanctuary. He felt unusually at peace in this place. He felt comforted and calm in the space. The one thing he liked most about it was the pulpit. The word was both read and preached from one place. *It makes more sense this way*, Angus thought.

The darkness was a mixed blessing to him, both serene and disturbing. He thought of the summers he spent in the coalfields with his dad. He remembered one summer in particular that inspired him to move toward his chosen profession.

The church had gotten a new pastor fresh from seminary in Edinburgh. Many of his parishioners were miners, so

Pastor McNeil decided to go down into the mine with the men to let them know God was with them.

This was an unusually safe mine. There hadn't been an accident there in over twenty years. It was also a very productive and profitable place for its owners.

But the day of the accident, it was as if an atomic bomb had exploded. A cloud of black coal dust so thick you couldn't see your hand in front of your face rose from inside the mine and enveloped the whole town like a pall on an ebony casket.

Angus and his father survived. The young cleric did not. For Angus, it was the beginning of a call to ministry. For his father, the funeral for the pastor and many of his friends was the last time he set foot in a church.

Angus had determined he would tell the story about the minister's sacrifice. The story about his father would remain safely locked away in his heart.

WORSHIP FLOWED like living water. They met in the chapel, a far more intimate and alluring space. Setting this service in the evening also lent it an air of mystery.

The opening words reminded Angus of a grand invitation. Paula began with a reading from St. John's Gospel. "*Jesus said, I give you a new commandment, that you love one another. Just as I have loved you, you also should love one another.*" What followed was a contemplative hymn, wafting through the congregation like incense. The scriptures chosen for the evening were always the same. The story of the first Passover from Exodus, then the story of how St. Paul passed on what he knew about the first communion, followed by the gospel account of Jesus washing the disciples' feet.

Angus chose to speak of Paul's instruction regarding communion. He reminded the worshipers that the church at Corinth was in the middle of a fight. Some people came drunk to communion, and Paul wanted to remind them of what they were doing. "So every time we eat this bread and drink this cup," said Angus, "we are in the presence of Christ, and as such, should behave accordingly." Angus finished by saying, "The paradox of the Christian faith is in the fact that we live when we proclaim Christ's death until he comes. For us to live is to die in Christ. We die to ourselves, to our own ego, to our own self-esteem. We die so we might live anew in Christ, able then to see a sister or brother in need, and know with certainty that we are one with them."

Next came the foot washing. The last few years of Pete's ministry, he had tried to introduce this ancient ritual to his church. It hadn't been easy. These were Presbyterians after all—quiet, conservative, private, and inward. But for Angus and Tom Branch, who assisted him, washing the feet of those few who came forward was very rewarding and humbling.

The service flowed from there into communion. Angus quoted the scripture from I Corinthians: "Hear the words of the institution of the Holy Supper of our Lord, Jesus Christ:

> *The Lord Jesus, on the night of his arrest, took bread, and after giving thanks to God, he broke it, and gave it to his disciples, saying: 'Take, eat, this is my body, given for you. Do this in remembrance of me.' In the same way he took the cup, saying: 'This cup is the new covenant sealed in my blood, shed for you for the forgiveness of sins. Whenever you drink it, do this in remembrance of me.'*
>
> *'Every time you eat this bread and drink this cup, you proclaim the saving death of the risen Lord until he comes.'*

Angus reminded them that this meal was once a feast, but because people forgot why they had come, now all that's left is a crust of bread and a thimbleful of grape juice, not even wine. As the sacrament shrank, so did the church.

The service ended in an unusual way. After communion, the congregation was invited to "strip the church," while Psalm 22 was read. Stripping the church is in preparation for the Good Friday service which remembers the moment of Christ's death on a cross.

AFTER THE SERVICE Paula and Angus straightened up the chapel.

"Does Hector see me as a suspect?" asked Paula, picking up the wine cups and the bulletins.

"Your name has not come up in conversations I've had with him. He surprised me when he made Charlie a suspect, so I wouldn't want to speak for what Hector does or doesn't think about you. I'd encourage you to talk to him, if you're worried for some reason." He let the last of that sentence trail off to see how Paula would react.

"Oh, no, I'm not worried. I know I'm innocent. I had nothing to do with this business."

"Nothing?" asked Angus curiously.

"Well, I had feelings for him, but I never would have acted on them. That would have been just too . . . wrong."

"You seem to have pretty strong feelings about the rightness or wrongness of your actions. I find that admirable. Many people wouldn't have that kind of self-control."

"Right is right, Reverend, and wrong is wrong." It's as though she underlined *right* and *wrong* by the way she said them. "And there is never any way to make one into the other."

"You sound rather definite about the difference between right and wrong."

"Oh, yes, Reverend. My mother taught us the difference, and I tried to teach it to my kids. Everything is all so relative today that people, and children in particular, just don't know the difference. I think that's just wrong. Well, I'll just go into the kitchen to clean up these glasses. If you want to leave, that's all right. Thanks for coming. Your presence these past days has meant so much to a lot of people."

"I think I have a handle on the difference between right and wrong, but every now and then, it does get confusing. Like when you withheld information about your feelings for Pastor Pete; that's at least impeding the investigation. Isn't that wrong?"

Paula looked a bit red in the face and couldn't look Angus in the eye. "Well, I didn't mean anything by it. It was no harm to anyone. It's not like I tried to kill anyone."

"No one is accusing you of that. I'm just trying to say that telling right from wrong is always easier for someone else than it is for you."

"I suppose so, and I get your point, I think. Well, I have to take these glasses into the kitchen to wash them. You don't have to stick around any longer. Having you with us these past few weeks has been amazingly comforting. Thank you for all your help." And with that she was gone.

ANGUS HEARD the crash of glass and turned to investigate the noise. It appeared to come from the sanctuary which by now was a dark, shadowy place. Angus was guided by the few security lights over the exits. He passed between shadow and light like a pilgrim on a quest, unsure of what he was looking for.

He got to the communion table which was on the floor level of the sanctuary, right in front of the chancel steps. There had been a ceramic chalice and a plate on the table, but now there was only a plate. The chalice lay in pieces on the hardwood floor. The communion set was a gift to the church from Pete and his wife on the third anniversary of his ministry there.

Angus bent down to pick up the pieces when he heard footsteps. He looked up but could not see clearly in the darkness. The figure was silhouetted by the security lights in the back, and his shadow draped over the pews and the front of the sanctuary.

"Hi, Angus," said the figure as he approached the kneeling man.

Angus tried to squint through the darkness into the light to see. "Mr. Branch, it that you?"

"Yes, it is, Angus," he said as he came closer.

Angus stood and faced him with the pieces of the chalice resting in his hands. "Someone deliberately broke this chalice to get my attention and get me into the sanctuary."

"Why do you say that? Maybe there is another explanation. Maybe it was an accident. I've been in the office all this time." Tom shrugged. "I heard the same noise you did."

"Did you see anyone?"

"No, I didn't. But I heard a door close."

"Which one?"

Tom showed Angus which door he thought it was, the one closest to the kitchen. The light from the kitchen would not be visible from the fellowship hall, so anyone leaving the building by that door would not have seen a light on in the kitchen.

"Did you see who it was?"

"Well, no, Angus. I didn't."

Angus got the broom and dustpan from the kitchen and was heading back to the sanctuary. Then it hit him like a mad mule braying in annoyance. Tom Branch was the one who hated Pete, who was jealous of his popularity in the town, who maybe was having an affair with his wife, if Ruthie was to be believed. Beth had tried to tell him as much, but he wasn't paying any attention.

But it was Maureen who just didn't fit in any of this. Several good suspects would work in this puzzle if it weren't for Maureen. Her death just didn't make any sense. But still, everything else...

He cleaned up the mess around the communion table and there, on his hands and knees, he thought of Jesus washing the disciples' feet. This wasn't about them and what Jesus wanted from them, although he told them to love each other. It was about him sharing who he was with those who mattered most. It was about risking being vulnerable at the very point in his life when he needed all the strength he could muster. How in the world could he do such a thing? *What an incredibly strong person he was*, thought Angus. *How strong he is*, Angus corrected himself.

"Angus?" Tom was in the kitchen. "I'm going now. Paula's left, and everything's locked up. Do you need any help?"

"Yes, Tom, I do." He came toward Tom. "I need some advice."

"About what?"

"About talking to someone that I think had something to do with Peter's death."

"Well, I wouldn't talk to him without someone else there. You never know what they might do without a witness."

"That's good advice, Tom, but in this case I'm going to have to go ahead."

"Why?"

"Because now seems as good a time as any."

"You mean me?" Tom pointed to himself, looking around, knowing no one else was there. "You think I killed Pastor Pete?"

"You hated him, Tom. You were jealous of his popularity in your town. You were having an affair with his wife, and he was in the way."

"It seems you have it all wrapped up in a neat package, Pastor, but I'm sorry to have to unwrap it for you. I was out of town when he was killed, and I can prove it. My affair, while I'm surprised you knew about it, was coming to an end. I love my wife and have decided to dedicate myself to making it work. Just call me an old-fashioned guy."

"This was all out of my own head, Tom. And Hector knows all the stuff we've talked about. We'll check out everything you've said."

"Angus, I thought we could be friends. I can't have you accusing me of murder."

"I think the same thing, Tom. And if you didn't do it, you don't have anything to worry about."

"The next time we talk, Angus, will be in the presence of my lawyer, unless Hector finds out who did this."

"I'll remember that."

Tom turned and walked out.

WHILE HE was talking to Tom, Angus had moved toward the kitchen. He turned back to retrieve the broom and dustpan from the sanctuary where he had left them. He didn't see it coming out of the darkness, glinting in the soft glow of the security lights. The gold cross came crashing down on him and knocked him to the ground unconscious. The shadowy figure retreated toward the kitchen door, opened it, and stumbled into the arms of Hector Chavez coming up the back stairs.

"Why, Jan," he said smiling, "you're just the one I wanted to see. I am arresting you for the murder of Peter Anderson and Maureen Sullivan, the attempted murder of Beth McKinley, and that's just the beginning."

Jan Smith, dressed all in black, hands behind her back, was straining against the handcuffs. "They're all lies. I didn't do a thing," she snarled. "You can't prove it."

Chapter Thirty-One: The Perfect Lure

THE LAKE SHONE brilliantly, white and green and blue in the misty haze of an early spring morning. Angus watched Hector cast his lure in a high, majestic arch almost to the other side of the lake. Then Angus cast, and his lure plunked six feet from the boat.

"I haven't been fishing as much as I would have liked," he said sheepishly.

"You know what they say, 'A bad day fishing is better than a good day doing anything else,'" said Hector.

"I am so glad you showed up when you did the other night. It was such a stroke of luck to catch Jan in the act."

"Don't thank me, thank your wife. She's the one who called and told me there might be trouble at the church."

"She is a clever one, isn't she?" Angus smiled to himself.

"When you cast, let go sooner. You're holding on to it too long."

The next cast was clean and long and high, gleaming softly in the hazy dawn. Angus smiled. Hector said, "There you go. Now we'll see if we can catch some fish."

"I still can't believe someone would kill just because of a thrift store coming in next door."

"We're all sinners, aren't we, Reverend?" Hector asked with a smile.

"True enough. Kids kill to wear someone else's tennis shoes."

"The thing that stumped me for the longest time was the power plant connection. I just could never put the stuff going on at the church together with the death of Maureen," said Hector.

"That's because the two of them were in it together. Jan did it to keep the riffraff from her store. Steve killed Maureen to avenge her squealing over the embezzlement charge. Steve told us he had been down-sized from the plant. That was only partly true. He was the only one let go. I called the plant later to confirm that. And Maureen is the one who spotted it and told her bosses about it. That's why she had to die."

Hector jerked up his rod with a violent motion. "I got one," he said through clenched teeth. He fought the fish for several minutes, and then Angus witnessed a wonderful sight. The fish gathered all its strength and leaped into the air, spraying water as he went.

Hector kept reeling it in. He got it to the side of the boat. "That's a good fish," he said. He reached down to bring it aboard, but before he did, the fish broke free of the hook, hesitated for a few seconds, and swam away. "Damn!" said Hector. "I'm sorry, Angus."

"No need. That was my sentiment exactly."

They talked about the experience for several minutes, reliving each exciting moment. Finally Hector said, "the one that got away."

"Just like this case. Steve Smith is still at large. I just never figured they would be in this thing together."

"And Jan already admitted to being the 'man' Ben Irwin saw on the roof of the church. But we'll get Steve. The FBI said they have solid leads on where he might be headed next. And they keep talking to Jan, pumping her for information. It seems that Maureen was the target all along. Steve really didn't like what she had done to him."

"And so Pastor Pete and Beth were afterthoughts?" said Angus. "They went to a lot of trouble to set up Peter's murder and killed Maureen with a scarf. What's the deal with that?"

"We spent so much time on the people in the church, we didn't look far enough outside to see who else had a motive. That's why they did it that way. And Jan also figured, with Peter out of the way, the chances of the church going ahead with a thrift store would be remote."

"I also found out," Angus interrupted, "that Steve had a preacher father that he hated, and this brought all that up again, and gave him extra incentive."

"How did you find that out?" asked Hector.

"I asked," smiled Angus. "I talked to Pete's widow yesterday. She's so relieved this whole thing is over so the town can move on."

"What's she going to do?"

"She says she may just stay right where she is. It's home to her and the kids; it's all they know. Personally, I think that's a good idea."

"Oh, and Angus–we checked out the house on Oak. The notorious cat has disappeared again!"

They fished for the rest of the day. Most of the time what they caught, they released. They kept enough for the two families to have a fish fry that night.

LATER AT HECTOR'S house, Angus looked at Hector laughing at a joke his son had told and thought of the last line of *Casablanca*. He raised his beer bottle in Hector's direction and said, "I think this is the start of a beautiful friendship."

Hector smiled, and they clicked their bottles together.

Born in the Chicago suburbs, Mark W. Stoub, like his protagonist, Angus McPherson, has been a Texas transplant for over ten years. He received his B.A. from Maryville College in Tennessee , his M.Div. from Louisville Seminary, and his D.Min. from McCormick Seminary in Chicago. A Presbyterian minister for over thirty-five years, he still pastors the good folks in Bay City , TX where he lives with his wife, Jane, and their two cats, Max and Katrina.

81706047R00186

Made in the USA
Columbia, SC
07 December 2017